Praise for Laurie Graff's debut novel,
You Have to Kiss a Lot of Frogs

"I never knew bad dates could be so good."
—Kelly Ripa

"A provocative and intelligent look at the ways that people search for a meaningful life."
—*Publishers Weekly*

"More than just a catalogue of loser guys and bad relationships, Graff's smart and funny novel shows just how hard finding the right man can be and how easy it is for a relationship to fail."
—*Booklist*

"Graff's debut novel is funny, hard to put down and may cause other authors to ask, 'Why didn't I think of that book idea?' "
—*Romantic Times*

Praise for the novels of Caren Lissner

"Woody Allen–hilarious, compulsively readable and unpretentiously smart."
—*Philadelphia Weekly* on *Carrie Pilby*

"Lissner's heroine is utterly charming and unique, and readers will eagerly turn the pages to find out how her search for happiness unfolds."
—*Booklist* on *Carrie Pilby*

Scenes *from a* Holiday

Laurie Graff

Caren Lissner

Melanie Murray

RED
DRESS
I N K
™

SCENES FROM A HOLIDAY

A Red Dress Ink novel

ISBN 0-373-89537-2

© 2005 by Harlequin Books S.A.

The publisher acknowledges the copyright holders of the individual works as follows:

THE EIGHT DATES OF HANNUKKAH
© 2005 by Laurie Graff.

CARRIE PILBY'S NEW YEAR'S RESOLUTION
© 2005 by Caren Lissner.

EMMA TOWNSEND SAVES CHRISTMAS
© 2005 by Melanie Murray.

www.RedDressInk.com

Printed in U.S.A.

Laurie Graff, a writer and actor, is the author of *You Have to Kiss a Lot of Frogs.* The sequel, *Looking for Mr. Goodfrog,* will be published in April 2006. She lives in Manhattan.

Caren Lissner lives in Hoboken, New Jersey, and works as a newspaper editor. Check out her Web site at www.carenlissner.com.

Melanie Murray lives in Brooklyn with her boyfriend and bulldog.

CONTENTS

THE EIGHT DATES
OF HANUKKAH
Laurie Graff

On the First Date of Hanukkah

It wasn't just because Nicki Heller was a Sagittarius, although Sagittarians were known to love the pursuit of love more than the actual act. They were also well known for being incorrigible flirts; their self-image had them believing absolutely everyone found them attractive. But let's face it, everyone she ever went out with *did* want to marry her. Hey, the truth was the truth.

The list had even included Davey Horowitz, who had sat behind her in the third grade. Since 1974 was not a time when boys dipped girls' pigtails into ink wells when they had a crush, Davey had twisted the head of her first-night-of-Hanukkah gift, a brand new Mod Barbie, until it completely disconnected from the body. The proportions of that body would have been 36-18-32 on a real girl—and, despite her infatuation with Barbie, the eight-year-old Nicki already knew they were proportions she'd never have and, believe it or not, would never even aspire to, thank you very much.

Davey had detached the doll's head from its ridiculous body so he could throw it across the room to Tony Morelli, who said he would give it back to her after school. But instead, Tony had thrown it down the sewer outside P.S. 276, their public school in Canarsie. He'd given Nicki a Hanukkah *aynhoreh*—the Hanukkah evil eye—by never, ever giving her back her doll.

So it wasn't just the mad memories of Mod Barbie that made her think twice after she said yes to Mark last week, when he brought up "the dinner date." And it wasn't just because a true Sagittarian would always put off till tomorrow what could be done today. No, it was not just for those reasons that Nicki Heller did not want to meet Mark Baum on this first night of Hanukkah for dinner at that quaint little Italian bistro down on Carmine Street where they'd had their first date fourteen months ago.

It was that tonight Nicki knew for sure Mark would want to right the Hanukkah wrongs of yesteryear by placing a diamond ring on Nicki's butter plate and proposing.

Nicki already knew she would say no because she was as finished with marriage as she was with her first husband, and to tell you the truth, she just wasn't in the mood for another one.

To this day, Nicki wasn't quite sure why she had gotten married in the first place. Especially so young. It wasn't just because Jay was cute. And it wasn't just because he really liked Nicki, though he did like her, instantly in fact, when he met her at college that December, the middle of their sophomore year. They were the only two that had gone back for seconds of the godawful totally *goyishe* macaroni-and-cheese casserole with the big, brown pieces of sausage baked inside.

"My grandma Ida would have a coronary if she saw me eating this," Nicki had said, putting her plate on top of the industrial-steel counter, watching as the woman behind it with the hairnet dipped a big industrial-steel spoon into the orange-colored mass and plopped a chunk of it on Nicki's plate. "My grandparents live downstairs from us, one of those two-family houses, talk about reach out and touch someone. And they used to bring their own dishes up to my mother to try to stay kosher, but it became such a hassle that now they just try to forget about it."

Grandma Ida also had to give in to having two granddaughters who were not named after a deceased family member, the traditional way of naming a Jewish child. Nicki, a derivative of Nicole, got her name because Nicki's mom had always loved it. Three years later when Nicki's younger sister was born, she was named Cyd after the dancer Cyd Charisse. *Gants gut meshuggeh,* Grandma Ida would say. Craziness. But over time she had come to accept her daughter's modern ways.

"Kosher shmosher," Nicki told Jay, jabbing her fork right past the noodles and straight into the sausage.

"I agree. Hey—I like your boots," said Jay, indicating with his head that they should mosey out of the kitchen.

"Thanks. My mother sent them to me. For Hanukkah. Tonight's the first night," she said, following him into the dining hall, past the table with the girls from her dorm. Past the one with her current roommate and her newest current boyfriend. Past just about everyone, until they found a spot where they could be alone.

"Happy Hanukkah," Jay said, making a space for them to put down their trays. "I wish my mother would send me a Hanukkah present."

"I'll give you some of mine. My mother will send me one for every night."

"Wow, that's great. What does she do for your birthday?"

"It's tomorrow. Be here. Same time. Same place. And I'll let you know!"

The next night Jay showed up at the dining hall with a menorah, Hanukkah candles, birthday candles, a package of Ding Dongs, a dreidel—just in case Nicki liked to play the holiday's gambling game—and a poster of the poker-playing dogs sitting on a commuter train. And that's how simple it was with Nicki and Jay. They fell into something. Maybe there was a little trouble, but nothing so terrible—so they stayed.

They dated throughout their sophomore year and then moved off campus together, where they remained until graduation. After that they moved down to New York, and a few years after they married they moved out of the city and into a house.

Nicki disliked the suburbs. Nicki liked the city and that's where Nicki wanted to stay, but Jay kept pushing and Jay wanted to leave and Jay felt he was entitled because Jay felt the move was going to move their life forward and besides, wasn't he the one who was always waiting for Nicki?

But Nicki loved Jay. He was the first, he was good, and he was crazy about her. She knew she added color and spice to his life, and while, quite frankly, it often felt like Jay was holding her back, somehow everything would always fall back into place. It always did, and everything would have been fine *if only*. If only Jay hadn't practically demanded they move out of the city, and if only it hadn't been to Westchester, back to his roots just a few blocks from his mother. If only Jay hadn't insisted Nicki meet him every night at Grand Central so they could make the 6:23—a train Nicki told him over and over again was impossible to make when you ran your own events-planning business and you had to show up at the events that were mostly scheduled at night…if they weren't on weekends. If only Jay had understood, and if only Jay had not forced her with the baby ultimatum.

Nicki wanted a kid. She did. Really. And she was going

to try to have one. *When* she was ready. Which she wasn't yet. Her business was doing so well, she barely had time to make dinner, let alone a baby. It would be when it would be.

She was only twenty-three when they married, and she still had plenty of time. Plenty! If Jay had had a couple more interests, something a little more social going on in his life than waiting for Nicki at home and collecting comics, well, maybe then Jay could have given Nicki more space to do her thing. Jay might have understood better if he, too, ran his own business, instead of working for the government. So, okay, he was a lawyer. A city attorney. But mainly he was a nine-to-fiver—he practically punched a clock for God's sake.

Jay liked routine, but Nicki did not. Jay was a neat freak, and Nicki was not. He was tight, she would splurge; he was punctual while she was late. They were different, and Jay had always liked those differences. And now Jay did not. Not now, not anymore. Something had changed and now Jay wanted what Jay wanted, and mainly it was for Nicki to not be Nicki anymore. Jay felt uncompromising and Jay was a noose around Nicki's neck.

She didn't really want to, but then she had to—she wasn't given a choice. It was a double whammy. The biggest Hanukkah *aynhoreh* yet. Nicki's marriage ended on December 11, her thirtieth birthday and, that year, the first night of Hanukkah.

"I'm tired of the Nicki Heller show," shouted Jay.

"Well, that's just tough! Because it's not going off the air!"

She took their dog, Bandit, the Honda, a bunch of clothes, and the pictures of the dogs playing poker and riding the commuter train, and she commuted out of Westchester and down to the city for the very last time—because when the sun rose the next morning, Nicki "never changed her name" Heller would also rise, and begin again.

★ ★ ★

"I know the reservation's for seven but I just don't think I'm going to be able to get out of here on time," Nicki said into the phone while looking at her computer screen. She was so glad that she had finally got one of those big flat ones. It took up much less room on her desk and that was a really good thing because there was so much stuff on it she could barely see.

It must have been piling up for a while, but she hadn't realized it until this morning when she interviewed that nice communications major from NYU for the spring internship position. Nicki knew she'd be able to teach her a lot, and hoped the girl didn't have her heart set on an internship at a big-shot magazine, a hot-to-trot publishing house or some advertising agency.

"The detail that goes into event planning will be primary to anything you do. You'll have to be a list-maker whether you go into marketing, public relations, publishing or TV production," Nicki had told her once they finally got into the interview. Perhaps not for the girl, but for Nicki, who liked anything off-beat, it was an auspicious beginning.

The girl had banged on the door, thinking that no one was there, while Nicki was pulling on the doorknob to open the big, gray industrial door that was so thick the girl couldn't hear Nicki yelling, "Hang on, I almost got it!" When the door finally did open, the momentum caused the doorknob to fall off into Nicki's hand, which led the girl to fall into Nicki, and the two of them to fall backward into a big box filled with soft throw pillows for next week's Japanese-style singles soiree.

"I bet you didn't expect to enter the corporate world like that," said Nicki, getting up, shaking out her own long dark curls, and untangling her pale purple pashmina that had got caught under her gauzy, flowy skirt.

Brushing off her camel-haired coat while smoothing her long hair back into place, the NYU girl followed Nicki out of the entry room and into her office via a maze of cartons, videotapes, chairs, clothes, papers, magazines, newspapers, books, toys, gadgets and more and more cartons of stuff. Nicki stepped over each item effortlessly, like the route was a hiking trail she knew by heart.

"You want some coffee?"

"Thanks, a cup of coffee would be great," the NYU girl said.

"Yeah, it would, but the one thing I can't find is the cof-feemaker, so let's forget it," said Nicki, and instead picked up a bag of salted sourdough pretzels that had been lying on a nearby file cabinet and tossed them to the girl, before clear-ing a spot for her on the couch with one big karate chop.

"There ya go. You can fit. You're a skinny minnie!" Nicki took her seat behind her desk. She loved her office. She stole a quick glance out her ninth-floor window, right in New York's garment center and just a block away from Macy's.

"I used to do all kinds of events, but now I team up with organizations and specialize in singles events. You get to meet a lot of guys. It's a perk of the work," she told the girl, omitting that she had developed Single Not Soul-O: Sin-gles Events for Like-Minded Souls after her divorce as a way to get herself back out there without actually having to go. "I'm busy all year round. Being single isn't seasonal, believe me. And working here is especially good if you hate to date…like me. Unless you already have a boyfriend."

"I bet the girls in my sorority would come to every event, too," said the prospective intern, suddenly looking a lot more interested and standing up.

"Sit down, relax."

"Well, it's just that…I can't see you. I, uh…I can't see over those, uh, stacks." Piles of paper covered every inch of Nicki's desk.

"Oh, so why didn't you say so?" Standing up, Nicki took a big chunk from one stack and threw it on the floor, then took a bigger chunk from another stack and threw that down, too. Their mutual laughter let Nicki know a deal could be sealed.

Nicki wanted to call her now and settle it before the holiday. A girl like that would be good. Smart, well-educated, pretty...

What time *was* it? She looked at the time in the lower right-hand corner of her computer screen. How could it already be six o'clock?

"Mark, I'm sorry, I really am. But there's no way I can be downtown in an hour. Can you change it? Can you make it for eight?"

But at seven when Mark called back, Nicki asked if he could make it for nine. And at seven-thirty when he called back, she thought for sure she could be there by nine-fifteen, nine-thirty at the latest. But when he called, yet again, at eight, she wondered if they could just maybe skip it and do it tomorrow.

"Oh, wait. Wait a minute, wait," she said, climbing over a couple of things to get to her calendar posted on the bulletin board. "Tomorrow is that Matzo Ball thingy."

Not to be outdone by Christmas, the Matzo Ball had become one of the biggest annual celebrations in the city for Jewish singles. Tomorrow night a big synagogue on the Upper East Side was sponsoring one. The Jewish singles business had been good to Nicki, and over a year ago she had even nabbed Mark at one of the evenings she had planned for her neighborhood JCC.

It was just one of those flukes that people call fate. Nicki had organized a singles seminar around the latest how-to, *What's Love Got to Do with It?* The speaker needed three men to do an exercise. As those events had the tendency to attract more women than men, they were short one man. That didn't pose a problem for Nicki. She walked out of that classroom and into the next, a class on photography, and asked for a volunteer.

Mark said later that he heard bells when he saw her—of course he'd volunteer, what else did she need? And the rest, as they say, is history. By that point Nicki had been out of her marriage over six years and had already had two and half boyfriends, okay, maybe three—but while the first two were crazy about her and talked about marriage and families and all that, she just wasn't ready. And then that third one—well, he seemed kind of great, until he disappeared after three months.

Nicki heard women complaining about that very thing at singles events, but stuff like that had never happened to her before, so she decided that guy just didn't count.

By the time of the class it was already a couple of months since that *experience,* as she would come to think of it—as if having plans to go to London for a week and then waiting at Newark Airport for a no-show boyfriend was an *experience.* It was more like a devastation, if you asked her, but nobody ever did because she just told everyone that at the airport she broke up with him.

Anyway, that first night was enough time for Nicki to see that Mark Baum—forty years old, divorced, no kids, science teacher at Stuyvestant (a great, smart, high school in Battery Park City, where he also lived), graduate of Cornell, raised in New Jersey, kind, reliable, low-key, funny, still had hair— was just the right temperament for Nicki. And just like with Jay, she and Mark turned into *something.* When their something had hit a year, Mark made it clear it was time for it to turn into *something more.*

Why? Why did he have to go and try to "take it to the next level"?

★ ★ ★

"How do you think it can go on like this, Nic?" asked Mark. "How many times do we have to go around the same block?" He walked around his apartment while talking on his cell, staring out the window that faced where the Twin Towers used to be.

He'd never forget that day. The chaos at the school, explosions so loud they all thought they were going up in flames. On a day like that you thought if you came out of it alive you'd never ask for anything again. But then, when you were lucky enough to find something you wanted, a day like that made you want it even more. It made you want to put down roots and have something you could call yours. Something you could come home to. It made you want to do better than you did in your first marriage. He laughed with Nicki as much as he loved. He even laughed with Bandit, or at him, the wide black French bulldog who always looked like he'd prefer living in Paris and spending his afternoons at a sidewalk café.

However, Mark was beginning to worry that Nicki was stuck.

He tried to reassure her, over and over. "We'll never have to leave the city. You'll be able to go back to work once we have a family. You can still do events at night. But it will be different and you will have to compromise—somewhere, somehow, sometimes. And if you can't start tonight, on a holiday… And for goodness' sake, Nic, it's not just Hanukkah tonight, it's Christmas Eve, too. *No one* is working. You shouldn't even be in your office building that late tonight. There's no security. What do I have to do to get through to you?"

She had seemed relieved when, two weeks ago, her birthday had come and gone without the proposal. Thirty-eight. Women were having babies into their forties. Maybe Mark could wait two more years. When she hit forty. Maybe then she'd want to slow down…a little. Maybe. Maybe not. But it became clear he was only waiting to have "the dinner date" tonight. Hanukkah. The first candle.

"Nicki. Are you there?" Mark sat down on his couch and opened the black velvet box that held the ring. She wasn't a big one for jewelry. She was so easy to please in so many ways. All you had to do with Nicki was be there and love her. And give her her freedom. All the time.

Not that she liked to hang out alone. No, Nicki needed someone. She needed and needed and then she would run. He knew there had to be something else she was terrified of, but every time he thought he had found the key it never opened the door.

During the summer they broke up for two weeks. And while his heart wasn't in it, he went out on a blind date— with a colleague's niece he had heard so much about. She criticized everything from his unstylish attire to his wire-rim glasses to his choice of restaurant to his career.

Nicki wasn't like that. She didn't complain about a teacher's salary…she had once dated a partner in a law firm that had made a lot of money, someone who took her on trips—something about almost going to London, more than that he had never learned—but she told him the lawyer guy was no biggie. Money was not the hook into Nicki. Her heart was big. She loved animals. Her family. And him. So what was it? *What was up?*

"Mark, I've gotta go. You want to come by here later and you can do stuff on the computer and then we can go back to my place? I've got a menorah around here somewhere, too. We can light the candles. Okay?"

Okay? Should he say yes? He had no willpower with her. He was going to say yes. Why not? It was okay. After all, it wasn't like she was rejecting him. But she was rejecting what he wanted to offer. And he was tired of how that made him feel. Tired that he was unable to see his life a year from now, or two, or three. His first marriage was short-lived. Meeting in Europe shortly after college they had eloped, but once they were back in the States it was clear they had made one big giant mistake. Mark was cautious. Reliable. Mark was one of those rare birds who knew his mind. He was ready, and if she wasn't able to commit now—

"Then I'm afraid, Nic, I'm really sad, actually, that you never will. I don't want to lose you but I don't want to look back and have lost my opportunity for a family by waiting for something I'm not sure you'll ever even want."

There was a giant pause on the other end. Nicki was sitting at her desk taking some of the pretzels and breaking them in pieces over the desk before she ate a couple. She was hungry, she sort of missed Mark, she hated being alone, she loved him. This time it really did feel right, but what if…what if it turned out to be the same thing all over again? She knew it was time to leave work. But she just couldn't deal with it, she just couldn't—

"If you get in a cab now, Nic, we can both be there in twenty minutes. It's only eight-fifteen." He paused before he asked again. "Okay?"

She didn't answer. She walked with the cordless phone out of her office into the main entry room. Accept a marriage proposal by nine o'clock or lose Mark. It was too late, now, to contact the intern. It was Hanukkah and it would be Christmas tomorrow. He was right. She should get out of the office. But—

"Okay? Nicki? Are you leaving now?"

"I don't know what I'm doing, Mark," she said, searching for the stepladder so she could climb up to the top shelf of the closet to search for that menorah. "Can't you just come here and we'll figure it out?" she asked, spotting the ladder across the room, folded up next to the other file cabinet with all that info on good, cheap catering. Tonight might be a good time to go through some stuff and get organized for next year. "Settled? You'll come?"

Mark looked down at his glass coffee table and closed the lid on the small velvet box. What could he have been thinking? She was completely loyal and she loved him, but she would not let him in. And so he was going to have to go. It's funny how a day you thought would bring so much joy could turn around and do just the opposite.

"No, Nicki. I'm not coming. I'm not going to be able to see you anymore. I'm sorry. I want to be your husband, not the guy who you meet up with after you finish everything else that came first. I hope you'll find what you're looking for. Don't stay too late."

"Wait a minute, Mark." Nicki was suddenly more than a little nervous here. She hadn't expected it to come to this. What could she do? She could say she'd meet him after all, and get it back on track, except that she knew she couldn't. Her mother, her sister and her grandmother now, too, had been driving her crazy about this, but she just wasn't ready. Why couldn't they understand? Maybe she should hop the L train and go sleep in Canarsie tonight. She could have bagels and lox in the morning with her dad and Grandpa Bernie. People who wouldn't ask her anything about anything.

"Okay, Mark, then, I'll see you…well, I mean, I guess I won't," she said. "If you change your mind tonight or anything, I'll probably be here." She paused, knowing she was making a mistake, but like a snowball rolling down a hill it was gaining speed, getting bigger and bigger till it ran off on its own. "'I'll miss ya," Nicki said, and then she hung up. She made sure she hung up first.

So. Nicki walked over to an empty desk and opened a holiday tin of butter cookies someone or other had given her. It wasn't over, she thought, as she bit into the hard, sweet cookie. He wasn't going to let her go. Mark was going to get into a cab and show up at her office in twenty minutes and hang out and wait for her and everything would be fine, and they could figure it out tomorrow. Maybe she would even make a Hanukkah dinner—but first she had to order party favors for the Japanese thingy. Maybe she'd go down to Chinatown tomorrow. Was anything open?

Nicki climbed the stepladder and began rummaging through the closet, pushing wrapping paper, boxes, ornaments, hanging files, printer ink—oh *that's* where that was— off to the side. Hanukkah candles. *Aha!* That was a start, she thought, tossing a box down to the chair below. And right behind the candles was the big, clunky menorah.

She loved it. The menorah had come over on the boat from Roumania with her father's parents—it was a family heirloom and one of the few things that Mal Heller had inherited from his parents, both of them gone. She was up on her tippy-toes to reach it, stuck in the back on the top shelf of the closet, the gold and silver metal gleaming, when she heard the banging at the door.

She had *known* he would come! Was she right or was she right! Of course there was no reason to think that she and Mark had really broken up. Of course they hadn't. Nicki had known Mark would hop a cab and come over. Okay, this was important. Nicki was super happy that he was here, but she didn't want to step down off the ladder and open the door. Aside from wanting to get the menorah, she didn't want Mark to think she was *too* anxious.

"I think it's open," she called down from the stepladder, thinking it probably was, since it had no doorknob and she hadn't bolted it on the inside all day. She had found a steel poker on the shelf and was using it to pry the menorah forward—she wanted it in her hands when Mark walked in the door. Diamond shmiamond! They'd celebrate Hanukkah here, and then maybe go uptown and get some Chinese. The menorah was coming to the edge of the shelf slowly but it was not quite there, not yet, but it was closer to the edge of the shelf and almost within reach—when the door opened. But it didn't just open. It forcefully threw itself ajar, slamming itself against the wall.

"Aaaah!" Nicki screamed. The sound made her jump, almost causing her to almost slip on the stepladder as the poker jumped up and moved the menorah forward—

"Aaaah!" She continued to scream, quietly in her head, as she regained her balance on the ladder. She was shocked to see a man that wasn't Mark standing below her, a man in a black ski cap that almost covered his eyes, a man wearing a dirty worn-out brown leather jacket and a mean expression, a man who was holding a knife.

"Don't move!" he shouted. His voice harsh and angry.

Nicki didn't. She didn't know what to do. She was suddenly scared. Vulnerable. Mark was right. He had said not to stay at work so late. What was wrong with her? Why had she pushed the envelope? Mark was right. Mark. *Mark!* How could she have been so dumb? Right now she could have been sitting in La Trattoria with Mark and an emerald-cut diamond, and instead… Ohmy*god,* what was going to happen to her now?

"What the fuck! My partner was already here?" asked the man, glancing in disbelief around the office that looked like it had been ransacked. "I just saw him and he said he didn't have *nuthin'* from this floor."

"Nah, it always looks like this," Nicki shouted down from atop the ladder with all the bravado she could muster. If she came down from the ladder, he would kill her. If she stayed up on the ladder, well…he would kill her. If she offered him something maybe… She looked around her office but from this view, well, who could find anything? It was *such* a mess, she had to admit, although the new angle did allow her to finally locate that coffeemaker.

"So the only thing here is you, huh?" he said, slowly walking toward Nicki. "What are you doin' here anyway so late on a holiday? You have no boyfriend or nuthin'?" he said, talking slow, walking slow. "You're not so bad," he said, getting closer, causing her heart to beat faster, tears welling in her eyes. She was not going to look scared, dammit, she was not.

She didn't take her eyes off him, but from behind her back she got a tighter grasp on the poker. She felt her hand on the bottom of it and knew it was facing straight up. If she could whip it around, quickly, maybe she could stab him the very moment she felt him come near. And he was so close…

With no time to count to three, she whipped the poker around to the front, but instead it banged into the top shelf and the menorah, the beautiful, metal menorah that had been dangling at the edge, started to fall. She knew it was falling on top of her, and she wanted to jump off the ladder, but the guy was standing below her with the knife, and she didn't know what to do, and before she could decide, the decision was made for her—the menorah toppled off the shelf, landing on her head.

And before Nicki could no longer see, there were a few things that Nicki saw: the burglar's feet scurry out of the office, the poker resting itself against a case of champagne, the red cardigan with the black embossed *N* she had been looking for, stars and a Hanukkah *aynhoreh* so big and so bad, Nicki knew she might never see another Hanukkah again.

On the Second Date of Hanukkah

Nicki opened the box of Hanukkah candles sitting on the gray swivel chair and wondered where they had come from. Had she picked them up at Odd Job Lot on sale? She always liked to make a big deal about choosing the colors. Tonight the menorah would be lit up in purple, red and blue. She chose purple to be the *shamas,* the lead candle that would light the other two.

When she was little, each night after they lit the menorah, she and her sister Cyd would be given a gift. The presents would be hidden around her house—upstairs, or sometimes they'd be hidden at her grandparents', downstairs. Once Nicki found a gift in the basement, and one year when it was unseasonably warm her father hid the packages out back in the little enclosed cement yard.

Nicki took a few steps back to look at the lighted menorah and was struck by the fact that she didn't trip over anything. Then she looked around her office. What the—?

Something weird had definitely happened. When, she wasn't sure, because Nicki had no recollection of the first night of Hanukkah except to know it was over. It was *definitely* the next day. The menorah was next to the computer on the small desk in the entry room, and the date on the computer screen confirmed it. So did the date on the newspaper that was neatly folded and—wait a minute, what paper was that? Did the *Times* change their masthead?

Lifting the paper, Nicki looked up and was amazed by what she saw. Or rather what she didn't see. The room was spotless!

With everything filed and put away Nicki could see why her landlord wanted to raise her rent. There was a lot of square footage here. Who knew? She looked at the big geometric area rug, beige walls, potted plants, framed pictures, curtains… Curtains? She hadn't even gotten around yet to putting up curtains in her apartment. Her apartment! When was the last time she had been back to her apartment? When was the last time anyone had walked Bandit?

Nicki was bolting out of the entry room and into her office to grab her coat and go uptown when she was greeted by Bandit, in a red bandana, lounging on a beige chenille throw on the two-seater couch in her office. *Her* office? Wait a sec, it no longer looked like her office! Who could have done all this? Ida, at eighty-six, didn't have the strength. Her mother, maybe? Mark?

Yes. Mark must have arranged to give her one of those makeover thingamajigs for Hanukkah. *Extreme Makeover: Office Edition!* It was practically the perfect gift, except she wasn't sure if she'd ever find anything again.

Nicki entered the pristine little bathroom and fixed herself up, knowing she was about to come face-to-face with the crew that had pulled this together, and, of course, with Mark, who *had* to have signed off on it. Talk about going room to room to find your Hanukkah gift!

She went for her black wool coat, but instead, on the coat rack, found a thigh-length cotton sateen trench in off-white. Okay, why not? She threw her cell phone into her purse, her purple pashmina over her shoulders, and, putting Bandit on his leash, she walked out of her office, into the hall, and over to the elevator to ride downstairs and be received.

"Oy veissimir," said Ida, grabbing another tissue from the box to dry her eyes as she sat in a chair across from Nicki, whose head was all bandaged and now lay so still on the big hospital bed. Ida had spent the night in that orange chair after they had gotten the call. *The call.*

They all knew Mark had been planning to propose. When the phone rang and it was Mark, Ida only hoped Nicki had said yes. She couldn't understand her granddaughter. Thirty-eight—she should have children by now, like Cyd. True, it wasn't like it was in Ida's day, but at least in her day when you got married you stayed married. For better or for worse. What? Life with Bernie was a bed of roses? Sure, with a couple of thorns—not that she was complaining. But nowadays? Ida watches TV. She knows. Nowadays marriage was never for worse, just for better, or until something better came along.

But who cared about that? Nicki's marriage to Jay was long done with, finished, and this Mark was such a nice boy. Such a mensch. And he was supposed to propose, for goodness' sake. And he would make Nicki a wonderful husband—not that any of that mattered anymore.

To think just yesterday at this time Ida had imagined the worst thing ever would be if Nicki said no to Mark. Could she have imagined an accident like this? Could she have imagined that heavy menorah falling on Nicki? And to know she had been burglarized! The menorah might have saved her from—

Ida shuddered to think what might have happened if that

derelict had gotten his hands on Nicki. Someone in the building called the police. Somehow Mark had shown up. Ida couldn't remember details. She had gone numb when they got the call. Nothing but Nicki mattered. And nothing would ever matter again if her Nickala didn't wake up from this coma. And soon.

Nicki walked out of her office building, excited about the big reaction shot that would surely be caught on film by the show's camera crew. She hoped they had taken before pictures so they could put them up on the screen with the afters, side by side, her favorite part of all those shows.

"Hey, watch it!" from some guy in a hurry, however, was all she heard when she stepped out onto West 35th Street. And while there was no crew to be seen, the street was busy, filled with people walking like they had someplace to go, all of them in a hurry and all of them walking alone.

Nicki looked across the street at Macy's. They always put up lots of Christmas decorations, with a little tribute to Hanukkah, but now the entire front of the store was decorated with blue and white electric bulbs that created a menorah, a dreidel and a Star of David. Sweet, thought Nicki, looking down at Bandit doing his business and then doing a double take, because the street sign that had always said Broadway now said something else. In big letters, and as clear as day, the sign said Dreidel Way.

Nicki picked up Bandit and ducked inside the nearest pizza parlor—there was one on every corner. Instead of big, burly Frank standing behind the counter cutting the pies, there was a scrawny guy with glasses.

"Hey, I've gotta ask you something," said Nicki, looking around the restaurant crowded with single women and their dogs, all sitting at different tables, alone, eating pizza. "But first I'll take a slice." As she watched the guy go to heat it up in the oven, she put Bandit down and he immediately ran over to an animated white Maltese that looked slightly aloof.

"Charlie, be friendly, okay?" said the brown-haired woman. She smiled up at Nicki. "He loves people, but he's not so crazy about other dogs. Sorry."

"It's okay," said Nicki. "It's just that—"

"Pizza's ready, miss. Come get your slice."

"One sec," said Nicki, looking at the pizza guy and then back at the woman. "Can I ask you something?"

"Oh," said the woman looking at her watch. "I have a show tonight and I'm running late. Could someone else help you?" She threw her empty paper plate into a nearby garbage bin.

"No problem," said Nicki. "What's your show?"

"Here. Maybe you'll come," said the woman, whipping a green flier out of her bag and handing it to Nicki before leaving, Charlie leading the way.

Nicki looked at the flier. "'Frogaphobia,'" she read aloud. The show was playing at the Maccabee Theater. Nicki thought that must be a new venue. "'Just when you thought it was safe to date! Look back on fifteen years of bad dates in the life of single, Jewish actress Karrie Kline.' *Oy.* Better her than me," said Nicki, tucking the flier into her pocket, then going to the counter to pay. But when she opened her wallet, all her money was gone! Nicki fished inside, but all she found was some Hanukkah *gelt.* "Look," she said to the pizza guy, "I don't know how this happened or where my money went, but..." She showed him the *gelt,* the chocolate-covered coins wrapped in gold foil, and put two of them on the counter.

"Take this back," he said, pushing the second candied coin across the glass counter. "Pizza only costs one."

"Okay," said Nicki, completely frazzled now, expecting to snap out of this any second, even pinching herself to help make it happen. But nothing happened. Nothing changed.

The only thing that felt familiar was that she was starved.
Nicki sprinkled some hot pepper onto the slice before she
took a bite, but it tasted a little too good for a dream. She
must have been hungry. Now that she was eating, everything
would be okay, she thought taking the slice and Bandit out
to the street. But when Nicki got to the corner the sign still
said Dreidel Way.

"Can I ask you something?" Nicki said, marching up to a
redhead who was part of a group of three women around
her age. "When did Broadway become Dreidel Way?" she
asked, pointing up to the sign. "Who's responsible for that?
Bloomberg?"

The women giggled, giving one another meaningful
glances before one of them said, "Welcome!"

"You must be new here," said the redhead.

"I've lived in New York my whole life, thank you very
much."

"New York? New York is over," she answered. "This is
Menorahville! Where every day is Hanukkah and everyone
is single! The only way out of here is to meet someone and
get married. We've been trying for what feels like forever.
We keep going to the same singles events over and over, but
we meet all the same *shmegegees* who are too cheap to go
out on a date, let alone go out and get married. So good
luck." She hurried away, seemingly uneager to befriend the
competition.

"Wait," yelled Nicki, chasing the women, who were now
jaywalking to get away. "Where do you have to go for the
singles events? Where do you meet the men?" Nicki stood
on the curb, hopeful they would tell.

"Oh, what the hell?" said the brunette. "Tonight's the
Matzo Ball. Come with us. But you're on your own once we
get there, okay?"

They hailed a cab and got in. The cabbie tried to hit on

all four of them, but after an informal interview it became clear that Alan Cohen, devoid of any professional aspirations greater than driving a cab, would not be a suitable fit for any of the women.

"I can give you my e-mail in case you change your mind," said Alan, as each of the women paid him in *gelt* before entering the Chyatt Hotel.

As promised, the women disappeared the second their tickets were taken, leaving Nicki to fend for herself. But she couldn't care less. Everyone Nicki had ever met had wanted to marry her. Hell, she could be out of Menorahville by midnight!

The huge room was flooded with people, and a big, silver ball in the middle of it spun round and round while the disco music blared. Nicki couldn't believe what she saw. With hundreds of people there—three, even five…who knew, maybe eight—there had to be *someone* she could marry. And with that thought a pain sliced right through her. She missed Mark.

Nicki looked around. This was awful. This was a scene. She'd never ever had to do anything like this, *ever,* to meet a man. What would she have to do now?

"Can I buy you a drink?" The voice sounded like gravel.

Nicki looked up and saw it belonged to a rotund man in a dated double-breasted navy blue suit, who flashed his yellowed teeth to show his very practiced, very easy yellow smile.

"I, myself, like a good scotch," he said.

Okay. He was not much in the looks department. To be honest, it seemed like the looks department had closed its door on him altogether. But she doubted he had women lining up for him. A date with this guy would be a piece of cake.

"I'll just have a club soda," said Nicki.

The guy waved the bartender down before resting his hand on the bar, allowing Nicki to observe his thick, pudgy fingers and his pudgy pinky adorned with a gaudy gold ring. On second thought—

"You know what?" she said, his pudginess so close she could almost feel it on her. "Maybe we should add a little vodka to that soda. What do you think?"

As soon as Nicki took a sip of her drink, he put his heavy hand on her back, pointing her in the direction of a table. "I'm Howie Goldenberger," he said, right into her ear. "And you, so lovely, who might you be?"

Nicki shouted her name as she followed him to a little round table, where she took a seat on a little round chair. Howie stared at her—God, he was practically salivating. Meanwhile, all around Nicki people were screaming at each other over the music and exchanging business cards before moving on to someone new.

"So, what brings an attractive woman like yourself to a place like this?" he asked, his predictability exactly what Nicki was counting on.

"To tell you the truth, Howie, I haven't got a clue!" she said, bringing her drink to her mouth, her sip quickly turning into a gulp as the truth of the statement landed. "What about you?"

"It's been so long, I can't even remember anymore," he said, his brown eyes dancing as he flashed his yellow smile.

But that didn't bother Nicki. In fact, she was going to see past all that and get right into his heart, right into his soul, and right out of Menorahville.

"I don't care much for these events," said Howie, placing the empty scotch glass down on the mosaic-tiled table. "It's a little too noisy for me, you know." He sat back, surveying Nicki. "I know a great little Mexican joint. Enchilatke. It's a little ways uptown, but I've got a car. What do you say we get out of here?"

With Bandit in tow, Nicki was out of the Matzo Ball and

onto the street before you could spin the dreidel. She followed as Howie unlocked the door of a car whose interior smelled of stale cigar smoke. Nicki immediately began to cough and blew on the overflow of ashes in the opened ash tray, causing them to fly up and spill down.

"What do you think of this, baby?" said Howie, now sitting behind the wheel and lighting up a cigar while turning on the engine. "I mean, why buy new when you can keep a girl like this? I got this car when I graduated dental school and I haven't traded her since."

You haven't cleaned her, either, judged Nicki, even though she thought, all things considered, she shouldn't be one to judge.

"There's nothing like a Macanudo," Howie said, before placing the cigar back into his mouth, slowly inhaling. "Hand-made, hand-rolled and full-bodied." Howie was sure blowing a lot of hot air. "Hey, Nic, how's about a little getting-to-know-you kiss?"

"How's about not?" she answered, leaning out the window, lapping up the air. She longed to be out of here and home. If only she could see her way home. And to Nicki's surprise she almost did, because as they drove up Menorahville's Latke Lane, she couldn't help but notice that it looked a lot like West End Avenue, her street on the Upper West Side.

"What?" she shrieked, as they drove past the corner of 81st where a sign, Single Apartments Available, hung outside the modern residential building with the sparsely decorated lobby jammed with singles! "That's where I live. My building. Or at least it was."

"You'd be surprised just how many singles are in Menorahville. But the real beauty of it is that most of them don't drive, so you can always get a good spot," said Howie, jubilant as he parked right in front of the restaurant.

The menu looked great. Howie was leaning over it and

staring into Nicki's eyes as the waiter took their order. They chatted and crunched their way through two baskets of chips, a plate of chicken tacos and an order of chimichangas. By the time they got to the flan, Nicki was certain that Howie had fallen for her. Far. She decided it was time to close her eyes and go get 'em.

"Fabulouso," said Nicki, never much of a drinker, gulping down the last of the sangria so she could get herself to do what she knew she had to.

Howie reached into the breast pocket of his jacket to pull out *another* smoke. "You should know, Nicki, that I love a good cigar after a good meal, and also after a good—" Instead of finishing his sentence he lit up and took a puff. "I don't want to be impolite to a girl like you, although you are definitely sexy."

"Go on, be impolite, How," said Nicki, taking his hand, ready to get this all over with, ready to take the plunge. "You can be impolite today, tomorrow…" She leaned across the table in search of his lips. "Take me, I'm yours!"

"Hey, wait a minute, wait, wait, hold your horses," said Howie, standing up and pushing Nicki back to her place. "Let's slow down here a minute."

"Sorry," she said, suddenly confused. "I thought we were clicking." After that pitcher of sangria, Nicki sure was.

"We were. We are. You're the only girl I've really clicked with since I got here. You're the first girl I know I could really be with. And believe me I've been around every block in Menorahville, so I know."

"So, good. Let's go for it. And let's get out of here," said Nicki, thankful, thinking she wouldn't miss a thing about Menorahville—except that so far the food had actually been pretty good.

"It's not that easy," said Howie. "I…well…"

"What?"

"Well…I, uh…you know, I'd want to be sure."

"You're here so long you can't even remember and now you need to keep dating to be sure? How many times do you have to go around the same block?" Nicki asked, getting a flash of something or other about Mark but she didn't know what. She just knew she wanted to get back. Howie was her shot. "So?"

"So it's like this," said Howie, exhaling the rest of his hot air before he spoke. "If I marry you, Nicki, if I get out of here, then, well…well I lose what I've got."

"Yeah, but so what? Isn't that the point? What have you got here that's so good?"

"It's like this," said Howie, sighing, finally putting out the damn cigar. "I usually don't have to spell it out with all the others, but—"

Others? "What others?" Nicki had assessed this overblown *nebish* with the absolute certainty that he hadn't had a girl even glance his way since he got here. "You have a girlfriend? You seemed like you were available."

"I am. That's the beauty of it. You see, Nicki—" Howie leaned across the table to whisper his very personal secret "—I'm in the mix."

"In the mix?"

"In the mix."

"What the hell does it mean to be 'in the mix'?" she asked, not even bothering to go for more sangria, getting the distinct feeling it wasn't going to help.

"I can, uh…how shall I say it? Continually rotate," said Howie. "And, uh, right now my dance card, as they say, is full, so I can't add on any more." He punctuated the sentence by flashing the palms of his pudgy hands as he smiled his big yellow smile.

"How many?" asked Nicki. She couldn't believe it. A guy like this had a stable?

"What?"

"You said you rotate. So at any given time, how many?" She had figured a guy like this to have been alone for years. She had figured pudgy-handed, fat-lipped, cigar-smoking Howie had had no opportunities, *nada,* none, and surely that was the reason and the only reason he was still here.

"Right now I'm down to three," he said.

"*Down* to three?"

"Yeah."

"Wait. Let me get this straight. You mean you have three women you rotate doing what with? Dinner?"

"I told you, I'm in the mix. The *mix!*" He seemed so perplexed that he had to explain. "Sex. I rotate sex with three women. But only three. All of whom like me very much, by the way, and all of whom think that someday *some*thing will happen between us. But nothing ever will. Why should I give up a good thing? I put in a fourth last week, but three's my limit, so I had to let one go. You really caught my eye so I had to check you out. I might have dumped another one for you, but I can see you're not a girl I could just continue to fool around with, so I told you the truth. But hey, I can have it every day of the week if I want it. I'm *in the mix!*"

Nicki stared across the table at Howie. Unavailable Howie. Howie in the mix. The mixed nuts, if you asked her. But Howie was in, and Nicki could see that getting out of Menorahville was going to be a lot harder than she had thought.

On the Third Date of Hanukkah

"I was afraid that the two of you were starting to go around in circles," Helene told Mark while they sat in her daughter's hospital room, waiting for any sign that said that Nicki was back, hoping for anything more than the slow steady breathing.

But thank God, at least, for that, thought Mark. If not for that… He couldn't even let himself think about that.

"Well, we were," he said, "but then I—" Mark stopped talking. He felt as if it had been his fault. If only he had been there. If only he had said yes, and met her when she had asked. The one time he stood up to Nicki—and look what happened, he thought as he sat on the edge of her bed gently rubbing her feet. Nicki had always found that annoying. *"Go away. Stop. Cut it out."* What Mark wouldn't give now to hear that whine!

"I know what you're thinking," Helene said to Mark as she watched Nicki from the orange chair on one side of the bed. Grandpa Bernie slept in the green chair on the other.

Today Ida had stayed home, and Mal had gone to the store for a few hours to check on things. Mark knew this was his busy season, as Mal would say. Everyone needed cardboard boxes, gift wrap and cards.

"At least we heard it from you, Mark," Helene said. "And you were *there*."

It wasn't to patch things up that he had shown up at Nicki's office. Mark had hung up the phone and put on his coat, and the next thing he knew he was riding the train uptown to Rockefeller Center to take a look at the tree. The sight had always filled Mark with holiday spirit and hope, two things he felt were greatly lacking lately. And how he got off at 34th instead of 47th and wound up in front of Nicki's office building, he didn't know.

But when he got there, out of all the things he expected to see, Nicki knocked unconscious and carried out on a stretcher was the last. The guy on the floor below, the one in the T-shirt business, had heard the ruckus and called 9-1-1, and, thankfully, not a moment too soon. Mark rode with Nicki in the ambulance to Mount Sinai Hospital and stayed while she was settled into a room. From her eighth-floor window was a beautiful view of Central Park. Nicki loved the park, and Mark was hoping, somehow, that it was a view she could see.

Nicki was running with Bandit in Schlepp Meadow in the park. He was off the leash—dogs in the park in Menorahville were allowed. *Finally,* thought Nicki, remembering all the tickets she had accrued each time Bandit was caught, *sans* leash, during the day when she thought no one was looking. Offhand Nicki could account for five, maybe six tickets, at forty bucks a pop. That was a lot of *gelt,* she thought as Bandit, suddenly the center of attention, was surrounded by a pack of dogs and now moseying up to a cute little Yorkie.

"Bandit's got it made in the shade here," Nicki told the

Yorkie's mom. There were so many pretty women out with their dogs it looked more like a typical afternoon for desperate housewives than stranded singles. "Where do the *guys* go with their dogs?"

"They don't," said the Yorkie's mom, a thin put-together strawberry blonde with a clipped nervous way about her speech. "Hardly any of the guys have dogs. Too much responsibility! I ask you, how the heck are we ever going to get out of here if they don't even want to take on the responsibility of a dog? Camille," she said to her little Yorkie. "Play nice with Bandit. Stop teasing. Or on second thought…maybe start! Play hard to get. What do *you* think about that?" she asked Nicki.

Suddenly from behind her, another woman stepped forward. Nicki recognized her as the actress from that pizza place, the one in the show about frogs.

"Hi there. I'm Karrie. We met before, remember? This is Jeanine," she said, pointing to the strawberry blonde. "I know you met Charlie," said Karrie, pointing to her little dog. Content to have the full attention of the women, Charlie jumped up on his hind legs to greet Nicki, allowing Bandit to have Camille to himself.

"I'm Nicki. Hi, Jeanine. Hi, Karrie. Yeah, I definitely remember you," she said, though the pizza place already felt like a lifetime ago. "So, Jeanine, tell me, because I was never good at games and I want to get out of here. How do you play hard to get? How does that one go?"

"It's easy. Just act like you don't want them and then they get hooked," she said, just as Camille left Bandit for Charlie. "See, everyone likes someone who likes someone else!"

The three women watched Bandit's eyes droop when he lost Camille to Charlie, whose indifference in turn gave Camille a renewed interest in Bandit, who was now aloof to her and back on the prowl.

"Or not," said Karrie, pointing to the dogs as evidence to the contrary.

"But if everyone here is supposed to marry somebody, I'd think you have to just go for it!" said Nicki, wincing as she remembered last night and Howie.

"Well, I sure haven't figured it out. But I guess anything's worth a try," said Karrie, gathering up her bag and Charlie and saying goodbye.

"Wait up, Kar," said Nicki, running to catch up. She felt they were simpatico—she and this petite blue-eyed woman who was a little older than herself, and she wondered if, somehow, Karrie could help her. "Are you seeing anyone here?"

"No," said Karrie. "Fortunately the only engagement I'm required to have here is at the theater."

Hearing the word *engagement* Nicki felt a pang of guilt and thought about Mark. But then, she had gone for it with him. Right? She just hadn't gone for *all* of it. Not yet, anyway. If she had, would she be here now? And when she got back, would he be waiting?

"So you don't have to be here? You're kind of…jobbed in?" asked Nicki.

"Yeah, I'm on tour with my show and when my run is over, I'm gone."

"That's interesting," said Nicki, the wheels in her head beginning to turn. She wasn't here long, but she already missed working. Could she somehow do it here—?

"Hey, listen," said Karrie, interrupting Nicki's thoughts. "I just got an idea. I ran into an ex of mine here. A photographer. His name's Elliot. Maybe you'd like him. He's coming to my show tomorrow. I'll arrange for you to sit next to each other. Like a blind date. What do you have to lose?"

"Sold," said Nicki, stopping for a sec so Bandit could sniff a fire hydrant. What was so good that they were always sniffing?

"I've got to run. But come down and see the show. With Elliot. It's at eight. Eight shows a week. One for each candle!"

"I think I will. He's allowed in, right?" she said, pointing to Bandit.

"Hey—in this place single women and their dogs are the longest-lasting relationships, if not the only relationships." Karrie stepped off the curb into the street and stuck out her hand to hail a cab.

"Thanks," said Nicki, looking around and wondering what she should do next. "Hey. Any ideas about where else I can go?"

"There's a church on Latke Lane," Karrie said as she opened the cab door so Charlie could hop in first.

"A church? Latke whatayacallit? Where?"

"The old West End Avenue, 86th, you can't miss it," Karrie called from the cab window as the driver made a U-turn and they sped away.

Nicki headed north. But as she and Bandit walked the crowded streets she couldn't help but notice that everyone they passed looked preoccupied; everyone was so busy worrying about how they were going to meet somebody, they missed every opportunity to go up to someone they could easily say hello to on the street and meet. Nicki saw a couple of men and a couple of opportunities and she tried to say hi, but no one could hear her. One guy was singing with his Walkman, another was talking really, really loudly on his cell and another was oblivious to everything, looking in only one direction, down.

However, when Nicki looked up she realized Karrie had been right when she told her she couldn't miss it. And it was a sight for her sore eyes because it was even familiar. Hundreds of people stood outside on the steps, something Nicki used to see every Friday night, because this place was just a few blocks from where she had lived. But instead of the usual five hundred, now there had to be well over a thousand.

Mark had suggested more than once that they go for Shabbat services, but Nicki was never into it. Yet now, when she entered the beautiful old church that also functioned as a synagogue, the warmth of tradition washed over her and it felt so good, she wondered why she had always made such a big deal about it.

She and Bandit found seats in an upstairs pew. Taking a quick look around, Nicki was seized with fear, grabbed a prayer book and, for the first time ever, began to pray. After looking at the men around her she knew she was going to need all the help she could get.

Okay, put on the brakes. Look at it differently. Let's say Nicki *had* to marry someone from here. Let's say this was it. Now or never. Who would it be? After Howie, she sure wasn't making any more assumptions. Looks counted, and Milquetoast didn't necessarily mean open to marriage. She let her eyes search. Row by row, seat by seat. Too old, too young. Bad hair, bad outfit. Taken—holding hands with girl. Taken—holding hands with himself!

"We know that all of you out there are single," the rabbi said, talking on a microphone from the pulpit, his wise voice filling the hall. "Now, week after week many of you come to me, unhappy. 'Rabbi, I want to meet someone. Help me. There's nobody out there to meet.' Now if there's no one to meet in Menorahville, well, there's really no place else to go! So what should you do?"

You could feel everyone in the sanctuary shift forward in their seats, as this sermon surely spoke to them.

"I stand here looking out and see all of you searching, but no one is connecting. Every week the numbers here grow and grow, our congregation gets bigger and bigger, and still no one is meeting. There are people all around you. Take a moment and look."

Oy. Did she have to? Nicki looked around. Again. Too bald, too boring, too disengaged, too weird.

"We, here at the synagogue, think men and women are not properly communicating. So we are inviting all the single people in the congregation to come to a commitment workshop we're starting this week. As a society we need to understand why we can't connect, but you need to examine for yourself what you want, and have the faith and the ability to go forward."

Self-examination. Nicki hadn't spent much time on that, she'd admit. But there was never any time, and besides, there was no point. Everything in her life had been going along fine. Clipping along. Except for that one time, all that with Jay, all *that.* She didn't even want to think about *that* anymore, but she didn't have to, because that was long gone....

Or was it? Most of the time Nicki felt fine. She felt she had moved on from Jay. Water under the bridge and all that. But every time she thought she was really free, memories came rushing back to haunt her. Forget *that,* she thought, and, turning her head, she locked eyes with a man with glasses sitting a few rows behind her. His hands were tightly crossed over his waist, and she thought he smiled at her, so she smiled back, but in a matter of seconds she saw that he was really seeing right past her and that what she had witnessed was just a nervous tick.

"Tonight, when you go downstairs to the Oneg, after you've taken something to eat and drink, make an effort to really socialize. Talk to someone new, someone you would otherwise ignore. Open yourself up to be surprised."

Nicki agreed. Wholeheartedly. She was going to open herself up so big that there would be plenty of space to marry a man she met at the Oneg.

As soon as she got down the stairs, before she even had the chance to break a piece of bread, she felt a tap on her back.

"Can I pet your dog?" The guy bent down to reach Bandit, but Bandit was already across the room on his expandable leash. "Larry Kellerman. Travel agent. And if you want to know what business is like in Menorahville, I'll tell you. Busy. I'm busy. Really busy. People are booking trips all the time—*optimistic planning,* we call it—but no one can get out of here, so they never get to go. Cancellations are a very big business, too," said Larry. He spoke quickly and with a nasal New York twang. Larry was wearing a Mets baseball cap and a long black leather coat. "And it's not just regular trips, either. You'd be surprised how many honeymoons we get to book and cancel. Cancellations. Big business. Very, very big. Names. His first. Then yours."

"Bandit down there, and I'm Nicki Heller." Larry bent down again to pet Bandit, who had returned and immediately growled. The dog practically groaned when he looked up at Nicki, who now knew for sure that this fast-talking guy was one she would not be going out with.

"That's cool. I'm tough. I can take anything," said Larry. "Dog doesn't like me. Big shit. Let me introduce you to my buddy here." He pointed to a guy walking toward them. "Nicki Heller, meet my bud, also my roommate, fresh off the boat from Anchorage. Meet Alaska Man."

Alaska Man looked to be in his thirties. His weathered face, shaggy hair and pointy features made him not actually good-looking, but not bad. He was carrying a big plate of food. Enough for everyone to share.

"I'm Albert Aronson," he said, extending the plate.

"I like Alaska Man!" Nicki said, taking in the guy while taking a chocolate doughnut. "How's it going?"

"I just sublet a room in my apartment to this guy," Larry explained.

"Is he fun to live with?" Nicki asked his new roomie.

"Only when I'm stoned."

"You still get stoned?" Nicki looked at this Larry. What was up with that? He had to be at least her age. He could even be forty—and he was still getting stoned?

"Don't get so excited, Nic, it's not *every* day, just once in a while," said Larry.

"Glad to hear it."

"What about you?" she asked Albert, the Alaska Man. "You get stoned, too?"

"Are you kidding? I've got too much to do to waste it wasted. I'm in Menorahville for just a short time. And I *chose* to come here," he said. Proudly.

"Our Alaska Man has quite a job ahead of him," said Larry, reaching to break off a piece of doughnut from Albert's plate at the same time as Nicki.

"Go get your own," she said, stopping him. "I like this one. And the food's practically the only thing here that's keeping me going."

"Can't blame a guy for trying."

"So you two meet here or what?" Nicki asked, thinking it might be good to befriend these guys, who could introduce her to some others.

"We met when I went on a Jewish singles cruise to Alaska," said Larry. "One that I'm apparently still on, because when the ship docked and I got off, I wound up here."

"Wow, Lar, you really do get around," Nicki said. "And you?" She turned her attention to the warmer guy from the colder climate.

"First thing you should know about this dude is that he's a big entrepreneur," Larry said, definitely talking up this Alaska Man.

Nicki had the feeling he just wanted his apartment back.

"He owns the Ice Café, a chain of Internet cafés in Alaska."

"Oh, so you're here for a little expansion?" Nicki asked him. "Just in time, too. Since I've been in Menorahville I haven't seen one Internet café!"

"No Internet café," said Albert. "I've got a tougher job. I've taken this short-term sublet on the West Side and I have eighty-eight days to go to every singles event in this place until I find myself a Jewish bride and bring her back to Alaska."

"Wow!" said Nicki, contemplating for a whole half second whether this was a bride she could be. But what if you didn't get to go back to your other life when you got out? What if you really had to stick with the marriage you made? What if you could never ever... She couldn't wrap her head around any of that right now, but she knew wherever she was headed, it sure wasn't going to be Alaska. Forget that. Alaska was like the end of the world. Dank, cold. Ice and frozen tundra.

"So what do you think about that?" asked Albert, making it seem more like an inquiry than genuine interest.

"I think it's sad there's a shortage of Jewish women in Alaska, and even sadder to tell you I'm not your girl," said Nicki, putting both of them at ease. "I'm from the Upper West Side and once I get out of here I don't even want to go to New Jersey. To tell you the truth, after this I'd even have trouble relocating to the Upper East Side. But..."

But what? What if Nicki got stuck here? Would she? Nah. Not Nicki. Of course she'd meet someone and get out. She was just starting to lose her marbles without work. What was it already? Two days? Three? Three days of running around all day just looking for a guy. Not for her. Why, even at home, hadn't she met Mark on the job? She *had* to work. Wait a minute. Karrie was here just for work. Albert *chose* to come here for work. A job. Could that work?

Nicki wondered if, somehow, she could work herself out

of Menorahville. It was worth a try. She still had her office, right? And she was in the singles events business, right? What better place to do an event than here! All Albert needed was one fabulouso singles event…and so did she!

Everything looked better once Nicki was out of the Oneg and back in business. She pitched idea after idea to Albert while they walked, with Bandit, down Latke Lane. Nicki was trying to figure out how to create the most scintillating singles event—one that would unite Albert with a girl he hoped would dig him enough to not mind digging a little snow. As each idea clicked, Nicki felt more and more alive. So much for the self-examination.

"So what have you done since you got here, Al? Tell me what events you've already been to. How many dates so far? Any bites?"

"I took out a personal ad in the *Daily Candle*," said Albert. "Listen to this. 'Alaska Bound? Jewish Gal Wanted!' All in bold. What do you think?"

"Responses?" asked Nicki, who in regard to Albert was already ruling out creative types.

"None."

"*That's* what I think!" said Nicki. "Listen, just because this place is flooded with available Jewish women doesn't mean it's easy to find one who's going to go freeze her tootsies off for you."

"So what do I do?" asked Albert. "Do you think someone special will want out of here badly enough to move to Alaska?"

"My grandma Ida always says, Every pot has a cover. You know what that means?"

They had been walking and talking. It was springlike and the air smelled like candy. The night was still young. An hour ago that was upsetting, but now she could walk back to her office and pull an all-nighter doing work. All she needed was a little… Nicki looked across the street and saw exactly what her heart desired. Some Chinese takeout to take in and she'd be all set.

"Hungry?" she asked Albert as they crossed.

"Wow," he said. "Six Chinese takeouts all on the same block! You know, in some ways Menorahville is amazing."

"Yeah," said Nicki, walking down the street and arbitrarily picking one. "In some ways it's no different from New York!" Nicki looked at the menu hanging in the window to confirm this to be true. It was. Moo-shoo pork, sweet and sour soup, cold sesame noodles.

"Hey, Nicki, here's my card," said Albert, handing it over.

"Great." She tucked the card into her coat pocket. "Tonight I'll draw up a contract and—"

"Oh, definitely," said Albert, cutting her off. "And don't worry. Do whatever you want. Money's no problem for me. What's *gelt* here I promise will turn into real cash when we get out."

Everything was falling into place. Nicki had a plan. Two, in fact. Plan A was to go the traditional route: marry and get out of Menorahville. And now Nicki had a backup. Plan B. She would work and plan Albert's event, and when he met a bride she'd get out of here by going back with them to plan their wedding! Why not? She was sure it would work. And she needed it badly enough to put in the effort to find out. Not to mention the motivation of the money that would be waiting on the other side.

"Let's talk tomorrow," said Albert. "You can call my cell."

"It works here?" Nicki asked. She realized she hadn't made any calls, since she didn't have anyone to talk to.

"Yeah, just dial 8 before the area code. Listen, it was wonderful meeting you, Ms. Heller." Albert took her right hand and kissed it. "I feel we have entered into a commitment, and I will follow through. You have my word. I have high hopes."

"And I have chutzpah! Don't worry, Al. Somebody's going to want to rub noses with you. Get a good night's sleep and I'll call you tomorrow." And with that, Nicki waved him goodbye and spun around to open the restaurant door.

But just then, out of the blue, someone was there. Okay, people were everywhere, so it wasn't that. Someone was walking out of the takeout just as she was walking in. Someone knocked into her and it knocked her out. Not cold, not like that—it wasn't that, it was who. This one, this someone made her heart flutter and Nicki's heart wasn't big on the fluttering thing, so this took her by surprise. In that brief awareness that one might call love at first sight, Nicki felt happy, and, for the first time, happy she was here. He smiled at her, and she beamed back.

"Do I know you?" he asked.

"Not yet!" He was tall with dark hair, a goatee and almond-shaped green eyes that looked kind. He was wearing a dark green turtleneck under a brown leather jacket, and carrying a soft attaché case and a brown bag of Chinese food. Nicki hoped he'd ask her to share.

"Excuse me," the man said. "I thought for a second I knew you. I'm sorry. I smiled because I thought you were my friend Lauren."

"Oh," said Nicki, unruffled on the outside, her blood rushing quickly on the inside. "I smiled because I thought you were cute!"

"Really! You thought I was cute? Today? After the day I had? Wow!" The guy kind of relaxed and indicated they should walk so they could talk. Following the scent of the food, Bandit came, too. "I'm Marko," he said, "but please call me Dave." The cute, tired guy reached into his attaché case to produce a business card with both names. Marko Dave was his pen name and Dave Marko his personal. Both were on his card.

"Are your books sold here?" asked Nicki, wondering where that eighty-four-dollar order from Amazon she had placed would wind up now. Talk about free shipping!

"I'm really a columnist and I'm looking for a job here," said Dave Marko/Marko Dave. "I just got a lead and have to go home and prepare a pitch."

"Hey—funny, I just started to work here, too!" In that moment Nicki felt she could stay forever. She reached into her handbag for her business card to give to Marko, er, Dave. The words *Single Not Soul-O* suddenly meant a lot more. Something magical was happening within her, and for the life of her she couldn't understand it.

"But of course it—the job, I mean—would only be temporary," he said. "I mean, this, all this is, well…" Dave seemed to indicate with a gesture that so was Menorahville.

"Hey, the way the job market's been going, everything's temporary these days!" She didn't know him but she had a feeling. A big one. Only she wasn't going to act like that. Nicki was not a flirt, she was a friend. She'd never gotten the hang of the flirty thing. With Nicki, what you saw was what you got.

"Yeah." He smiled. He paused. "Hey, how would you like to go out with me? How would you like to have tea? There's this little place called Tea-Lights down the street."

"I'd like that," said Nicki. "I think I'd like that better than coffee!" A writer, a columnist. Someone creative, someone suave. No *let's meet for coffee* with this guy. This guy was much classier than coffee. This guy was tea!

"Great," said Dave. "Okay, listen." He stopped again, and looked at her. "I have to go because I have this deadline to meet, but I'll call you. Okay?"

"Great," said Nicki, saying only what she meant and nothing more.

"Okay, then," Dave said sweetly. Nicki waved as he walked

away, then she tugged on Bandit's leash and turned toward the restaurant entrance, but she heard Dave call her name.

"If I really get motivated and finish, can I call you tonight?"

"Get motivated," she yelled as she turned around and flashed a big smile at Dave Marko/Marko Dave. "Call me," she said, then strolled into the restaurant, excited about her date, and making a mental note when she put in her order to tell them not to include the tea.

On the Fourth Date of Hanukkah

The audience was laughing. They were in stitches. Karrie Kline was up on stage, doing her show, talking about one bad date after another. Telling her tales about kissing frog after frog, none of whom turned into princes. In fact, as the show went on, Nicki hardly even thought them frog-worthy. At best they were just plain old toads. Pond scum. Creepy crawlers. Bugs!

When the curtain came down Karrie received a standing ovation. Mainly from the women. A few men in the audience seemed to hang their heads in shame. This included Nicki's date, Elliot. Some date. The first thing he said when she showed up was, "Oh… Can we just be friends? I can tell already that you're not my type." Nicki had never had anyone treat her so dismissively. And then Elliot chewed her ear off about Karrie.

"So basically when I got here I figured out that I did everything wrong with her. Every time we started to get close I pulled away, and then she couldn't take it anymore. All that time we went out I really was kind of a brat. I really was. Not that she was perfect, either. But it was great to see her here."

"So marry her."

Last night was really hard. But when Nicki woke up this morning she wanted to be optimistic. She had actually been hopeful about this blind date. She had thought, since it came through a reliable source, that maybe…just *maybe* she'd have a good time and *some*thing would be possible. But Elliot was quickly turning out to be even more unavailable than the others.

"Marry Karrie? I can't marry her. Oh no, I don't want to marry her. I would never want to marry Karrie," said Elliot. "I like her and I miss her and I think about her a *lot,* I mean a lot, but once I start seeing her I don't want to see her anymore. But then, she doesn't want to see *me,* so I try to do better, but then whatever I do it's not better. Uh-uh. It makes her *so* annoyed with me, you have no idea. I know I'm here because I'm supposed to marry somebody, but I don't want to marry just anybody, I really would want to marry someone like Karrie, but I definitely can't marry her. Nicki, do you understand?"

After her brief non-date date with Elliot, Nicki was able to see how Karrie had culled enough material for a show. Nicki watched him and a few others staring at her during the Q & A. She didn't know Karrie well, but well enough to know that the only thing these guys would get to be with her was fodder for another show.

"The question is," said Karrie, onstage, perky and lively, repeating the question for the whole audience to hear, "why didn't I do a show about a girl who got a ring?" Karrie paused. "I guess that would be inspirational in a place like Menorah-ville, but, how does that saying go? Write what you know!"

The women cheered. They finally had someone they could identify with—someone who took all her dating *mish-*

igos and turned it into entertainment. Something to be taken lightly. Something that wasn't the end of the world, but at the very worst could be a story that ended hopefully ever after. But that was okay if you were home. If you weren't stuck here. If Nicki had seen this show in New York she'd have thought it funny. If she had even seen it when she first arrived in Menorahville, she was sure she would have laughed. But now it drove her crazy. She had never understood the panic that went on among the women she'd meet at her planned singles events. The same conversations would repeat themselves over and over.

Do you think he'll call me? When do you think he'll call me? Should I call him? What if he doesn't call? Do you think he's calling someone else? Why isn't he calling? Why doesn't he call me? What if he just never, ever calls?

Nicki had never gone through any of that. Okay, there was the stuff with Jay, but they were married. And she had never counted that whole thing that went down at Newark. She and that lawyer guy actually went out for a while. They went out long enough to plan the trip he stood her up on. Compared to all this, that was pretty good. At least that relationship got off the ground. Not like here. Not like the stuff with these women.

She wasn't immune to the women's feelings. Nicki was compassionate. Whenever she spoke with the women at events, she cared. Besides, it wasn't a bad thing, at least from Nicki's point of view. Let's face it, she was in the singles events business, and in order to stay in the singles events business she needed single men and single women to come to the events. The men's inability to follow through was almost a guarantee she'd stay in business! But now, shoot. Now it was affecting her personally. Now she really got it. Because now Nicki was one of these women.

"Yes, you." Karrie pointed to a guy in his midthirties sitting a few rows in front of Nicki. He stood. His glasses fell down to his nose and his belly fell down to his toes. It was hard to understand him, his speech was so garbled. "Can you please repeat that?" Karrie asked from the stage.

"How do you break up with someone?" he asked. He looked like he should be having a hard enough time getting anyone to say yes, let alone having to plot how he should say no.

"You have someone in mind?" asked Karrie.

"Well, I go out with these women and then I don't want to see them anymore. What should I do?"

"If it was just one date and you don't want to go out again, I think you can just let it go—that's pretty harmless," Karrie explained. "Is that what you're referring to?"

"Uh…no. I want to know how to break up when—" The guy stopped.

"When what? Two dates, three? Three months, six? What situations are you talking about?" asked Karrie.

"Well." The guy took a deep breath and looked around at the audience before he answered. "I want to know how to break up with a girl after you've gone out with her, like, three times and you've already had sex once or twice. Is it okay to just not call her again?"

"*Booooooooooooooooo!*"

"*Hissssssssssssssssss!*"

"*Booooooooooooooooo!*"

"Well, after asking that question here tonight, you may never get another date, so you might not need that answer after all!" said Karrie.

Even Elliot grimaced. Boy, thought Nicki, watching Karrie lightly roll from one question to the next because she knew she didn't have an answer that could fix it. Nicki had been shocked that a guy like Howie Goldenberger was able to score, and so high, but, boy, he was like Prince Charming

compared to this *schlub!* This guy had his pick of the pantry—and still, he didn't want to commit to loving anyone?
What the heck was going on here? It all made her feel even
worse. She'd been trying to forget about last night, but she
couldn't, because in addition to her profound disappointment, she was afraid there wouldn't even be a next time. For
the first time, ever, Nicki was afraid it wouldn't be so easy to
meet somebody. She was afraid she just might get stuck.
Here. In Menorahville. Alone. She tried to push the thought
to another part of her brain, but the message took up most
of it, replaying itself in her head.

Armed with Chinese food and the Albert idea, Nicki had
waltzed into her Midtown abode last night feeling a tremen-
dous wave of optimism. The place was so comfortable and
so clean! She loved that. Who'd have thunk it? She felt that
in Menorahville she could corner and conquer the market
on singles events planning, and now she had Dave
Marko/Marko Dave. They didn't have to marry right away.
They could stay on for a while, have fun and build their new
careers. Okay, maybe she was putting the cart before the
horse—she hadn't had the date yet, but later she would, because the light on her answering machine was blinking and
then the machine announced that the message was from him.

Nicki opened the brown take-out bag, bringing a pair of
chopsticks and the cold sesame noodles with her over to the
little two-seater in her office, expecting that before this day
was over it would be fully occupied. She felt better than she
had in a long time. As if she was getting a brand-new beginning. A fresh start, without any baggage. And yes, she did
mean that literally! Yeah, she definitely missed home, her
family, life as she knew it, and Mark, but she had just found
something else. That feeling. Nicki couldn't remember the
last time she felt so jazzed about going on a first date. Every
relationship she'd ever had, she'd sort of fallen into. They

had never really started dating—they just starting being a couple.

Nicki had never understood all that before she got here. This business with the dates and the calls, who's available and who's not. When a potential couple had issues she sometimes wondered if maybe the girl was at fault. Maybe those women weren't really nice to the guys or maybe they were too nice. In a desperate way. Nicki had always thought there had to be some reason the guys were so flaky.

Before Menorahville, Nicki had never encountered such difficulties. Now she had to wonder why. She had always thought love was easy, but people had told her she was lucky. She hadn't seen it that way. Compared to the experiences these women had, though, she had been. And in a few short days not only was she seeing the despair around her, but after listening to Dave's message last night and then watching this tonight, Nicki was feeling it, too. Like it was contagious— she was catching the dating disease. She only hoped it wasn't terminal.

"Hi, Nicki. This is Dave. Dave Marko. You remember me…Marko? Dave. Well. Hi. I just wanted to call you as soon as possible because it was really really nice to meet you and I wanted to tell you that. Umm… I hope you like the Chinese food. I like the prawns and broccoli a lot—to tell you truth the food in this place is really very good. Anyway, uh, about tonight. I know I said it would be nice if we got together for tea. And I'd like to do that. I mean, you seemed very nice and I think it would be fun. But I feel I really have to tell you this, up front. I mean I called you right away because I want you to know that in all probability that's all it would be. Tea. Just tea. It's just that I've been in these situations before and you think, hey, wow, this is cool, let's have tea, but then when you get there it's like it's supposed to be more. Like it's supposed to be the beginning of something incredible, you know. And it won't be. I want to be straight, you know. I want to be up front, okay? So I don't want you to think it's going to be the beginning of anything, because it won't be. All it'll be is tea. Just tea. Okay. Good. Maybe you think it's weird, like I'm a moron or something running on and on like this on your machine, but I decided I need to be really clear. You seemed sweet, so, if you do want to go out for tea, I mean *just* tea, call me."

She didn't.

"What's the matter? What happened?" When Cyd got to the doorway of Nicki's room she could see that everyone was shaken up. Like something had happened. Had *just* happened, she thought. She was only gone a second, well what— five, ten minutes at the most—bringing the kids downstairs for Jonathan to take home. She needed to stay here longer, she didn't want to leave her parents. And now when she walked in, they were crying?

"Come outside here in the hall," said Mal, taking her arm and guiding Cyd out before she'd even had the chance to walk in. "Let's talk outside."

"What happened? What, Daddy? What happened with Nic?"

Cyd pushed her bangs out of her brown eyes, which were already filling with tears. She was emotional. Slight. Blond. Different from Nicki in every way.

"The doctor. He used the word *retreating*. I don't know that he meant anything by it, but he shouldn't have said it. Not in front of your mother, anyway."

"We've got to reach out to her, Dad. We have to try harder. Bring her back. Talk. Engage her. You know Nicki— we have to keep her entertained."

"How? What are you going to say to her?"

"I don't know. It doesn't matter. Just let me go talk to her,

Dad." Cyd shot past him into the room and pulled up the chair next to her big sister's bed. Nicki. So peaceful. She never saw her this quiet. In her wildest dreams she couldn't even imagine her sister this quiet.

"Nic, it's me, Cyd. Listen, I can't believe you're one to hold a grudge. I mean, I never thought you'd go this far to make me confess. You were right. You didn't lose those orange Jellies after gym in high school. I took them. I borrowed them out of your closet and they ripped. Well, they could've gotten lost in your locker. I mean, Canarsie High's probably still finding artifacts from your locker."

"I remember that episode," said Helene. "High drama. You were crying, Nicki, because you couldn't find the shoes, Cyd was crying because I wouldn't buy her a pair. The constant fighting over those ugly plastic shoes. I remember!"

"I don't," said Mal. "Where was I?"

"Working!" Cyd and Helene answered together.

"Well, we know who Nicki takes after," said Helene.

"Yeah, Dad. You worked so much you were hardly ever around."

"Wait a minute. Give me a break. Retail, I'm in retail. You can't make a buck if you're closed. You have to be open."

"It's okay, Mal. We're just talking here, no one's criticizing you."

"Anyway, guess what, Nic?" said Cyd, not wanting her parents to get into *that* right now. "I found you an identical pair on eBay. I have them. It's your Hanukkah present. It was supposed to be a surprise but, hey, I think this year we all got enough surprises. I got you a matching Jelly Kelly bag, too. In orange. And if you don't wake up soon I'm keeping the stuff and you'll never get it back."

"Remember," said Mal, laughing. "Remember when she got that job at the Gap, over the winter vacation. Hey, Nic, remember your first job?"

"She's always so enterprising, such a hard worker, so different from Cyd."

"Hey—why are you picking on me? I had jobs, too, Ma. I used to babysit, for God's sake, and look at me now."

"All I said was the two of you are different," said Helene. "That's all I meant. Nicki thrives on work in a different way. She loves it, she hides behind it. She's like your father. Listen, we're just talking here, no one's criticizing you."

"I'm talking here," said Mal.

"So talk," Cyd and Helen said together.

"Okay. Nic came home that first day and she said she quit, and I said, 'Why'd you quit? I thought you wanted a job.' And Nicki here said—remember, honey? She said she couldn't work there because she didn't want to fold the clothes." He looked directly at Nicki now. "You said you didn't do it at home and you weren't doing it there. And I said, 'It's the Gap, what did you think you're gonna do there all day?' And you said you could never be that fussy about it. It was like doing origami with a sweater." Mal paused. "I loved that. Origami with a sweater."

Nicki went up to Karrie to congratulate her after the show. She was surrounded by a group of women asking her what they should do to meet a guy. Elliot was hanging around behind her. Elliot wanted Karrie back, but he only wanted her back because she would be leaving Menorahville. He knew this, she knew this, and now Nicki knew it, too. Go know!

"Kar, come here," said Nicki. "I want to ask you something."

"Sure." Karrie put up her index finger to indicate to the women that she'd be right back.

"You're not really here, right? In Menorahville," asked Nicki. She needed to get this right, because the answer to this question would mean everything. She was nervous, and held Bandit's leash very tight. "I mean, after your run you get to go back, right?"

"Yeah. Thank God."

"So, do you think if I work here, too, I'll be able to get out also? I mean, you came here to work and I just kind of landed. But if I worked with someone like you, someone who also didn't *have* to be here, who could leave…" Nicki didn't finish the sentence as she suddenly started thinking about Albert. He had been so excited when she talked to him today. The event was going to be spectacular, and she was calling it The Ice Princess! That was the theme. Albert loved it. He had said he would meet her tonight to sign the contract, but she still hadn't heard from him. Well, she'd deal with that tomorrow. Right now she wanted to see if anyone could guarantee her Plan B to be a sure thing, before she said good-night and went back to work.

A few days and Nicki was already duplicating her patterns from home. If something happened she didn't like, she fought it—but not from her heart, from her office. She wasn't a quitter. She'd just have to let it wait because suddenly she'd have more work. She always had work. And she always found more. Even when she quit her first job. What was that? Oh yeah, that dumb job at the Gap where she had to fold all those sweaters. Such a pain in the neck. She told her father it was like doing origami with sweaters. Why'd she think of that just now? But anyway, she just went to the mall and found herself another job, in a bakery. Much better benefits, too, if you asked her.

"Nicki? Nic—"

"Sorry, Kar, I just went somewhere for a sec—"

"You think I'm crazy?" said Mal. "I swear to God she heard me. I really think she did."

"No, Dad, we don't think you're crazy. We saw it, too. Didn't we? Didn't we, Ma?"

Helene nodded silently. On the one hand she'd barely

been holding on, but on the other she'd been surprisingly strong. She turned to look at the electric menorah that had been sitting on the windowsill for the past few days, untouched. Helene turned the orange bulb in the center, and then she turned four more. The bulbs cast an orange hue, a little light, a lot of hope.

"You wanted to ask me something?"

Karrie's question brought Nicki back. "You have someone waiting in New York?" she asked, out of nothing more than curiosity.

"Nope," Karrie said, shaking her head. "You?"

"Yeah. But I don't know if I will when I go back," she said.

"If that work plan doesn't pan out, you mean? And if you go back married to someone else? Because I don't know how it works, Nicki, but maybe once you're back you don't have to stay with the guy. Or maybe you want to. Or maybe you just become the new and improved version of you or something. But to be honest, I'm not really sure."

"Nah, it's not that. It's just…" Nicki paused. She was going to tell her. She realized in telling Karrie the truth she'd be facing it herself for the first time.

"I did what some of these guys do. Sort of. I'm divorced. The first one ended, well, I don't have to get into it, but partly because I wasn't around as much as I could've been—not that he was such a prince, either. And Mark, my boyfriend now, wanted to ask me to get married but, well, actually I don't know what happened because now I'm here, but I do know I was, uh…I kept putting him off."

"How come?" Karrie seemed interested.

"I don't know that, either. But maybe—" Nicki hadn't even had a chance yet to think, but maybe…

"What, Nicki?"

"Who knows? You think maybe that's why I'm here?"

"Could be. And maybe I'm here so you can teach me how to meet guys I actually like who want to marry me!"

At that, Elliot approached Karrie, which Nicki could see was not exactly what either of them had in mind, but served as her cue to leave.

The women said goodbye. They both felt for sure that at some point they would meet again. Someplace else. Hopefully home. And then she didn't know what happened, but Nicki felt a little better. She was feeling okay. She was in Menorahville, and she was going to work. She was doing The Ice Princess event, but she was also going to start doing something else. She was going to get out there and date. Nicki "hate to date" Heller was going to pick herself back up, and, dammit, she was sure as hell going to try.

On the Fifth Date of Hanukkah

"If you're serious about wanting to connect, you've come to the right event." The short, stout man spoke into a hand mike so everyone in the room could hear. Sitting inside the gymnasium of a local Y were exactly one hundred people. Fifty men and fifty women.

"Bait-a-Mate is a proven commodity. Many people marry who meet at Bait-a-Mate," said the guy, talking a mile a minute like he couldn't get to the end of the speech fast enough. "I'm going to tell you how it works, but first, take a quick look around. Believe it or not, and if I were you I'd believe it, your soul mate could be sitting in the chair right next to you!"

Give me a break, thought Nicki. She had organized how many singles events? And she never heard anyone lay it on *that* thick, she thought, fiddling with the scorecard and pencil she had been given when she arrived. A scorecard! Some way to set the tone for romance! She was also given a white name tag to wear with the number 084 written in black Magic Marker. It looked just lovely smack-dab in the middle of her sheer black silk blouse. She had no idea where the shirt came from, but to be honest, when it came to clothes she couldn't complain. Her closet in Menorahville left nothing to be desired. Silk blouse, gauzy skirt, pashmina—her favorite outfit—hung in her closet in eight different colors. Okay, so maybe it was the *only* outfit that hung in her closet in Menorahville, but Nicki wasn't a big one for variety, so it suited her just fine.

Besides, that should be her worst problem, because coming to this singles event tonight—an event she had not planned—an event she had come to with the high hopes that she'd be bait enough to catch a mate, Nicki felt that her best match, so far, was to every other female in the place. For the first time in her life Nicki felt just like all the women she'd seen at her events, and she didn't like the feeling, not one little bit.

"Okay, so here's how we throw our rod into the mating hole!" The seats were all arranged in rows and rows of a giant U, and the leader stood in the center, turning to face different parts of the crowd as he spoke.

"You'll have thirty seconds to introduce yourself. When you stand up, tell us your number." He pointed to the name tag. "Tell us who you are, something engaging about yourself, what you do, or rather what you did—we sure know what you have to do to get out of here!"

He chuckled, and then chuckled again, but he was the only one. "We have a very high success rate in Menorahville, so don't despair. Business is great, so I sure don't. Okay! When you see someone you'd like to have a date with, color in the oval box on your scorecard that corresponds with their number.

"After everyone has introduced himself or herself we'll

walk around, shmooze, have a little nosh—there's a nice spread in the back, so no matter what happens the evening shouldn't be a total loss. Maybe after you talk to some people you'll decide to add a few numbers to your card. Maybe after a little shmooze you'll eliminate some. Just bear in mind, the more numbers you color in, the more you increase your chance of a match! Because later you will hand in your scorecards and we'll run them through our computer, and every time two people list each other's numbers, you'll have a match!" He smiled triumphantly.

"At the end of the night," he continued, "we will hand you your matches hot off the printer. Talk to your match before you leave tonight and make a date. For that matter, make one for tonight! There is only one rule at Bait-a-Mate. If the two numbers match, you *have* to go on the date. Okay? You *have* to go. Good. Any questions? You!"

He pointed to an anorexic-looking woman sitting off to the side in the back. "Can you please speak up?" he asked her, while Nicki wondered if the dating police would come and arrest you and put you behind bars for failure to date if, instead, you just went home.

"What if nobody you write down writes your number?" asked the woman in a quivering tone. "What if you can't get a match?"

"Then come back tomorrow!" said the guy, anxious to get this going. "A new crowd arrives every day in Menorahville. Just because you have no matches doesn't mean that nobody picked you. It just means the people you picked all picked someone else! All righty? So…let's go!"

Nicki had really pushed herself to get here. She had been completely absorbed in the planning of Albert's event. It was going to be held on the eighth candle. The eighth day of Hanukkah, the miracle night. The miracle being that Albert would find his bride at this event, and Nicki would leave

Menorahville with them so she could plan the next one. Their wedding. The Ice Princess would be like one of those reality shows, except this one would unfold at a dance.

Nicki thought a ballroom dance would be a fantastic way for people to meet Albert. And today she had the great stroke of luck to secure Reba Martinez, owner of Orbit Dance, which sponsored Menorahville's premiere dance parties. Their slogan was The Romance Of Dance Takes You Out Of This World! (Just how far out was still a surprise!) Reba agreed to give Albert a crash course in ballroom dancing before the party. Albert was not only ready to roll, but also to bankroll the whole event. The guy was loaded. He green-lighted every expense! Nicki figured she was going to get one fat check when they got back.

But as fast as Albert had said yes on the phone, he was slow when it came to dropping by her office to sign. Nicki considered putting everything on hold until he did. But the wheels were in motion. Besides, Albert seemed trustworthy. Nicki was just a little nervous. She had a lot riding on this event. But if she put her energy into coming through for Albert, he'd surely come through for her.

Nicki looked up from her unmarked scorecard, suddenly realizing a few guys had already stood up and introduced themselves and she hadn't been paying attention. Work sure took her mind off things! But, alas, here she was, entrenched in Plan A where all she had to do was connect. Something she had initially thought would be a breeze. Well, that was still easy enough, right?

Wrong.

"I'm 022. Hello. I don't know what to say about me. I work. All the time. I mean I used to. I mean I might. Work. A lot. Again. When I get out of here. I mean, if, when, whatever, just pick me. I'm a lawyer."

"Hi, just call me Double-O-Seven. Only kidding. I'm

077. You got that, girls? 077. Get it and get it right, because even though I really want to leave here in time to watch the game, I won't walk out the door if I meet that special woman tonight. Oh, by the way, I'm also a lawyer."

"I can be silly *and* I can be serious. And when I'm not stuck at work every night till eleven, I can even flirt. 062 and a lawyer."

"Hey there, men! Take a good look. I'm not your typical lady lawyer. I'd like to meet someone and be smitten, and ideally you'll even feel the same way about me!" Wink. Wink. "Number 093. See you in my office!" Wink. Wink.

"055. I have only three things to say: Yankees, ethnic food, lawyer."

"From here on, in to save time," the leader interrupted in an announcement over his mike, "we will just assume everyone is a lawyer, so only let us know if you're *not*."

"I like travel, rock concerts, restaurants…"

"I like restaurants, travel, long walks on the beach…"

"I like long walks on the beach, concerts, dining out…"

"Dining in, watching TV, going to the movies…"

"Seeing movies, eating out…"

"Eating out, ordering in…"

"Sleeping in…"

"I'm looking to have kids, looking for someone emotionally stable…"

"Looking for someone special…"

"Someone special, someone stable…"

"Only people who are emotionally stable. No therapy patients, please…"

Nicki's scorecard was blank. The only one who appealed to her at all was the female lawyer, but she wasn't desperate enough to go thataway. Not yet, anyhow.

"I was in a relationship but then I got divorced. I was a lawyer and now I'm not. I'm an actor. So far in my fledgling acting career I've earned a grand total of ninety-six dollars as a non-union extra on *Law & Order*. I took a guitar lesson before I came here. I'm 098. Thanks."

As soon as it was time to shmooze, Nicki made a beeline to 098, knowing after the disclaimer of his income, he would be, just as she suspected, standing by himself. And to her delight, she found him, right in front of the mini Danish. Nicki first went around to the side, taking some cheese, a prune and a cherry and putting them on a plate before approaching 098.

"Want to share?" she asked the guy who, baseball cap off, was clearly bald. Up close she could also see that his skin had been left pocked by what must have been an acute bout of teenage acne.

"Thanks!" 098 reached across to her plate and popped the cherry into his mouth. He smiled as he chewed. "Write me down!" he said, pointing to his name tag that was hanging off its side on his navy blue fleece sweatshirt.

"Already did," said Nicki, wiping her hands with a napkin before reaching for his. "084. Nice to meet ya!" Whew. Great. Nicki was back. This was it. Easy. Both of them raring to go.

"Where do you want to meet after they do the matches, you know, so we can make the date?" asked 098, wiping his hand on his jeans before shaking Nicki's.

"Right over there," said Nicki, pointing to the platters of cakes, cookies and her favorite chocolate-covered doughnuts. She didn't care what anybody said, they were definitely better than Krispy Kreme. "How about over by the Entenmann's, okay?"

It seemed like an eternity while everyone waited for the computer to work its magic. Nicki had written down six men, already juggling and figuring out how to set up dates with the other five without being too obvious in front of 098. She figured 098 would have more matches than just her, too, but all of their additional dates would only serve as backup. They had already made a pact. She could tell 098 was offbeat, quirky, whimsical, and wanted out. She was going for it. She thought she'd even kiss him tonight if it felt okay. And if *that* felt okay, well, who knew how far she'd go!

But when they called out her number and she retrieved her matches Nicki saw that 098 was her *only* match, that the other five guys she had written down had not written her number, that it was 098 or nobody, so she zoomed over to their meeting place and grabbed what was left of the Marble Loaf *and* the All Butter Loaf—as good as Entenmann's was, she swore they did something to food here to make the good stuff even better—to find her date and seal her fate. He was waiting.

"You're the only match I got," said 098, taking a piece of the Marble Loaf off her plate.

"Me, too," said Nicki. She smiled, watching him eat. They had a lot in common. "So," she said. "Tonight?"

"You know," he said, reaching over and picking up another piece, "tonight would be good, but I kind of want to watch the game, too. Is that okay?"

"Sure," said Nicki. She could wait a day. She could do some more work tonight, and besides, with 098 in the bag maybe she could even relax a little. "Tomorrow?"

"Great," he said. "Tomorrow's great. What time is good? Wait, wait…" He scratched his head like an answer was going to come out of it. "I have my session at the gym tomorrow. Early."

"No problem. How about the evening?" asked Nicki, smiling. Still smiling. Not acting like she was catching on. Already. She was already learning to see the signs, and fast.

"I swim in the afternoon."

"Oh.

"I have dinner plans with a couple of guys at night."

"Okay."

"I have guitar lessons after."

"I see."

"Already bought a movie ticket for after that."

"Hmm…"

"Personal trainer, lunch, swimming, basketball, nap time, jazz concert…"

If you listened to 098 you'd have sworn he was vacationing at a Superclub on some Caribbean island!

"Can I call you?" he asked. "Can I call you later? Tomorrow? Or maybe the day after?"

Nicki took the last two pieces of the two different loaves before she turned around and walked away, across the floor and up the stairs to exit the gym. As humiliated as she felt, Nicki really felt for the people who got back an empty scorecard and were standing on the sidelines all alone, watching the clusters of matches making lots of noise. The clacking and yakking about dates and times surrounding them. She continued on out—even as she passed the teary face of the anorexic girl, and even as she heard 098 calling after her. His speech sounded garbled, and Nicki suspected he was only squeezing out his words between bites, and more bites, of cake.

"Are you okay with last minute? Can we leave it like that? How about that? How about I just call you on the spur of the moment? Maybe if you tell me where you live, I can just drop by when I have some time. Would that work? Let's do that. I really want to see you. So how about this? Someday when you least expect it I could just show up and ring your bell. Would that be okay? Hey, wait. 084. Wait, wait up. What do you think about that?"

On the Sixth Date of Hanukkah

"Don't you think that people really don't give each other enough of a chance?" asked the small, square accountant facing Nicki on the small, square velveteen couch in the corner of the library in the back of Le Nosh, the quaint coffee house that was hosting the HastyDate event.

"Don't you think that one should try to see past physical appearance, past the concept of chemistry, and instead concentrate on the mutual goals of lifelong friendship, trust and sharing one's life? Don't you think people put way too much emphasis on looks? Don't you think so? Tell me, Nicki. A pretty name. That is your name, isn't it? I've spent so many years working, Nicki, and now I'm comfortable. I'm ready. I can put all that aside. I'm ready to fully give of myself. What are you looking for in a soul mate? And tell me, Nicki, do you have the patience to stick by somebody until the chemistry comes? I know this is a lot to ask and even more to have to answer in just eight minutes."

"Hey, don't worry about it. I'll do my best!" Nicki looked at her watch. "Even though time flies and all that." She really didn't know what to say to the guy, but was thankful two out of the eight minutes were already gone.

"Eight minutes just isn't enough," said the small square man who, Nicki thought sadly, resembled a eunuch.

And sometimes it was eight too many. *Oy*. Nicki smiled at him. She didn't want to be mean or anything, it was just so incredibly *yechy* being in this position, being forced to look at this man like he could possibly turn out to be somebody. Depending on what was going on, eight minutes could be a very, very long time.

HastyDate had guaranteed eight eight-minute dates. The women remained seated in different spots around the room, and every eight minutes the leader blew a whistle and the men rotated to talk with another woman. You were given a number and a scorecard—hey, what was with these events and scorecards? And then having to wait and see if the people you wrote down also wrote you! If you wanted to go out with someone, you always got a chance to talk to them at the event. So why the hell didn't the two people just make a date and go? What? You needed to write it down and wait to see who came in? What was it? A horse race?

Nicki didn't even bother to look at this guy's name, or number for that matter. She was just babbling away until the whistle would blow and this date would be up. The hastier the better, she thought, while wondering if, perhaps, the eunuch and that anorexic might be a match. Nicki figured that right about now she probably felt just as crummy as any woman who had ever come up to her after an event and complained. She always used to say something cheerful and hopeful; it was easy for her to be nice when afterwards she got to shrug it all off. Because after her events she'd just call Mark to come meet her. What would he say if he could see her now?

★ ★ ★

"So how did you two meet?" Mark asked Bernie and Ida. Grandma Ida had brought potato latkes to the hospital. Tonight Nicki's whole family was there. Mark thought she had sounded so cute when she said that she'd peeled the potatoes herself, no Manischewitz mix for her! She was never one to just add water, she told him. Her latkes were the real deal, and her Nickala's favorite. Was it too crazy to think the smell of the food, the aroma, the warmth from the family, from her own oven, yet, might actually reach her granddaughter? Mark listened to Ida, smiling on the outside while his heart broke on the inside.

"Well," said Bernie, his plate piled high with the flattened, fried-potato pancakes. "I worshiped Ida, here, from afar."

"Ooh, Grandpa," said Cyd. "That is *so* romantic. Did you worship me from afar, too?" she asked her husband.

"Yeah, from as afar across the selling floor as I could be until you caught me," said Jonathan, who owned the women's clothing store where Cyd had once worked as a salesperson.

"You caught *me*," said Cyd.

"I don't care who caught who, Mark wants to hear the story," said Mal.

"So don't you interrupt," said Helene.

"I'm not interrupting," said Mal. "I was just saying."

"So don't say," all three women said together.

Mark laughed. He had gotten to know the Hellers better than he'd ever expected in the past week. Well, almost. Almost a week. Not quite. But quite a week.

"I won a beauty contest in Roumania when I was eighteen years old," said Ida. "You should have seen me," she said to Mark. "I was really something in those days. My hair so long, dark, curly...much like Nicki's and—"

"I was telling the story," said Bernie.

"So tell it!" Ida, Helene and Cyd spoke in unison like they were trained to come in on cue.

"So Ida, here, was engaged to somebody else," he said.

"I never knew that, Grandma. You never told me that, Ma."

"What was to tell? Just listen to your grandfather."

"I was working as an apprentice barber at that time, and she would walk by the shop every day around lunchtime, and I couldn't take my eyes off of her—what a beauty! And my father used to say, 'What are you looking so much? A girl like that will never give a second look to the likes of you!' But then, as luck would have it, Ida caught her fiancé cheating."

"You're kidding!" said Cyd.

"And in *those* days! A very big scandal," said Helene.

"Oh," said Ida. "It was. It was a very big deal. A real big *gedillah*," she said. "Anyway, I was lucky to get rid of that louse before we tied the knot, believe me!"

"So how'd you snag her, Grandpa B?" asked Jonathan.

"I pursued her and pursued her until she paid attention to me, and then finally I married her. Twice! First in Europe by a rabbi. But your grandmother, here, applied for a visa under her single name, so when we came over we got married again on the boat!"

"Our story is much less glamorous, right, Mal?" said Helene, going over to light the menorah. It had become her unofficial job. Only two candles left. "We met on the subway."

"The L train," said Mal. "It takes forever from Union Square to Brooklyn. By the time we got to Sutter Avenue, I think we were engaged!"

Mark laughed along with everyone else. It all sounded so easy. Why hadn't it been so easy with him and Nic? He didn't understand. He felt Ida's eyes on him, like she saw something, or knew something he didn't. He glanced over at Nicki. What are you thinking about during all this, Nic? What's going on in your mind?

★ ★ ★

Each eight-minute date seemed like an eternity. One guy was worse than the next. It used to be so easy. Nicki would just live her life and in her travels she'd meet somebody and *bam!* A relationship. Not like this. Nicki couldn't believe how hard it was just to meet someone! Fortunately, the whistle blew, but her heart dropped when the next guy sat down.

"So my name is Joshua and I'm your HastyDate. My number is 4598 in case you want to write me down after. I hope you'll write me down after. Let me tell you about myself. I really like my job. I love what I do. Or what I did." Joshua paused. "I'm a mailman."

And the whistle blew…

"I voted Republican in the last few elections," the darkhaired, olive-skinned guy with the glint in his eyes told an intensely leaning-to-the-left Nicki. "I believe in everyone's right to own handguns."

"Do you, uh, have a, a handgun?" asked Nicki, whose heart had sunk, yet again, once he started talking, initially having found some attraction to his dark, swarthy looks.

"*A* gun?" The guy burst out laughing. "I have *five* guns."

"*Five guns?*" Nicki screamed and then got quiet, scared even. The light of the candle flickered, illuminating the glint in his dark eyes. In this new light he resembled a terrorist. Just to clarify, she whispered, "You have *five guns*?"

"This is a problem for you? Why? What do you think I'm going to do? Shoot you?"

And the whistle blew…

"So my theory is that the reason men and women can't connect is that the only thing men are really searching for is that warm, fuzzy place where no one will ever bother them. Somewhere that feels much like it felt when you were in the womb. Now even though I'm a man, I feel I am man enough to admit this, and man enough to tell you…."

Nicki took those eight minutes to tune out and recap her day of work. Albert's event was coming together unbelievably well. Plan B was moving forward, thank God, because Plan A was falling apart here at the seams. Today Nicki had cemented everything with the newspaper, radio and TV stations in Menorahville, all the local syndicates, and the hype was big! It was fast becoming the hottest talk around town, and getting so much attention that everyone wanted to be that lucky Jewish gal who was crowned the Ice Princess.

Nicki was psyched when she called to give Albert the news, but felt somewhat disappointed that his reaction had not matched her own enthusiasm. She guessed he was just so humble and sincere in his desire for a bride that he didn't get carried away by the bells and whistles. But Nicki had pulled out all the stops, because the big news was that the event was going to be televised.

Albert was coming by tomorrow to put his pen to paper. It was all systems go! And as the whistle blew and Nicki faced her next HastyDate she only wished she was already gone.

On the Seventh Date of Hanukkah

"Okay, thanks, Mom… No…. I don't know what to tell you," Helene said into the hospital phone. Ida had called four times already and it wasn't even three o'clock. "All right… I will… Yes… As soon as anything changes… Me, too… Tell Pop we love him."

Mal watched his wife as she spoke. This was not the way it was supposed to be. Not at his age. At his age your parents were lying in the hospital bed, and you were on the phone consoling your children. Not the other way around.

"What'd she have to say?" asked Mal, when she hung up. Could either of them ever have imagined anything this devastating?

"Cyd dropped the kids off and went to do errands. Jonathan's at work. Pop took Bandit for a walk."

Today was a week. Seven days. When it was just a day, a few days, Mal could almost take it. But a week. A week could turn into two, into a month, into a year. Years.

"He was just talking, Helene," said Mal, reaching his hand across and placing it on top of his wife's. "The doctor." He had told them this morning that a coma did not usually last more than a few weeks, but was concerned that one had already passed. And if she did not come out of it, Nicki could lapse into a...what did he call it? A persistent vegetative state.

"No bedside manner to speak of," said Helene as she wiped the tears from her eyes.

Mal shook his head, silently agreeing. The clinical way that the doctor had told them Nicki should have woken up by now seemed heartless. Mal had always found a way to take care of his girls. What in the world could he possibly do now?

Bandit pulled Nicki as she held on to his leash, making their way west on Miracle Mile, an area strikingly similar to New York's meat-packing district. What better place to hold Smooch&Pooch, an event tailor-made for singles with pets. From down the block Bandit could already sniff out his cronies, and was rushing to the door as fast as his four legs would carry him.

It was so dark when Nicki entered the club, she could hardly see which way to go, but she immediately overheard two guys talking.

"Hey, man, want a toke?"

"Hey, dude, I'm already high!"

She sincerely hoped this would not be indicative of the rest of the night's prospects. Catching the eye of the bartender who had already spotted Bandit, Nicki was pointed in the direction of an alcove with long rows of white crystal beads as a curtain. Bandit charged ahead of her, bringing them both to the other side of the beads. It was a whole new world. And not such a small one, after all! Two gigantic, stuffed, battery-operated boxers barked on cue at their entrance, and sat on either side of a curly haired woman with glasses. Nicki handed her a piece of *gelt*.

"This is a high-price event because it's so specialized," the woman said, pushing the piece of *gelt* over to the side, opening her palm on the table and indicating that she wanted more.

"Okay," said Nicki. "How much?" She dug into her purse to locate more chocolate coins. She hoped she had some left to spend and hadn't eaten it all. This *gelt* business was the best, not to mention a great little snack to have on hand.

"Three," said the woman, her palm still open. Nicki looked at the sign next to the woman's hand: "I read Palms and Paws—Pet Psychic—So what, they don't talk! You still can know!"

Nicki handed over three pieces, hoping she'd have enough *gelt* to get her through tomorrow. Tomorrow was the eighth day and then Hanukkah would end. But, she was told, not for long, because in Menorahville it would always begin again, and with the new beginning she would receive a whole new batch of *gelt*. It kind of reminded her of that Club Med vacation she went on with Mark where they gave you beads to spend instead of money. Only, when that week was over, you got out of Club Med and went home.

"The pet's not free. Three for you and three for him," said the ticket taker–pet psychic, while Nicki looked over at Bandit who, as per usual, was surrounded by an adoring group of dogs, causing Nicki to wonder about the possibility of changing species.

She left Bandit to mingle as she walked away to get a drink. Cubes of ice floated in a big crystal bowl that was filled with pink La Pooch punch! She poured some into a pink glass with *Smooch&Pooch* scrawled across it in big, black script.

"Cute party favor, don't you think?" said the young girl next to her, refilling her glass. "Enjoy it, because I think that's about the only thing you'll get to take home with you tonight!"

Nicki surveyed the room and to her immense disappointment she saw nothing but women. Women sitting alone with other women because all of their dogs had run off together. Women trying to have fun with each other while their pooches chewed up the town!

"Why am I not surprised?" said Nicki, who in spite of herself really was. She took a seat at a nearby table and scanned the room. Her eyes stopped at Jeanine, the strawberry blonde from the park, the one who must have been right when she told Nicki that men didn't want the responsibility of a dog, the one who planned to play hard to get. Judging by the crowd it wasn't a game she'd get to play.

"Welcome, welcome... *Ladies!*" said a tall, affable blond man in a striped blue-and-white polo shirt. "We're so glad you came. As I look around I'd have to say that while *you* may not meet someone, tonight, your dog definitely will!" He turned to look at his partner, a female version of him, dressed almost identically in a matching blue-and-white polo. She smiled with the slightly smug look of someone that wasn't stuck here, a look that Nicki was coming to recognize all too readily.

"If you'd like, we can play the ice-breaker game, anyway. It will help you to make friends with the other women, and if I were you I'd think that would be a pretty good idea."

The women looked at each other as the striped-polo-shirted pair slipped in and around the crowd distributing two sheets of paper. One contained a bunch of questions and the other had a big square that resembled a tic-tac-toe game. Nicki took a pencil and the two sheets of paper, noting that however this might be disguised, she was still receiving another scorecard.

"Now I want you to walk up to people and ask them these questions. Put an *X* when you get a yes and an *O* when you get a no. For every tic-tac-toe you make, you'll see why you ladies aren't in relationships! Just kidding!" He pressed his tongue against his cheek before he looked back at the crowd. "Seriously, for every tic-tac-toe you make you'll get another ticket to enter the raffle! The more tickets, the more chances you'll have of winning wonderful prizes. Maybe not the one you want, but let's be honest here, are you really in a position to be so picky? Okay… Go ask!"

The women began rotating around one another in circles. Questions, laughter, questions, squeals, questions, questions, and snorts of indignation jumped back and forth and up and about the room. Nicki stayed put at the table. She hadn't moved once she'd read the questions:

Does your dog have a personal trainer?
Does your dog sleep in your bed?
Does your dog stay in the room when you have sex?
Did a relationship ever end over your dog?
Do you take your dog on vacations?
Does your dog have better outfits than you do?
Do you think you look like your dog?

The women around Nicki were hysterical with laughter. She was surprised to see that even Jeanine and her group of girls were having one helluva time. But this was not the life Nicki wanted. She'd rather be alone, working, than to be here for one more second. She left her tic-tac-toe sheet on the table along with her empty Smooch&Pooch glass, before grabbing Bandit from his tête-à-tête with a cockapoo and marching them both to the door.

"What about the raffle? You don't want to miss the raffle, do you?" the female polo shirt called to Nicki when she saw her heading out. "We have an all-inclusive spa weekend for you and your dog at Canine Ranch!"

Nicki didn't care. She opened her date book, crossing out Smooch&Pooch and looking to the event written down under it. This one *had* to be better. She promised herself she would try absolutely everything before leaving it up to fate.

Nicki hailed a cab to take her to Breakfast and Bed, a cooking class for singles. Bandit jumped in the back. As sad as he was to leave, Bandit always knew there was a new sniff at the end of every block. Nicki instructed the cabbie where to go and was met with a snort.

"What day is this?" he said, "The seventh candle? Seven days doth not a week make in Menorahville. But almost."

"So you remember me!" said Nicki, when she looked up and saw it was the same cabbie she had driven with on her first day here. "I made such a great impression?"

"Well, that, and…" Alan Cohen continued driving while he spoke, making eye contact with Nicki in his rearview mirror. "Your voice. That sound of panic! And now the cooking class. Everyone saves that event for last. Like the men here really want to learn how to cook! But you'll try anything, right? Everyone goes through the same things as you for a while, but then it goes away, you know. You get used to being here. Alone. You settle in and, to be honest, once you do, it's really not so bad."

They stopped at a red light and he turned around to face Nicki. The whiff of his flannel shirt practically knocked her out. She didn't know how long he'd been settled in, but one thing he hadn't settled into doing was his laundry.

"I'm getting out of here," said Nicki, hanging all her hopes on Plan B—on The Ice Princess event tomorrow. "Tomorrow. I will. I know it."

"Oh, yeah?" said Alan, and seizing his chance, jumped out of the front of the cab and into the back with Nicki. "Ya sure you don't want to go out tonight with me? I'll be your date. The longer you stay here, the better I'll look. Besides, I like you feisty Brooklyn girls."

Nicki looked at him with a combination of low-grade fear and incredulity. She had never told him where she was from!

"Midwood section," Alan pointed to himself. "Takes one to know one!" he said, answering her nonverbal question.

The light turned green and all the cars behind them started honking.

"Wait," said Alan, getting out to return to the front.

Nicki didn't. With Bandit in her arms she quickly unlatched the cab door and ran out into the traffic, running the rest of the way down the block and up to the cooking class that was already in progress.

"*Bonjour!* You are in luck! We have one oven left," said the French cooking teacher, dressed in yellow and wearing a head piece in the shape of a menorah with seven bulbs on top of her head all aglow. "Won't you join us, *s'il vous plaît?*"

In every nook in every corner of every cozy kitchen was a woman. Not a man to be found. Nicki, who only liked to make reservations, lost the little interest she had had. "What are you making tonight?" she asked, stalling a moment, trying to be polite.

"A chocolate soufflé!"

"Sorry. I'm allergic," she responded, turning on her heel, somewhat regretting her choice. Chocolate soufflé was among her favorites. But she suddenly realized the best place of all to meet someone. Sorry she hadn't thought of it earlier, Nicki made a dash for the subway, hoping she wasn't too late.

She and Bandit flew through the closing doors of an 8 train headed uptown. They got off at 86th, then ran down the block through the crowd to Latke Lane, where Nicki raced up the steps to the synagogue just in time for the closing minutes of the rabbi's commitment class.

"We will meet again next week," he said, "and we hope that the attendance is better than tonight."

Nicki was breathless when she arrived and didn't know what he meant, because she could feel that the place was full.

She could feel the heat of bodies all around her. But now, after catching her breath and looking around the sanctuary, she saw there was not a man to be found.

"Perhaps if we tell them they can watch the game when we meet we might attract a few good men?" The rabbi, trying to be upbeat, laughed at his attempt, but Nicki no longer found any of this to be a laughing matter. It was hard to really click with someone, it was hard to get something going and it was harder still to sustain it. But the women kept showing up. The women tried. The women wanted it. And the men, sadly, were absent. The men were unavailable—they simply did not follow through.

Nicki turned and saw a group she sort of recognized. She overheard them say they were going out for dinner. Nicki thought she should go up to them—she knew she'd be welcome to join—but something stopped her. It was more than that she'd be lousy company. She felt she was losing her faith and her ability to remain upbeat...no matter what. That was always one of her strongest assets. She decided maybe it was best to be alone. She thought she'd sneak off and wait for everyone to leave, because she wanted to linger. It was time Nicki made time for a little self-examination. And she wanted to pray.

On the Eighth Date of Hanukkah

Subject: The Ice Princess Event Coverage
Date: The Eighth Candle
Send To: assignmentdesk@foxynews8.menorahville.orb,
assignmentdesk@vh8.menorahville.orb,
lifestyleseditor@dailycandle.menorahville.orb,
dailydateshow@wdate8radio.menorahville.orb
From: nicki_heller@soul-o.menorahville.orb
Hi there!
It is so exciting that just about every major outlet in Menorahville has agreed to cover tonight's event. Your coverage is sure to put Menorahville on the map (whatever map *that* is) and, without a doubt, the terrific promo work you've done all week will get every eligible female down to the event where Albert is certain, tonight, to crown one his Ice Princess!
Here's the lowdown:
6:00 PM   Arrive at venue for setup
7:30 PM   The women arrive

8:00 PM   Albert's arrival
8:15 PM   Let the dance begin
10:00 PM   Albert crowns his Jewish princess
I'm sure Albert and his newly betrothed will be happy to hold interviews tomorrow before they leave to plan their wedding—an event you might even get to cover if you can get out of here. Background info on Albert is attached. Tonight will be a miracle, and a *mazel tov*!
Looking forward!
Nicki Heller
Event Planner
Single Not Soul-O

Nicki gave her office/apartment a final once-over before she left for the event. She needed to take the Ice Princess file with her so she'd have it in her bag, just in case she was instantly swooped back home to New York. She had no idea how it worked, and thought maybe it would be like that old TV show *Bewitched,* where Samantha used to wiggle her nose and wind up in an alternative universe, or in the office of Dr. Bombay. Nicki didn't know how she had gotten here, so she didn't know how she'd get back. Albert had called earlier to apologize for not coming by and signing, but they'd just do it later. She knew everything would be okay.

Plan B was going to work! She had heard it last night—at the synagogue. Nicki had felt the communication as strongly as if she was receiving instruction for a surefire plan. Albert's wedding was the thing that would surely bring her home.

"I just gave her a new name," explained Bernie that morning when he walked the rabbi out of Nicki's hospital room, just as Helene and Ida were coming in. "I did it last night, and he just came and said the prayers and now it's official."
Bernie had had a bad feeling last night, a very bad one. He

believed he could feel Nicki. He could almost feel her coming to them, and then, just like that, he could feel her drifting away. And he was really feeling it, no kidding. Last night when it was time to go home, he couldn't move. Literally couldn't budge. Everyone said nothing was different, Nicki was just the same, but he could feel her sliding, lower than low, and he stayed and slept in the cot next to her bed just so she'd know she wasn't alone.

"So what kind of name did you give?" asked Ida, who had brought a very special eighth-day-of-Hanukkah treat for her granddaughter. As she talked to her husband she placed the big Tupperware on the movable tray that swung across Nicki's bed. It was filled to the brim with dozens of delicious little *sufganiyot,* the holiday's special jelly doughnuts. The doughnuts were still warm, and the sweet scent of the sugar and jam filled the room.

"I gave her a new Hebrew name," said Bernie. "I changed it. The rabbi did a special favor for me to come here."

"What are you talking about, Pop?" asked Helene.

"She wasn't named for anybody, Helene," said Bernie. "She was *supposed* to be named after someone so there would be a connection—a bond. Between her soul and the deceased. Then Nicki would have a guardian angel. But you named whatever you wanted—this one you named like a gentile, and the other one you give a name after a Hollywood starlet. And look at her." Bernie stared at the silent, still sleeping Nicki. "She has no one to look after her from beyond. She has nothing. *Gornisht!*"

Ida turned away from her husband and her daughter, and instead reached inside the Tupperware and took a doughnut.

"Pop." Helene dried her eyes before she spoke to her father. "We gave each of the girls a Hebrew name we thought meant something nice. Nicki's name is *Naamah.*"

"And it means bird and she's flying away, Helene. Listen,

listen to me," said Bernie. *Oy,* why couldn't he keep his big mouth shut? He didn't want to make things worse. "The rabbi came special, and we gave her another name. A new name! *Nesia.* It means miracle of God. Today is the eighth day of Hanukkah. The oil made light for eight days. It was a miracle. And today will be Nicki's miracle. *Nesia Naamah.* The miracle of God, our bird will fly home."

Nicki and Bandit entered Central Park from the south, making their way to Candelabra, the club that was holding the event and was located where the Boathouse Restaurant should've been. She had already been to the venue earlier today to ensure that it would be fabulouso. Albert had allowed Nicki to hire the best party decor team in Menorahville and they promised to transform Candelabra into something that would be nothing short of spectacular. The dance would be held inside. Since it was warm enough outside, the party people said that they would design something thematic, so the crowning ceremony could take place out on the lake.

Nicki had wanted to be involved in every detail, but Albert insisted she just stay on the local publicity, working on getting the girls down and playing up the whole princess thing to entice any woman attending to two-step her way with Albert back to Alaska. All this just to bring home a Jewish bride. Nicki wondered what he'd do for the wedding!

As Nicki and Bandit marched along the path in the park to Candelabra, a couple of pieces kind of came together. It was like when you did a jigsaw puzzle and you got up for a second and found you'd been sitting on the one piece you were looking for. Last night had been intense. She'd stayed behind to pray and, well, that was intense enough. But on the seat of the pew was a flier left behind from the commitment workshop. And on it was a line in italic. A quote, from an old Talmudic scholar, and it read:

"He whose face does not shine will discover that his soul is also immersed in darkness."

Nicki didn't know how somebody else might interpret that. But she knew what it meant to her. Nicki had been living in darkness. While she always felt she was a bright light, she only shone because of how she reflected off those around her. She had been lucky to have her family, and she was seeing, now more than ever, how lucky she was to have Mark. But now her light was going out. It was growing dimmer, fading. Nicki was alone, without, and it felt like she was going to have to stay that way unless she could escape Menorahville.

Bandit barked as he ran through the little courtyard leading to the front door of the restaurant. It was propped open by a big, black trunk as one of the camera crews unloaded their equipment. With Bandit leading the way, Nicki stepped inside Candelabra and shrieked with joy as she looked about, making her way through the glorious Winter Wonderland that had truly transformed the club. In the center of the room was a dance floor, and behind it, huge and glowing, was a giant floor-to-ceiling menorah, glittering, a vision in translucent little lights. The biggest lights, on top, were the eight days of Hanukkah, all glowing and sparkling. A fake-snow machine blew in the background, both indoors and out, and snowflakes would fall throughout the night. White candles were burning everywhere.

But the best was when she walked outside. The lake had been frozen over and glimmering on the glossy ice was a stairway that led up to a scaffold, all of lit in luminous white lights. Hanging high above the platform was the signage on a sheath of white silk with *The Ice Princess* in silver script. This was where the crowning ceremony would take place;

it was glorious, seductive. Looking at it, she prayed Albert would find his mate…so she could get back to hers.

Nicki stepped on the ice to walk towards it. The fake snow made it sticky enough that she didn't slide.

"So what do you think?" asked Albert.

Lost in wonder, Nicki jumped at the sound of his voice, causing her to slip and almost fall.

"Don't worry, I'm okay," said Nicki, taking her hand back from Albert, who had grabbed it to catch her. "Wow! Look at you," she said, looking up to see plain old Albert also transformed—into *some*body's prince. In a black tuxedo with the icy radiance of white behind him, he was a vision that was sure to melt some girl's heart.

"You look great, too," he said, pointing to her outfit, her usual outfit. Nicki looked down to see what color she had on today. Red. She opened her bag and pulled out a contract.

"This is everything we talked about," she said as she undid the little clips of a manila envelope, taking out what she needed to hand over to Albert.

"What is this?" he asked before he saw his copy of a typewritten agreement. "Oh."

"Okay?" asked Nicki. "It's pretty direct. No hidden messages." Nicki laughed. She was delirious. Plan B…finally! And on the dotted line.

Albert took a second to give the document a once-over. Nicki, someone not crazy about silence to begin with, filled it in.

"It just says that I, Nicki Heller, Single Not Soul-O, formulated the idea and created the entire concept for the event, The Ice Princess. I secured Orbit Dance and Space Eight, the team that decorated this place." As if on cue Nicki and Albert both stopped to take a look around—it was just that breathtaking. "And let me tell you, Albert, this event's going to be *huge,* because I totally hyped it and got tons of press."

"Well," said Albert. "You sure did a bang-up job of everything, too. I really think you are one terrific event planner and I am very grateful for everything you have done for me, Nicki." He folded the agreement in thirds and placed it in the inside pocket of his tux. Then he turned to walk away, causing Nicki to feel something in her gut, something like a small kick in the stomach, but thankfully Albert turned back.

"Truly," he said, checking his watch. "Now that I see everything is under control I'll just go away until eight. Thank you." And then, for real, he turned and walked away.

"Wait a minute!" called Nicki as she cautiously ran a few feet to catch up to him. "The contract."

"What about it? It looks fine," said Albert.

"Well, I did my part, and I need you to sign it, too, so I know that you're going to do yours."

He stood and stared, almost quizzically.

"All the stuff you said you were going to do for me, Albert." Forget her stomach, Nicki was now kicking *herself*. She should have taken care of this contract before she did *anything*. Had she been snowed? Would Albert really…? Nah. For God's sake she met him at synagogue! "I need it in writing, Albert. I'm on your ticket out of here with you and your bride. I plan the wedding, and I get paid. For real."

Albert smiled. A great big happy one. "Sure, Nicki."

Whew!

"Great, so…" she reached into her bag and pulled out a pen.

"Nicki, come on. You're making me really, really uncomfortable here. You don't have to act like some aggressive New York girl. We're in Menorahville. We made an agreement. We can just shake on it. That's how they do things in Alaska." But he stood still without even extending his hand.

"No one does it that way, Albert. Who are you kidding? Not in New York, not in Alaska and definitely not in Menorahville."

"Look. I want to meet someone tonight. You've done a great job—I think it'll happen. I have plenty of money. I *know* I'm going to be planning a wedding. Okay?" He winked when he said that. "Just chill till later, okay?" And before she could answer he was gone.

Nicki tried to stay cool. And she might even have tried to "chill" till later if not for Bandit chasing after Albert and barking his head off. Still Nicki tried to stay calm. She took a deep breath in and let another one out. There would be a tomorrow, the sun would come out. Nicki only hoped she wouldn't be squinting at it from Menorahville. Forget that. Bandit was barking because Bandit knew! And in her gut, so did she: she had to get to Albert and fix this before it was too late.

"I have never seen such a beautiful group of women!" Reba's energetic voice over the mike reached the lake, loud and clear. "Give yourselves a big hand, ladies, for looking so gorgeous and coming down here tonight. Let's hear it!"

Judging by the sound of the applause before the music began Nicki thought it was a good turnout. Her spirits lifted, she raced across the lake, up the terrace steps and into the club, only to be knocked out by what she saw. So many women. Stunning, elegant. Dressed up for the ball. Cinderellas on ice!

"Now, ladies, remember when you dance that you get to be led! And I can assure you, Prince Albert is ready to lead!" Reba was excited and animated, her brown hair and blue satin dress shimmering in the lights. "You only have to follow, and I'm going to show you a basic waltz step that will have you gliding all over this dance floor!"

With everyone dancing it was impossible for Nicki to get across the room; it seemed faster just to waltz her way there. Bandit was her partner as her thoughts kept time to the music. When she was almost there, Nicki was intercepted by a waiter handing her a drink with a silver umbrella from his tray. She took a few gulps—boy, was it strong—and quietly slunk her way over to where Albert was giving an interview.

Looking straight into the camera, Albert didn't see Nicki sneaking up from behind. But as she did she saw that the logo on the microphone held by the interviewer did not belong to any of the local syndicates that she had booked. In fact, it said ABC…7!

"Five, four, three, two, one… Action!"

"Good evening, and welcome to the debut of *The Ice Princess* coming to you live from…well, let's not get into *that* right now. Tonight I'm proud to introduce Albert Aronson, an Alaskan entrepreneur who is here to crown the Ice Princess! Tell us, Albert. How do you feel?"

Nicki stood in the back, unseen, unheard, and anxious to hear Albert speak. She was suddenly too stunned to speak herself.

"I can't believe I was picked to star in ABC's newest reality show, *The Ice Princess!* I'm very, very honored. And grateful. First, I must thank the network. Look around, you guys really did a wonderful job with this club. Of course, I guess that's what happens when you work with a real budget." He chuckled. "I feel very strongly that my bride is here tonight, and in just a few minutes I will go out there to find the woman to sweep off her feet and fly to Alaska. And yes, of course we will be happy to have you throw us our wedding and telecast it live. I can't think of anything more romantic," he finished, a teardrop dripping down and freezing under his eye.

Nicki felt hot. She felt cold. She felt humiliated, stuck, used, betrayed. She, she, she….

"Tell us, Albert," said Buddy, the host of the show, who looked incredibly familiar to Nicki. "I'm sure the folks back home are dying to know just how this *unbelievable* whirlwind of a story, this brave and brilliant idea, got to the network's development folks… from *here*."

Albert's white teeth glistened under the camera lights when he smiled, unashamedly, and said, "I think a stranger overheard me talking someplace and must have phoned it in! Who knows? But here you are, here I am. I'm ready for love, Buddy, so let's get this show on the road!"

Buddy ushered Albert away. This Buddy who looked uncannily familiar, who looked almost identical to, oh no…wait! Identical to *Jay?* Her ex? When had Jay become a reality TV show host? Last thing she knew about Jay, he was, well…Nicki couldn't think about that right now. She couldn't think about anything that would distract her. She really tried to focus as she ran after them, but she kept losing them in the crowd. Nicki's head hurt, she kept losing her footing—that drink…she felt woozy. She just kept falling, falling and falling, even though she was trying so hard, trying so very hard just to find Albert on the dance floor, but she couldn't keep going. She kept trying, but Nicki was tired. So very, very tired.

"She looks pale, Ma. Ohmygod, I'm scared." Cyd started crying, as did Helene. Helene had been strong but she couldn't take it anymore. Her two grandsons sat on the floor in the hospital quietly playing Centipede with her son-in-law. They were all there. They had said the Hanukkah prayers, lit the eighth candle, eaten the jelly doughnuts and waited. And now it felt like something was happening. And it was not, by any means, anything good.

Helene held on to Cyd, whose right hand held tightly onto Mal's. Bernie and Ida held each other, and Mark sat next to Nicki on the bed, waiting, watching and wanting, while stroking the wet strands of hair off her damp face.

Bandit licked Nicki's face to wake her up. Where had she fallen to? She stood shakily and he led her outside just in time to see Buddy up on the scaffold handing Albert a diamond tiara to place on a blonde. A cute, curvy petite one who looked liked she really dug all of this attention, if not Albert.

"Stop," cried Nicki from the terrace of Candelabra, trying hard to get to them before the tiara hit the blonde's head. "Stop. Stop. Wait!"

All eyes turned to Nicki, who couldn't get there fast enough. Pulling an empty drink tray out of the hands of a nearby waiter, she ran down the steps to the lake, sat down on the tray, and holding onto Bandit's leash, let him pull her like he was competing in a championship dogsled race.

Plowing across the ice, the fake snow flying in every direction, the two of them attracted enough attention for everything to stop cold as Nicki approached the stairway she knew would not be leading to heaven. She bounded up the stairs, two steps at a time, ran across the platform and grabbed the tiara out of Albert's hand, as the two of them came face-to-face.

"How could you do this? How could you betray me like this? You made a commitment. You gave me your word, Albert. How could you? I stood by you. I did. I did."

Albert did not flinch. And with all the innocence of a lamb he said, "I did what was best for me. And now, Nicki, I don't need you."

She let the words land. She watched them fall out of his mouth like Scrabble letters and arrange themselves on and around all the little glass lights that lit up the scaffold. Except that as they fell, they weren't falling out of Albert's mouth. They were falling out of *his.* The other guy. The host. The Buddy. The other betrayer. The real one. Jay. Jay. They were falling from the mouth of Jay.

They fell around the tiara and the microphones and the cameras. She saw them. She saw them fall down to the frozen lake. Letters that formed words. A N D N O W N I C K I I D O N T N E E D Y O U. Hurtful letters falling onto

Bandit's leash, her pashmina, her dreams. Falling, landing hard. Accumulating. Like the fake snow.

A
N
D
N
O
W
N
I
C
K
I
I
D
O
N
T
N
E
E
D
Y
O
U

And then more letters arranged themselves inside her head.

B
A
S
T
A
R
D

She had kept it a secret all these years. She would never admit it could happen. A thing like that should never happen. Never. Not to anyone. And not to her. Not to Nicki. But it had. It had happened, but since she never told any one after a while she could almost believe it never had. Nicki walked up to Jay with a rage she had suppressed all this time and went to slap him, but he was quick and grabbed both her hands, holding them hard.

"Let go!" she shouted to Jay. "Let go!"

And then Nicki heard Ida. Her grandma Ida, Ida the only one who knew. The only one who had ever known. Ida, too, knew the pain of betrayal, but she had gotten through it. She had met Bernie. She had let herself love again. Why couldn't Nicki?

"Let go of it," Ida would tell her granddaughter. "Just let go."

But Nicki wouldn't let go. She would not let go.

"Nickala, my Nickala, can you hear me?" Ida said between sobs. "Don't let go, you hear? Don't let go!"

Nicki had held on to it. For years. Since the day she had found out. Her thirtieth birthday, she even got home that night early, and when she walked through the door Jay announced he was through. He had had it. He had met someone else. At The Children's Place. In the mall. In New Jersey. Buying Christmas clothes for her kid. A widow. In the neighborhood. Yes, it was her. That blonde. The cute, curvy petite one. A woman alone who needed a man. A woman who needed Jay.

"Listen, Nicki," said Jay, still holding both her hands, holding tight. "I had to move on. I had to let go. I loved you, Nicki, but I didn't feel you needed me. You were always so sure of yourself and me...I couldn't even stay up unless you held me. I couldn't keep needing you like that. It was bad. It was bad for both of us. Forgive me, Nicki. I didn't mean to hurt you. I just had to let go."

And with that, he did. Jay let go of her wrists and Nicki slipped. She slipped on the platform and off the scaffold and fell through the air, the air of the fake snow, the air of princesses, of ice and make-believe, of events and dates and men not to be had.

And as Nicki began falling faster, she was suddenly swept up; she was lifted, and lifted herself, high. She lifted herself higher and higher still, until she flew, and then, suddenly, her eyes opened and Nicki soared. Her path was clear and she was flying, finally free, a bird on her way home. To her nest. Her needs. And her need to need them.

It always boiled down to a moment. An exact moment, a precise second when things changed. But even if the moment seemed small, the change was not. The change was big.

"Hey."

The voice was quiet. Weak. At first Helene looked at Cyd, but it wasn't Cyd who'd spoken. While Mal looked at Ida who looked at Bernie who looked at Jonathan who looked over to the boys, Mark looked straight ahead at a finally awake Nicki.

"Ohmygod," shouted Helene. "Thank God!

"Thank you, thank you, God!"

"Nickala!"

"What's going on here?" Nicki asked.

"Nic!"

"Aunt Nicki!"

"Nesia Naamah!"

"What's going on? It looks like a morgue."

"You're back!"

"Where'd I go?" Nicki asked everyone. Nicki asked Mark. *Mark!*

"Hi," he whispered. He was so choked up that the word, barely formed, blew out in a whisper as he leaned over Nicki and carefully lifted her. He propped her on the pillows, her bandaged head resting gently against them so she could sit up and see. Then, just as carefully, he told her where she had been.

And then came the exact moment, the precise second when whatever was going on, changed. For the longest time Nicki had thought and wondered, she speculated and she had hoped, until now. Now she finally knew.

"So it looks to me like someone never got her first-night-of-Hanukkah gift," Nicki said, staring at Mark. In earnest.

"So it's okay to—" he began. "It's not too soon? You don't think—"

"Don't think you're getting out of this so easy, mister. If I remember, and I actually do, you were going to propose!"

Mark beamed as he reached into his pants pocket and pulled out the black velvet box. Bending down on his left knee, he opened the box on Nicki's right.

"With your family as witnesses…" he began.

Nicki beamed at each of them before she looked back at Mark.

"Nicki Heller, will you be my wife?"

"What took you so long!" she said, extending her hand and her heart as Mark put the ring on her finger and a kiss on her lips. Sweet. Quiet. A hush.

Then, at once, Jonathan and the boys were making a pizza run while everyone else began making plans. Bernie and Ida were planning the engagement party, Cyd was planning the shower, and Helene and Mal were planning the wedding.

But Nicki and Mark remained in the hush, as their only plans were making up for lost time.

CARRIE PILBY'S
NEW YEAR'S RESOLUTION
Caren Lissner

One

A few things that I do are either really strange or completely normal, but I'm not sure which, because I'm too afraid to ask anyone. For instance, I often have a running dialogue in my head during mundane activities. Like when I'm shopping or flipping through the mail: "I wonder what this is. Oh, a letter from my congressman. What's this? Oh, bills. Why do they always come from Delaware?" I'd say these things to a significant other if I had one, but that person might just answer back and throw off the meter and rhyme. Sometimes I worry that the more I become accustomed to my inner dialogue, the more likely it is that when I finally meet someone interesting enough to join me in real-life conversations, he will only seem to be interrupting them. And if I finally do meet the person who is interesting enough to join me in real-life conversations, will *I* seem interesting enough to *him*?

Another strange thing is that when I wake up in the morning, there's always music in my head. Sometimes it's not even a real song—just something from my imagination. I always tell myself I'll make notes on my original ditty later or tape it, but by the time I'm up, I've completely forgotten it.

Maybe I should slide a questionnaire under my neighbors' doors:

PLEASE ANSWER THE FOLLOWING:
Having a running dialogue in one's head and awakening to imaginary songs each day is:
A)   Normal;
B)   Strange;
C)   Normal, but the fact that you are asking me about it is strange.

If the answer is C, are these the kinds of things that people admit only to their lovers? And if I don't have one of those, is it okay that I admit it to you?

Tonight is New Year's Eve and I'm feeling a little lonely. Last year, after escaping the "progressive party" my friend Kara invited me to, I ended up spending the night with a guy named Cy, which was sort of a big deal for me.

At the time, I was nineteen, and I had just graduated from college the previous spring. I skipped three grades in elementary school. You might not know that I am a genius if you met me—a consequence of having one's nose in academics for all of one's young life is slow burnout after graduation. But I still want to talk about things that are important, and sometimes I feel like I'm the only person who does.

Last year, I was trying to adjust to life in New York, and life in general, which was not very easy since I had never actually adjusted to it in college. I excelled at philosophy, art history and chemistry, but was dismal at socializing. I was only fifteen when I started at Harvard. While everyone else was drinking and trying to shed their morals as quickly as possible, I was trying to get straight As just like in high school. Getting good grades wasn't hard. What was hard was trying to figure out how to do the right thing when everyone else was trying their best to do the wrong thing.

I'm not sure what I expected when I moved back to New York after graduation. Maybe I thought people would be older and calmer than in college, or that in a city this big, I'd surely find *some*where to fit in. But I kept meeting people with low intellectual and moral standards, just like in school. Rather than risk further humiliation and frustration, I decided to stay inside my apartment as much as I could. After all, I was never out of place in my apartment and I was tired of feeling like I needed to get drunk or yap about sex constantly to be considered a fun person.

My therapist, Dr. Petrov, refused to see the wisdom of my decision. He came up with a five-point plan last year for me to socialize, go on dates and act more like everyone else. The idea was that I could learn to get along with people who weren't exactly like me. The last part of the plan was that I had to go out for New Year's Eve.

I tried to go out more during the weeks leading up to New Year's. In the process, I learned where I could compromise a little without giving up my personality completely. I also met two people I could actually call friends.

My first friend was Kara. I met her while I was doing temporary legal proofreading around the city. Legal proofing is fun: You get a call at eleven p.m. telling you to rush to some sleepy firm, and you dash to Midtown like a missionary, red pencil in hand, where a harried associate is waiting to shove a five-page brief at you so you can locate errant commas.

You spend the rest of the night staring at the walls, and by morning you've earned a cool hundred bucks. Since my father pays the rent on my West Village apartment (he feels guilty for skipping me in school and making me into a social outcast—and who am I to argue with that?), a hundred bucks a few times a week is fine by me.

Kara, who was a temporary typist there, saw me one night and noticed we were about the same age. All right, she's twenty-six, but everyone else there was at least forty-five. When Kara found out about Dr. Petrov's list, she decided she was going to corrupt me. She dragged me to bars and parties, and I learned that I could adjust to hanging around with people who are different from me, even if I never know the right things to say.

Kara is wild where I'm shy. Kara is loud where I'm quiet. She still hasn't corrupted me completely. I think my reluctance keeps her honest, in a way. Sometimes even people like Kara need a friend who doesn't change *too* much.

I will see Kara today, on the day before New Year's, because I have a legal proofing assignment from eight a.m. to four p.m. Kara is a regular part-timer at the firm now, and she's actually responsible for getting me a lot more temporary legal proofreading assignments than I normally would have.

The other friend I made last year was Cy.

Cy is thirty-one. He has a boyish face, a corny sense of humor, and a smile that can get him a callback for any audition. Which it usually does.

I met him toward the end of the year. He had just moved to my block in the Village after living with his parents in South Jersey since grad school. He and I used to bump into each other around the neighborhood. When I saw him on New Year's Eve—we both happened to be out on our fire escapes, ignoring the rest of the world—he invited me over. And when we got along, it was only too easy to spend the night. This wasn't my usual behavior (maybe Kara *had* corrupted me a little), but I couldn't complain. I liked him a lot: He had a clean-shaven demeanor that seemed from another time, and he reveled in kitschy things like 78-r.p.m. records and musicals and childhood games.

After we dated for about a month—during which time I decided that if I had him and Kara in my life I didn't need anyone else—he helped produce a play Off-Off-Off-Off-Broadway (which is somewhere around Queens).

A month after that, I found out he was into some guy from the play.

Kara told me I was naive.

"You're so naive," she said.

"Why?"

"He's an actor," she said. "He's in New York. He's single. He's thirty-one. He loves the theater…."

"Just because he's in New York, he's single and he loves the theater doesn't mean he's gay," I said.

"I'd agree with you," she said, "except the play he's starring in is called *Queerano de Bergerac.*"

"So what?" I said. "He didn't make up the name."

She looked at me.

"Okay, so he did. But that still doesn't mean anything. So what if he helped stage a play called *Queerano*?"

"*And* he plays Queerano."

"A fine point," I said. "But I thought he liked me."

Kara stepped back, studied me myopically.

"He *did*," she said. "Underneath your prudishness, intractability and extreme sexual repression, you actually have potential."

"Uh—thanks?"

"But Cy hasn't been in New York very long," Kara said. "He's sowing his oats before he has to settle down."

That's the biggest thing I don't understand about society. Why do people "have to" settle down?

Why aren't they born wanting that?

So it's seven-thirty in the morning and I'm walking across Bryant Park toward my über high-paying legal proofreading assignment on New Year's Eve Day, wondering how much better off I am than one year ago. I did meet Kara last year. I did force myself to go out more, and I learned to accept people in my life who were different from me. I stopped judging people by their IQ or where they went to college, especially since there are people who are very smart in ways that I'm not. I also learned that we sometimes get the urge to do things that don't quite make sense. I even have a drink now and then.

But I also got dumped by Cy. When that happened, I regretted leaving my apartment at all. When you finally meet someone who makes you believe that all the things you waited for really do exist—things people told you that you were naive to want—and you find out it's all a lie, how can you ever believe again?

My New Year's resolution this year is to find one person— okay, one guy—in the world who is like me. That shouldn't be too difficult, right?

Two

At eight a.m., I stroll onto the tenth floor of Dickson, Monroe. I'm in the word-processing area, where rows of typists toil into the night inputting changes to documents. Off to the side are a couple of boxy offices where proofreaders can work. When I step into the main room, the night staff is slowly returning to consciousness. Sections of the Sunday *Times* and *Post* lie open on the tables like tired sunbathers. The receptionist rubs her eyes, pushing her fingers into the space beneath her glasses.

A guy walks past me rolling a cart full of empty doughnut boxes from a breakfast meeting, and powdered sugar dances at the bottom. I take a good whiff.

The supervisor, tall Al, looks sleepy, too; he stands up at his desk ostensibly to greet me, but really to stretch. He tells me there's no work right now. The temp agency called me twice to make sure I'd be here on time. But on time for what?

That's why I love this job.

★ ★ ★

I wend my way around the typing stations to the first proofreading room. Inside, Nigel, the overnight proofreader slash actor slash British expat, is packing up his notebooks. I ask him how it's going.

"Two hours of mad work, and then they left me alone," he says. I notice that he has sketched a naked lady on top of a yellow legal pad. He sees me looking and covers it with his sleeve.

I settle into my seat, which faces the wall. Here is what's on my desk to play with: Four sharp pencils. A white legal pad. A naked pink eraser, a bit worn and brown on one end. I collected erasers for one month in second grade, because I wanted to experiment with the viscoelastic and dielectric properties of rubber, but Kenny Meltzer stole them out of my pencil box when I was home with the flu.

Right in the middle of all the supplies is the holy grail: the firm's "face book." Law firms have books full of headshots of the partners and summer associates. Ostensibly it's to tell who's who in a large firm. But really, it's so people who are spending a hundred hours a week at the firm can figure out who to hit on in the building because they're never allowed to leave. The books are also helpful to proofreaders, even though we rarely meet the lawyers. You see, we deface the photos of attorneys who give us problems, the ones whose scribbled corrections and arrows take hours for our weary eyes to decipher. Every boss should be an underling for a week so he can learn how to make it tolerable.

So I flip through the face book, seeking updates. There's only one new comment since I was last here. Someone has added a word-balloon to a lawyer named Janice and written inside of it, "I expect lowly temps to translate my bullshit chicken-scratch." Good show!

Kara is coming in at noon. That's almost four hours from now. But I can be patient—she told me she has big news for me. That could mean anything. It could mean a new boyfriend, or it could mean a pedicure. Everything is dramatic in Kara's world.

I hope it's not a new boyfriend. She's harder to deal with when she's dating someone.

I pick up the white legal pad and one of those fresh pencils and write at the top:

CARRIE PILBY'S NEW YEAR'S RESOLUTION:
   ★★Find someone like me★★

Then I draw a blank. How will I find this someone? I consider the qualities I'm looking for in the mystery person: I want to meet someone who enjoys books as much as parties, who doesn't make excuses for dangerous behavior and who wouldn't cheat on his girlfriend and say, "It's human nature." I'd like to meet someone in New York who sticks by his values, for a change, whatever they are.

On my pad I write:

METHODS:
1. Attend two events—one social and one intellectual—per week.
2. Talk to at least one stranger at each event (preferably male).
3. If one of those male people asks me out, go.

That seems simple enough. But I feel like I need a time limit, so I change "per week" to "every week in January." Two events each week possibly until the end of time sounds a bit daunting. And if my endeavor doesn't look promising by the end of the month, there's always Plan B: Get my father to buy my way into a college undergraduate program. Yes, I know, I graduated from Harvard already, but I'm only twenty years old. I wasn't socially mature enough to handle college back then—only smart enough. Can you imagine how much better I'd do if I entered college again as a freshman, with all of the experience I've gained in the real world so far?

Yeah, me, neither.

I'm getting an early start on my resolution tonight, on New Year's Eve. It's not with Kara, though. Kara has invited me to another "progressive party" where people go to different houses, drinking and eating, but it's pretty much the same party I went to last year that ended with me escaping to (appropriately enough) my fire escape, and meeting up with Cy.

I have no other offers aside from Kara's tonight. So I'm going to do a trial run of my resolution. I will head to a random bar, sit there for at least an hour, and see if I can meet people.

Granted, I hate bars, but they're the main way to meet people in the city, and even people like me who are quiet will sometimes force themselves to go out with friends. Besides, what if I'm missing something? What if I will realize fifteen years from now that I actually love bars, and I regret not going when I was young?

If I could meet someone who also has trouble fitting in, who also enjoys staying inside on New Year's Eve, my life would be fine. But in order to meet that person, I have to go out.

Isn't it ironic?

★ ★ ★

I swivel in my gray office chair. There are still no assignments for me, so I use the time to think about a lot of things.

I think about why, instead of shopping for antiques, old people don't just save what they have when they're born.

I think about why we still say we "ship" things, when we send them by plane or truck.

I think about man's place in the global ecosystem.

I think about what the past tense of *grandstand* is.

At precisely 11:59 a.m., Kara rushes in, out of breath, as I am falling asleep. Behind me, she drops her purse on what was Nigel's desk. I turn around and we face each other in our office chairs.

"Guess what?" she says.

"What?"

"I said, 'Guess.'"

I haven't heard that one since third grade.

Her eyes are shining. She pulls her long, sleek dark hair behind her shoulder. "Mr. DeKuyper called me into his office at the end of the day yesterday." She stops.

"And?" Kara always makes me beg for more.

"He has a job for me. Someone else bailed at the last minute, so he called me. It's apartment-sitting. For all of January, at a huge place on Central Park West!"

There are certain people in this city who get "jobs" that no one else ever hears about—which are more opportunities than jobs, and generally involve "sitting" for something that you'd want anyway, like a house or Jaguar.

"Who's the owner?" I ask.

"You know how some old people have a million friends and no kids, so they travel all over the world?"

"No."

"Well, she's a rich old widow who has a million friends and no kids, so she travels all over the world. She's going to Mexico for all of January. Her name is Judith Sarakin Green."

"Sounds like a writer," I say. "Or a child psychologist."

"No, just a woman with three names." Kara organizes her bags on her desk. With her back to me, she says, "Judith's husband was a partner in the firm before he died. All I have to do is watch her house and move her car around the block once a week. The car's an Oldsmobile from the nineteen-seventies that she's driven, like, sixty miles in her whole life."

"She doesn't keep it in a garage?"

She sighs. "You know how there are certain kinds of rich people who weren't born rich, so they take any opportunity to save a buck?"

I think these are rhetorical questions.

"Oh, we are going to have so much fun!" Kara says.

"We?"

"You'll sleep over once a week," she says. "We'll eat sushi and compare notes on boys. I'm going to stay there overnight to make sure everything's okay. She's got a whirlpool with a skylight, and a library and three huge bedrooms."

"A library?"

"You have such a one-track mind. What's on the paper?"

She means the legal pad on my desk. I reluctantly proffer it. She'll make me show her either way. "It's a list of ways to fulfill my New Year's resolution," I explain. "I'm going to start working on it tonight."

"This is what you're doing instead of coming to the party of the year?"

"I'm still recovering from the party of *last* year."

Kara reads over the list. "Do you really want to meet someone who's *exactly* like you?"

"Not exactly," I say. "But someone who is like me in the right ways. More into books and philosophy than parties." I point to my schedule. "I'm going to go to one intellectual and one social event per week."

"Ooh-la-la," Kara says, handing it back to me. "I know what else you're going to do at least once a week."

"What?"

"Sleep over at Judith Sarakin Green's apartment on Central Park West and eat sushi with me."

"You have such a one-track mind," I say back.

"You'll love it. Think about it. You'll be keeping to your schedule to meet boys. I'm going to try to meet someone, too. Each week we'll have dinner and compare our progress."

That actually could be promising. Suddenly, the new year seems a whole lot brighter.

Three

Before I leave for my date with destiny, otherwise known as my pledge to sit at a bar for at least an hour, I wander around my apartment. I love my apartment. My bedroom looks out on the quaint row homes and bright painted shutters of Greenwich Village. The ceiling has an ornate centerpiece with a fleur-de-lis and a bulb in the middle. Between the bedroom and kitchen is a small living room with wooden floors and shelves packed with books. Every once in a while I arrange them in different ways—by color, by political philosophy, by how many times I've read them. Sometimes I just close my eyes and run my fingers along the sturdy spines. The secrets to the minds and science of the world are contained in thin bound blocks of paper.

Why must I leave thee?

Because I'm twenty years old, I've been out of college for over a year and I never did the right things people my age are supposed to do, whatever they were. I sure don't know what I'm supposed to be doing now.

My appointment with Dr. Petrov is next week, so he can help me, although I think I entertain him more than he helps me, because I'm smarter than him and because the time he spends with me is forty-five minutes he doesn't have to be on suicide watch.

Finding a bar in the Village that lets twenty-year-olds drink is not as hard as you might think. Crackdowns only happen after some famous person's kid is found facedown in his own vomit on a Village sidewalk, and that hasn't happened in at least three weeks. So I have carte blanche.

As I wander west, I see things and people I have never noticed before: a little side street called Gay Street, a short diagonal alley that seems hidden and sex shops with windows boasting all sorts of condoms and colorful devices. I could never buy a sex toy, because if there were a fire in my apartment and the firemen came, they would find it and it would be embarrassing. Even if I was dead, I'd still be embarrassed.

Up the block are three bars right next to one another. If I used the Kara method of casing bars, I'd say, "Oh, too many guys in that one, too many girls in this one, too preppy, too loud, too quiet." I think that maybe everyone is really here because they think it's what they should be doing—it's not just me. I'm just the only person brave enough to admit the truth. Of course, if you point out the truth, people look at you like you have two heads. I wonder if I could create an alternative New York society where people hang out at libraries on Saturday night instead. The problem is, there wouldn't be liquor to alter their personalities. So I guess in order to be social, everyone has to drink. If so, why am I the misfit, if everyone else is having such a hard time, too? Maybe I'm just the only one who admits it.

The third bar has a long, wooden bar area with several empty stools. So I head in.

I take my seat. In the middle of the room are small square tables with drink menus, and behind that is a back room with a pool table and dartboard. Several groups of guys are clustered around the pool table, but not in the middle. I'm sure it will fill up in an hour or two for New Year's Eve. I already hear horns and whistles outside, and the clip-clopping of women's heels.

I'm just glad I don't feel compelled to walk to Times Square with these herds of clopping sheep, as I did last year. It was awful. Everyone was pushed together and reeking of beer.

"Can I get you something, sweetie?"

I look up. A pretty but older bartender is smiling at me through purple lipstick. People always call me "sweetie" when I go into a place alone, as if being alone is the saddest thing in the world. There are much sadder things in the world: having cancer, being homeless, stepping on your own glasses. Besides, how does she know I'm not waiting for my fiancé to meet me?

I'm going to pretend my fiancé is outside parking the car.

"I'll have a margarita," I say. One of the things I've learned is which drinks I can order to seem like I know what I'm doing even when I don't. As I wait, I smile to myself because my perfect fiancé, who surprisingly finds my nerdy hesitations insanely cute, is coming to get me after he parks the car.

"Salt?" she asks.

"Does that cost extra?" She shakes her head. I notice that a fiftysomething man four stools down is leering at me. That's the problem with opening yourself up to meeting people: You have to meet too many of the wrong ones in order to meet the right ones. And even if they're not right for you, you're a nice person, so you can't just blow them off. But it only gives you a whole raft of new people whose feelings you have to tend to, and you're no closer to finding the one who makes you happy.

I know, I know, I should be grateful for every new person I meet. And I am. I actually met some people last year who I liked and never would have expected to. And then I met Cy, and…well, had a fun month and told him every crazy thing that ever happened to me, and then learned how easily men can get bored with me after a while. Kara told me I gave up too much too soon. She said one of the things smart women believe is that a guy will want to hear everything they have to say, because they grew up getting praised for their intelligence.

"You mean, I'm supposed to play dumb?" I asked her.

"No," she said. "I just mean that guys don't necessarily want to know everything that's in your personal journal."

But why not? I would love to meet a man who had piles of journals going back to sixth grade. But men never keep them. What is that, God's cruel joke?

The bartender delivers my margarita. At least she doesn't call me "sweetie" again. I settle in and avoid glancing at the fifty-something guy. Now I can't move my eyes to an entire half of the room. Why does this have to be so complicated? The world really isn't fitted for people to be alone. The wrong ones seize upon you and the right ones are sitting alone somewhere else.

I focus on the bartender as the place fills up behind me. I wonder if the hour I've given myself to meet someone is enough. It is New Year's Eve; I should make an extra effort. Okay, I propose staying for ninety minutes instead. Done. See the benefit of being alone? Every vote is unanimous.

The more people come in, the more nervous I feel, even if they camouflage my aloneness. Behind me is a trio of loud guys in leather jackets. They order drinks from the bartender. They're practically on top of me. In a minute, I'll actually be in these guys' way, even though I was here first. Not quite fair.

In order to elude their attention, I keep drinking my drink. Unfortunately, it's mostly ice, and even my capillary-like straw has not stemmed my intake. The bartendress asks me if I want another drink. I nod. I have to make the next one last at least fifteen minutes.

I can hear every word the guys behind me say. I have to work hard to not be in their conversation. They're arguing over which of two supermodels has the better body: Korzika Korzurkonovich, or Borznaria Boznovinsky. Okay, so those aren't their real names, but that's what female models' names sound like.

One of the guys in the trio leans over the bar and his voice is practically in my ear. How many minutes do I have left? Seventy-seven. If I were legal proofreading, I'd have earned four bucks already.

I sneak a peek at the guy who is ordering, even though he is probably too loud for me. He has a leather jacket, gaunt cheeks and a pockmarked face. His hair sprays out, prematurely gray in some areas, yet boyish. He smells strongly of cigarette smoke.

I hear him say something that ends in "...*this* girl," and I feel the back of my neck get hot. Are they talking about me? I'll pretend I didn't hear.

Suddenly, he looks straight at me. His friends are looking, too.

"You don't look like you're having a good time," the guy says.

And I don't know what to say in response.

There is a generally accepted standard that if you're female, no matter what a guy says to you, you're supposed to know the most deft, clever, flirty and nonbitchy comment to issue in return. But I don't have that gift. Maybe everyone learned it in eighth grade, which I skipped.

Before I can think of something, he adds, "Your expression hasn't changed once the whole night."

Now I really don't know what to say. He's putting me on the defensive. He could have said something nice or asked how I feel, instead of making a negative statement. How am I supposed to respond and not sound awkward? What can I say that's sexy, flirty and at the same time unbitchy?

"Oh" is all that comes to mind.

The guys look at each other. I feel exactly like I used to in school when a kid picked on me and I scrambled to say something back, but knew whatever came out would just get me picked on more. There was one junior-high class that was so bad that for an entire month I was afraid to speak except to answer the teacher's questions. But in this case, these guys are theoretically being nice to me. So why do I feel like a target?

"That's it?" the gaunt guy asks me.

I take a breath and try to keep my voice steady. "I would have something more to say," I tell him, "if you'd said something nice instead of insulting me."

He steps back, holding up his hands, as his friends laugh. "Whoa, whoa, whoa," he says. "I was just being friendly." His gray eyes gleam at me.

"What if I'd come up to you," I say, "and said, 'Your expression hasn't changed the whole night.' What would you say in response?"

Gaunt One looks at his friends for support. He won't like me now, but at least I'll save the next girl from humiliation.

Most girls aren't willing to stick their necks out. Only their breasts.

"See," I report triumphantly. "You can't come up with a single thing to say in response."

Gaunt One cracks a slight smile. "I'm thinkin'...I'm thinkin'..."

All three guys really are concentrating on it. They look like three thinking chimps.

Finally, Gaunt One says, "Okay. Here's what I'd say."

We wait.

"I'd say, 'My expression *might* change if you'd buy me a drink.'"

Now, see? That is pretty good. But it only proves my point. It's probably the most clever, flirty thing one could say in response, but it took him five minutes to figure it out. If I could have had five minutes, we might be sucking each other's tonsils by now.

Is my job in life to prepare light, sassy comebacks for men? Geishas got taken very good care of for that.

"Good one, Kurt," one of his friends says, smacking him on the back. So the Gaunt One is Kurt.

Since Kurt was at least nice enough to talk to me, I figure I'll be honest with him. "Well," I say, staring at my margarita, "I'm just not good at coming up with lines like that. I can't help it."

Kurt actually seems touched for a change. He's looking at the ground and kicking the base of my stool with his shoe. Maybe honesty works?

"That's okay," Kurt says. He looks up at me coyly. "I'll bet you have other talents."

A flirty answer might be "That's for me to know and you to find out," but wouldn't I just be encouraging this game?

"I *do* have other talents," I say.

"Like what?" Kurt asks.

"Reading," I say. "And talking about philosophy."

He thinks. "Like, feminism and shit?"

"Uh…I guess that could be one."

The two friends have moved back to give Kurt space, but they occasionally glance at him. Is Kurt actually interested in me? Could I ever be interested in him? I'm talking to a guy, anyway—that's a start.

"So, Miss Feminist," he says, "what's your name?"

I give him my best shy smile. Might as well pull this off so I can meet my goal for the night. "Carrie," I say.

Kurt puts his hand to his ear for a second, then seems to have gotten it. Sound travels slowly through Amstel-soaked air. "So, Carrie, why aren't you having a good time?"

He's still trying to tell me how I feel. What he really means is that I'm not behaving up to his standards.

"I'm not going to jump up and down because you decided to flirt with me," I say.

He laughs nervously. "You know," he says, "you probably think it's easy for me to come up to girls, but it's not. It took me a half-hour to work on that 'Your expression hasn't changed' line."

"Then you should have said something that wasn't insulting, besides just telling me how I look or feel," I say.

He glances back for his friends, but they're not there. He has to deal with me himself. "Like what?" he asks, leaning closer.

Maybe I've been too harsh. Sometimes it's hard to tell friend from foe. Especially when they use the same pickup lines.

The girl on the next stool leaves with her boyfriend, and Kurt nestles onto it, swiveling a little. His hips are attractive.

"You could have been honest," I say. The bar is packed

now. "You could have said, 'Hi. My name's Kurt. Tell me about yourself.'"

He thinks about it. "That's fair," he says. He extends his hand. "Hi. My name is Kurt. Tell me about yourself."

I can't help but smile.

"Ha!" he says. "I got her to smile."

Talking about me in third person: not cute. The bartender delivers him another beer and me a margarita, even though I didn't ask for a third one.

"I'll bet you're a smarty," he says. "I can always tell the smart girls. They're more uptight."

Thanks. Since I again don't know what to say, I sip my drink. That's what drinks are *for.*

"I bet you could teach me a lot of stuff," he says.

Finally, I decide I'll give him what he wants. "Well," I say cattily, "I'll bet *you* could teach *me* a lot of stuff, too." There! Eureka! I've flirted! Give me an A and send me home for the day.

He laughs. "I could teach you a *lot* of things."

It is then that I get one of those feelings. The feelings that are not rational, the feelings that come from somewhere much lower than my brain. It's just that he has such a nice smile, and his ample hair is adorable. Even his gaunt, pocky face is sort of cute. So maybe he's not the brightest bulb in that little space under the sink where you keep all the bulbs and cleansers. I did come here to act like a normal person, right? He's being friendly, right? I can't criticize his pickup lines when I'm no good with them myself. I learned last year not to judge people too quickly, and talking to Kurt is a good way to prove the lesson stuck with me. Maybe I'll unlock the secret doors to his hidden, marvelous intellect.

"So what's your *last* name?" he asks me.

I know instantly that it's not my last name he really wants—it's my background or religion. People only ask this when they're very proud of whatever theirs is—generally Irish or Italian. "Pilby," I say. Before he can further inquire, I say, "My parents were born in Britain."

"Oh," he says.

"What's yours?" I ask.

"Haupt," he says. "H-a-u-p-t."

"Are you German?"

He sits up straight. "One-hundred-percent American!" he says. "Well, technically, I'm a quarter German, a quarter Puerto Rican, and half Italian. A mutt."

"Maybe I should call you Mutt," I say, thinking the chain around his neck is sort of like a collar.

He leans his face closer to me. He smells nice. "Woof," he says, taking advantage of his new nickname, "woof." His stubble brushes softly against me for a second.

"Down, boy," I say, but stubble is kind of a turn-on. I must already have had too many margaritas.

"So how long have you been in the city?" he says, but he sloshes the word *city*. He's starting to get drunk, too. Thank God. This will be funny. Right? I'll keep sipping my Mexican medicine.

"Um," I say, "what?"

"Happy new year!" someone yells outside, two hours early. I forgot about that already.

"How longyoubeeninacity?" Mutt asks.

"A few years," I say. "How long have you been in the bar?"

"Forty-five minutes," he says. "But my friends and I were at a different bar first."

"And it was so much different from this one that you had to switch?"

He laughs. The bartender brings me my fourth margarita, even though again, I do not remember asking. When I grab it, I look at the mirrored clock on the wall and catch Kurt checking out my behind. I don't know that my behind is all that different from anyone else's. Usually what boys like about me is that I look young. Maybe because I *am* young.

"So," Kurt asks, "how long have you been in New York?"

"Didn't you already ask me that?" That's the first sign of drunkenness: repeating yourself. That's the first sign of drunkenness: repeating yourself.

He shrugs.

"A year and a half," I answer. "Since college."

Then he looks worried. "How old are you?"

"Twenty-one," I say. "Almost."

Suddenly he laughs. "Am I committing a felony by talking to you?"

"Probably a misdemeanor." It's so much easier to flirt when you've been taking your Mexican medicine.

"I can deal with a misdemeanor," he says.

Someone must have just turned down the dimmer, because the bar suddenly seems darker. The candles on the square tables are lit, and a TV up in the corner is flashing Dick Clark holding a microphone. Mutt and I both watch him for a second. Confetti is flying around the screen, and everyone is smiling with all their teeth.

When Mutt and I turn back to each other, neither of us seems to know what to say. I guess two people who have nothing in common are good for nine minutes of conversation. Hopefully when I meet the person I'm supposed to marry, I'll be able to have a conversation with him for the rest of my life.

"So, Carrie," Mutt says. "Do you like sports?"

"Not really," I say.

"Me, neither," he says. "Do you like cars?"

"No."

"Me, neither." He laughs. "How are you on public displays of affection?"

"Hate 'em."

"Me, too," he says. He leans toward me. "So, since you're not into kissing in public, how about we go somewhere else?"

He's made his move. I'm kind of intrigued. Then he's squeezing my hand and leading me out of the bar. As I dodge people's shoulders and shoes, I think that he must have paid for those last two drinks, because I didn't.

The frosty air hits every unclothed surface on my body. I see people all around, bursts of smoke coming from their mouths and dissipating. It feels much later than ten-thirty.

Kurt puts his arm around my shoulders and starts leading me somewhere, and I follow. What's going on here? It's the Mexican medicine at work. So what? I'm having a good time. I'm not thinking for a change. I'm normal! Normalness is fun!

As we walk, Kurt says, "Should we go back to my place?"

I am still rational enough to know not to go back to his place. "I don't think that's a good idea."

"Why?"

"I don't know you well enough," I say. We stop walking, but the thick crowd pushes around us.

"Maybe you could just walk me home," Mutt says.

"Where do you live?"

"Brooklyn."

"Brooklyn is kind of far to walk."

He considers this for a second, then says, "I know you're

against public displays of affection, but can I kiss you right here?"

"In the middle of the sidewalk?"

"Of course not. Against the wall."

"Oh, okay." Before I can say anything else, or think, which is usually my biggest mistake, he's bringing me to the wall and pressing his body against mine and forcing his tongue in my mouth. I sigh. I can't help it. It feels good.

He stops and stares at me. He looks adorable right now, like a wounded mutt. Then he closes his eyes and puts his lips to mine again. His mouth tastes beery and warm.

Finally, he stops.

"I'll hail a cab," he says.

"Wait," I say. "Why?"

"So we can go back to my apartment."

"We can't."

"You want to keep standing in the cold?"

"We were doing fine."

"I thought you were against PDAs."

"I *was*."

He grins. "Before you met me?"

I nod.

"Because I'm such a stud," he adds.

"You are." Hey, whatever works.

He leans in and kisses me again, long and soft. I don't care who's watching. Okay, I care a little bit. He wraps his arms around me. At least he's protecting me from the other crazies.

"Okay," he says breathily. "Enough teasing. Time to go home."

"I can't."

"I just want to show you my apartment."

I wish he'd stop making this difficult and just kiss me in the street like any normal person.

"Come on," he says. "What are you afraid of?"

I hate that tactic. Making me sound like a prude because I don't want to go home with someone I just met. But I learned a trick from Kara last year: Always turn the tables when a guy is manipulating you. I say, "What are you afraid of by staying *here*?"

He ignores that. "You don't think you can trust me?" he says, pleading with his gray eyes. He looks sweet. "We can go to your place."

"Why do we have to go to anyone's 'place'?" I ask.

"Because I like you."

"I like you, too," I say. "So let's keep doing what we were doing."

"Come on," he said. "All I want to do is show you my apartment. You can sleep on the couch. Wait—Kurt, you're an idiot. *I'll* sleep on the couch. You can sleep in my bed."

"No."

"I'll tell you what," he says. "We'll kiss on my couch for a while, like we were doing just now, and then you can go to sleep in my room, lock the door until morning and not come out, and you can keep the key so I can't bother you."

"It's not a good idea," I say.

"Why not?" Kurt says. "You'll have my room all to yourself, and I can't even get in."

Why does he have to keep talking?

"Come *on*," Kurt says. "I'm not gonna date rape you or something."

Now, see the difference between a smart guy and one who's kind of dim? A smart guy, whether his intentions were noble or not, would know not to even offer up the possibility of date rape. If he was socially inept in other ways, he would still be smart enough not to say *that*.

But then again, why do I always have to use that standard? A smart guy wouldn't be making out with me against the wall, giving me hope that a normal guy would like me.

I say, "It's just not good for girls to put themselves in that situation." The honesty tactic, again. I must be really desperate.

"You're right," he says. "Kurt, you're an idiot. I have the perfect solution. I go into my room, I lock it, I give you the keys to the whole freaking apartment, you sleep on the couch right next to the door, and if you decide to go for any reason at all, you can leave the keys on the dresser and I won't stop you. You'll have carte bleach.'"

Carte *bleach?* "Well," I say, "if I go back there, I might not be able to resist doing bad things."

There! I've found it! The ultimate flirty, sexy, rejecting-without-being-bitchy response!

Kurt cracks a smile. "Bad things, huh?" he says. He leans toward me and kisses me again.

I keep my eyes open because I've never had my eyes open while kissing. He looks like a giant fish with a lot of pores. Okay, I've learned why not to keep my eyes open while kissing.

Kurt's chin is rough and it sends a tickle through my body. I love the warmth inside his mouth.

He stops and gazes at me triumphantly. "Now let's go home."

"What did you stop for?"

He gets down on one knee. "Hi. I'm Kurt. Tell me about yourself."

"That isn't going to work twice," I say. "Look, I *wish* there was a way we could go home. I really do, but it would be too compromising."

Kurt says, "How can I make it any safer? I told you—I'll give you the key, I'll sleep on the couch—"

"I can't."

He looks at me. "You're someone who doesn't trust her feelings a lot, aren't you?"

"Psychoanalyzing me is manipulative and it won't get me to go home with you. I like you, but I can't go home with you. We can kiss here, or you can give me a call another day."

"Look, Carrie," he says. "I just want to spend New Year's Eve with you. Why is that wrong?"

Why indeed? Why is it easy for other people to have one-night stands, while I can't even get a quarter-night-stand right?

"I guess I have to go," I say sadly. *Suggest something else, Mutt.*

"Wait," he says.

Good. He's thought of something.

"Do you know what it's going to look like to my friends if I have nothing to show for this?" he says.

Oh my God! "How old are you?" I ask.

"That's not what I meant," he says. "Kurt, you're a moron. I'm just trying to come up with a way to be with you."

Now I feel bad. Won't it be good for my New Year's resolution if I spend more time with Kurt tonight? But my resolution is to find someone who's *like* me, not just someone who *likes* me.

"We can be together another time," I say.

"She's blowing me off," he says.

"It's not you," I say. "It's really late."

"How old are you?" he says snottily.

I guess I deserve that.

He sighs. "Well, can I get your number?"

"Why don't you give me yours?" I say. Kara taught me that, too.

"Oh, right. You'll never call."

"I will."

"You won't."

"I will."

"You won't."

"I will."

"You won't."

"I will."

"Promise you'll call," he says.

"I promise," I tell him, and as I say it, he puts his finger on my lips, like Helen Keller. He knows how to touch so delicately. Hmm. Mmmmmm. Let's see. If he gives me the key to the apartment, and I lock the door, and he sleeps on the couch, is that really so bad?

He pulls out a pack of cigarettes, finds a coupon inside the clear wrapping and scrawls his number on the back.

"You're cute, Carrie," he says. "Don't let anyone ever tell you otherwise."

Would they?

He pushes the paper into my hand and clasps his hand over mine to make sure it stays. He leans over and gives me a kiss on the cheek, smelling of cologne and beer. I start to feel a little depressed. I can't even do wrong things right.

Kurt says goodbye and starts walking back to the bar to find his friends. I see his hair flopping as he leaves. Part of me wants to run and tell him I've changed my mind. Part of me wants to explain that I just take longer to figure things out than most people, and maybe we should find another bar so we can talk more before I go home with him. But I let him go.

I know there's a chance I'll get home and hear everyone celebrating and think I should have stayed with Kurt. I look back toward the bar again, but I don't see him anymore. Is he off to find his friends? To see some girl? The amount of practice I need in dealing with these situations is incredible.

Once Kurt sobers up, he probably won't care whether I call him, anyway. I know he wouldn't have liked me if he was sober. I probably did the right thing. A decent guy doesn't try to force a girl to go home with him two hours after they meet.

I stuff the number in my pocket and walk toward my neighborhood. It's eleven p.m. and it's New Year's Eve, and I'm in a neighborhood packed with young revelers, and I feel just as alone as I did two hours ago.

Four

New Year's morning is quiet. Everyone else is drunk and hungover and most of the stores are closed. But I thrive on the silence. It only makes me more creative. There is an endless variety of mysteries to unlock, even within my apartment. Most people don't look around enough. For instance, take a gander inside my pantry. What exactly is the difference between a string bean and a green bean? Do you know? Of course you don't, because you're too busy getting high. Etymology is a hobby of mine, and if you think that's nerdy, you probably don't realize that there are five conflicting theories on the origin of *nerd,* which used to be commonly spelled N-U-R-D, and may have been derived from "nut."

Now to answer our main mystery—compliments of the *Webster's* unabridged dictionary next door in my living room—a string bean is any green bean with strings that are removed. The green bean is the pod part that you eat. So a string bean contains a green bean but a green bean isn't necessarily a string bean.

Well, that killed five minutes.

I would not have been better off if I'd gone home with Kurt last night. Because right now, instead of entering excellent exercises in etymological archeology, I would have been waking up hungover and awkward.

I sit back on my bed and remote-control the TV. Football. Some preacher. Cartoons. A news magazine.

I stop there.

On the newsmagazine is a segment about a couple who adopted a developmentally delayed child and two disabled children. The couple doesn't look that old. The woman is swinging one of the kids on a swing. Her husband is fairly handsome, with dark hair brushed back.

Watching them, I think: It's hard enough to find a guy who likes a girl who is slightly different from everyone else, so who are these women who end up with a guy who has the patience and dedication to adopt kids with problems? You've got to have a lot of love and loyalty as a couple to undertake something like that.

It reminds me of something I thought of three years ago, when I was seventeen, the last time my dad and I went to church together. Embedded in the walls, and near some pews, were small golden plaques that said things like "Donated by Mr. and Mrs. Joseph Johnson" and "Donated by Christopher and Susan Ross." At the time, I thought, That's a real couple. That's a couple who spent their lives together caring about causes, and they even donated money together.

And when I was seventeen, I wondered if I would ever meet a guy who would do that.

Now I have another thought.

What makes me think I deserve someone like that? I've never done anything for anyone other than myself.

Maybe if I become a better person, I will deserve better men. Because up to now, anything nice I've done has been for someone I know.

I drag myself to my computer, which is by my window. It's sunny out but the temperature is below freezing; the sun is merely a red herring.

I sit at my computer and search for volunteer activities in New York. In the process, I come across several social groups: The Lunch Club, Mensa, Silent Parties, Team Trivia, New York Cares, New York Foodies, FAIR, and God's Love We Deliver. I get on the e-mail lists for all of them. I'll have activities coming out of my derriere!

I know that the easiest volunteer activity would be "soup kitchens," because several people on my floor at Harvard volunteered at the ones in Boston on weekends. One of those people was a guy in a campus Christian group who still had sex with three or four girls in the dorm. But don't get me started on the whole hypocrisy thing. I don't mind people who have sex a lot, but I mind people who lie to themselves about it.

I find dozens of soup kitchens in New York. I scroll down the list to locate one that has meals on Saturday—which is the day after tomorrow—and accepts volunteers. There's one that's located near Columbia University. I'll bet Columbia kids volunteer there! I might meet some smart students who are close to my age. And I'll be helping the poor, too.

I scribble down the number so I can call and ask if new volunteers can stop by. Maybe I'll do this every few weeks. How selfish I have been, sleeping away all my time!

Since I've made great progress, I take a walk outside.

It's one of those dead days in January when the only people on the street are those who were dragged there by their dogs. I shove my hands in my pockets. There's a woman ahead of me walking a dachshund, the trendy NYC pooch of the moment, both because they're small enough to fit in a tiny apartment and because everyone loves a wiener. There's a gourmet food store ahead on the corner that all the Yuppies like, but it's closed today, and I see people practically bouncing off the doors. They must sell some crucial ingredient in hangover remedies.

By the corner, I pass a group of pre-teen kids who are roughhousing in front of a bagel place. Suddenly the youngest-looking one lets out a shriek: "Help me, miss!"

I turn around to see the two bigger boys practically choking the younger kid. He is kneeling on the ground and cringing in pain. My inclination is to pretend I didn't see anything and keep walking, but here's my chance to do something good. "Get off him!" I yell.

The boys release their grip and start laughing, and the other one stands up and grins, too. It was all a setup.

"Stupid bitch," the young one says in a scratchy voice, and his friends pat him on the back. "Bitch," one of the others says.

I'm mortified but I don't look at them. I don't want them to have the satisfaction. I keep my eyes trained on the ground and walk ahead as I hear their laughter. Behind me, I think everyone's laughing.

Five

I don't even want to get up on Saturday morning. See what happened when I tried to do something good? I got laughed at. Why should I think going to the soup kitchen today will be different?

Well, I might meet a brilliant Columbia student today who will change my life. And I'll be helping people who really need help—not little brats who are faking it.

With this attempt at optimism I pull myself out of bed and get ready to give back to the community.

When I arrive uptown at the East District Mission, I see a red sign that reads, "Opening our hearts to the community since 1966." Good. A line of disheveled people in sweatpants and heavy coats stands against the side of the building. I don't see any volunteers around. But I'm being judgmental—maybe those are the volunteers. Still, I'm a little intimidated. I don't know anyone here.

But I'm not going to be scared. These are the people in my community, and I am going to talk to them instead of acting like an overprivileged Harvard girl. There's a guy in the back of the line who has piles of shirts on and a black wool hat but no overcoat. I walk toward him and say cheerfully, "Hi. I'm a volunteer. Do you know where I go?"

The guy's lips spread into a grin. "You're new," he says.

Behind him, a different guy shoots him a look and says, "She just wants to know where to go, Brian. You fucking moron." Then he points down the stairs and shakes his head.

Already I've caused a fight. I do more harm than good. But I won't give up yet.

I trot to the bottom of the stairs, thinking to myself, *have a positive attitude, have a positive attitude.* When I get to the bottom, a neat-looking gray-haired man in a painter's cap is guarding the door. I tell him I'm a volunteer, and he sends me inside.

I'm immediately assaulted by the smells of burnt coffee and salad dressing. The room looks like the cafeteria of my elementary school. The tables are long and flat, with attached benches. Posters on the walls alternate between religious mottos and directions to Social Service agencies. During the week, this room is used for church functions, not as a soup kitchen. In a corner is a kitchen area, where a few people scurry around. The volunteers are at one of the tables eating the food. The guy on the phone told me that the volunteers eat the food before the "clients" or "guests" do, to show that they're willing to eat the same meal.

About twenty people sit at the volunteer table—perfect! Some might be Columbia students. I get closer. Approximately half of the people are wearing identical blue shirts that say "YCCA Youth Group." Hmm. They look fourteen years old; there are eight girls and two boys. Okay, scratch those ten off the "possible suitors" list. Of the remaining ten, three are adults wearing red YCCA shirts—those must be the parents and chaperones.

This cuts the pool to seven, but those seven look promising. Five people are wearing Paine Webber painter's caps and shirts. Their company must require some social service work, or at least encourage it. Three of them are guys and two are women. The two remaining people are a man and woman in their late forties. I think the Paine Webber crew is my best bet.

And miracle of miracles, the only available space to sit down is in the middle, next to one of the handsome Paine Webber guys. He has sad eyes and a kind expression. Perfect!

I squeeze between two people and say, "Hi." Everyone is eating spaghetti and a soggy Caesar salad drizzled with bits of cheese. As soon as I sit, I realize the spaghetti and salads aren't on the table. Only pitchers of pineapple juice (pineapple juice and salad? Eww) and coffee are there, along with paper plates piled high with smushed croissants that some bakery donated. I say "Excuse me" and get back up.

When I reach the salad line, the woman says, "Oh, you came too late. We're getting ready for our guests."

Okay. I return to my seat and turn over the upside-down foam cup to pour pineapple juice into it, then grab a croissant.

Of the three twentysomething Paine Webber men, the sad-eyed one isn't talking, but the one across from me, with dark hair and a goofy grin, is keeping the table riveted with stories.

"So then she sends me this e-mail, and it says, 'I thought you were my *other* friend Brewster.'" Everyone laughs. I steal glances at the sad-eyed guy next to me. He really is attractive. There's a lull in the conversation, and everyone is eating their salad—actually, it's so soggy that it might be more appropriate to say they're drinking it—and I ask the guy, "Have you worked at Paine Webber long?"

He looks at me and smiles. In halting English, he says, "Not very long."

"He's from Poland," the girl to the left of me says. "He's here for a few days."

"Oh." The guy nods and finishes eating. The dark-haired fellow with the stories says, "So I have to tell you guys about the real estate agent from last night."

"Ohh," says the girl sitting on the left of me, rolling her eyes. "Don't get me started."

"She was like, 'You're buying the same house your parents had,'" the guy says.

"That's not what she said. She goes, 'You're buying the same kind of house that *adults* buy…'" the girl says.

As the conversation continues, I realize the two of them are a couple. They're engaged and they're buying a house together.

This is like every English course I took at Harvard: Every man is either taken or inappropriate.

But I am here to volunteer, not necessarily to meet someone. I close my eyes and remind myself of that. *You are doing good for the community.* I only wish I knew someone in the community.

When I open my eyes, at the end of the table stands the handsomest man I've seen in months.

He's watching us eat. He's clad in a white short-sleeved T-shirt over a dark-blue long-sleeved one. The white one says Spring Fling '01. It looks old and frayed, but not ratty. The layered look. I like it.

"All right," he says, clapping. "Most of you know the drill, but since I see one or two new faces among you…"

He is looking in my direction. I smile. It's a genuine smile. Just being in his presence will do it.

"I'm Tim, and I'm a regular volunteer with the East District Mission Soup Kitchen," he says. "I started volunteering here back when I was a freshman at Columbia and now I work in Social Services in Harlem and I oversee the Saturday afternoon meal."

And thank God you do.

He tells us the Mission's philosophy—"We don't weed out anyone, we don't disallow anyone, and as long as they show up by noon and stand on line like everybody else, they are entitled to a square meal"—and I listen intently.

"Some of them have told us, especially at the end of the month when their benefits check runs out, that this is the only meal they eat all weekend."

How sad! And it's just pineapple juice!

"Since it's the beginning of the month," Tim explains, "we'll probably be a little lighter today than usual, but I want to thank you all for coming, especially since Columbia's on winter break and so we have fewer student volunteers."

Drat. But I don't care. I've found *him*—and him is Tim.

I can't wait to tell Kara and Petrov that I met my New Year's goal in the first week: a smart guy who's kind and does things that are important.

"You've all been assigned jobs," Tim says. "After you clear your plates, please go to your stations."

Wait—I haven't been assigned a job. I feel like the last kid on the class trip without a partner. Then again, I always feel like that.

As everyone gets up, I'm a bit lost. But Tim will help me. The Tim Man. Rin-Tin-Tim. I walk toward him, smiling.

I know I look good today. I wore a tight sweater in case I met anyone. "Hi," I say to Tim. "I'm Carrie."

He cups his hand to his mouth. His eyes dart behind me. "Yo, Andrew, don't start letting them in yet. We need cups on the last table."

"It's my first time," I tell him. "I've never worked in a soup kitchen before." He doesn't say anything, so I continue. "But I knew kids at Harvard who did and I always wanted to?" Now I'm uptalking, but at least he knows I went to a prestigious school like he did. "I graduated last year and moved to New York City. And now I want to help out."

He looks me up and down.

Then he says, "You don't have a hat?"

I don't get it. "A what?"

"If you have long hair, you need a hat." He cups his mouth again. "Monica, can you show her where to get a hairnet?"

How am I supposed to be attractive in a hairnet? Wait— think of the poor people.

Tim has walked away without me even realizing it. He's heading to the metal coffee machine, which two fourteen-year-old church girls are struggling over.

I wander over to Monica, the girl with the hairnets. At least she smiles at me. I'll make a female friend. Female friends are useful sometimes, and they even smell nice.

Monica is the fiancé of that dark-haired Paine Webber guy. I should have poisoned her pineapple juice when I had the chance.

"Here," she says, handing me a hairnet. Then she walks over to a table, and I'm left alone.

I turn with my back to the shelf with the hairnets, lean against it and case the room. They're letting the "guests" in now. Most of them are men, and most are from minority

groups. Some of them are stooped over. It's a shame they
have to be so sick or disheveled. It's cold out there and I'm
glad they're inside. Suddenly, I feel good that I'm doing this.
I'll do it every week. So what if I'm alone? I'm helping people out.

Except, I don't know how to wear this stupid hairnet. It feels
like someone took the strings of metal from a Brillo pad and
stretched them into a grid. I tug it over the front of my hair
and the back bounces off. I pull it back and the front comes
off. I look around, but there's no one who can help me. How
come I have a genius-level IQ and I can't put on a hairnet?

With one swoop, I pull the front while I snap the rest
around the back. It's on for a second, then bounces off.

I position it a different way, with my hands around the
sides, struggle a bit, and finally I have it. Most of the "clients"
or "guests" are sitting down. Four church kids are serving coffee. Three Paine Webber employees and two church kids are
behind a counter doling out spaghetti and meatballs. Five volunteers are delivering the full plates to the tables. Two are
monitoring the line at the door.

It's amazing how many situations there are where aloneness becomes self-perpetuating. If I was with someone else,
the two of us would march over to a person in authority and
ask for a job, or at least we'd be noticeable enough that someone would help us. But alone, I don't have the guts to ask,
and no one notices me.

The truth is, they don't need me here. I could go home
and doze off and it wouldn't make a difference to the homeless and poor. Every coffeepot is being poured, every morsel
of food is being dolloped. (There is no soup in this soup
kitchen, by the way, although on a cold day like today it
wouldn't be such a bad idea.)

Suddenly, Tim is behind me. "You need something to do?"

"Yes," I say, smiling.

"Okay," he says. "Hold on one second." He heads into a storeroom, finds a T-shirt and walks briskly across the room to give it to a guy who was waiting. I guess the guy asked for free clothes. Now I feel good again. This really is a useful service they have here.

I wait for Tim, but he seems to have forgotten about me for a second time. One of the guys monitoring the line has called him over and they're debating something.

It's selfish of me to feel sorry for myself when there are four dozen homeless people in here. I will find my*self* a job. Tim is busy. I see the spaghetti sauce splashing on the serving counter, and there are some wet rags and sponges around. I grab a rag and wipe off the table in front of people. "Good girl!" says one of the church mothers. Tim chooses this moment to appear again.

"We need you over there now," he says, almost scolding.

Hey, guy, we're volunteers. Lighten up.

Tim brings me to the exit and asks me if I can hand out oranges and apples as people leave. "Sure," I say. "It'll be like comparing apples and oranges." He doesn't smile.

But when my first pair of diners comes to the door for an orange and apple, I feel useful. "Can I have an extra orange for my kids?" the woman says. "Sure," I say happily, and plop one into her hand. We've got three boxes of oranges. Now more kids in Manhattan will get their vitamin C.

The responses I get as I give out the fruit are interesting. One man shakes his head at the apple and says, "That's instant diarrhea." Another puts his hand up to reject it, showing me he has no teeth.

Then I hear a voice say, "No." It's Tim. He's walking briskly toward me and he isn't smiling.

"You can't give them extra," Tim says. "Because then everyone will start asking."

"What?"

"Someone saw you give a woman two oranges."

"She wanted one for her kid…"

Tim rolls his eyes. "They all say that. If she had a kid, she'd bring him here. We have to stick to the rules." I know that I should be glad he's so dedicated to the soup kitchen, but how come Mutt on New Year's Eve was attracted to me, and here's a young Columbia grad who can't even smile at me? I'm young, and I have long dark hair and glasses—I'm not ugly or anything. Just socially inept.

I distribute fruit for an hour. Some people thank me for the meal, as if I created it myself. It's really humbling. I hope Tim saw how humble I am.

Six

"Who the fuck cares about string beans?"

That's Kara, never holding back. She jabs at the call button for the elevator that will take us upstairs to her temporary Central Park West apartment. I thought everyone learned by the time they were eight that repeatedly pressing elevator buttons doesn't help. Well, if you live in a *city,* you learn that. Kara grew up on Long Island.

The doors slide open. Someone gets out who looks familiar and walks toward the street.

"Is she someone?" I whisper.

"*Everyone's* someone," Kara whispers back.

Kara could potentially be famous someday—she's an actress. But she hasn't gotten a commercial or a play in a while, so she does the part-time legal proofreading.

Once we're in the elevator, I turn around to watch the numbers rise. There are nine floors in total. We're heading to the top. I don't think I've actually ever been in a penthouse apartment before, even though I've been in some pretty nice spaces on account of my father. He analyzes investment opportunities for foreign companies, and he travels a lot.

"*Are* there any famous people in this building?" I ask.

"I'm not sure," Kara says. "I guess *we'll* have to become famous."

"You're an actress," I say. "What can I do?"

Kara shrugs. "Write a novel about dating. I can write the sex scenes."

"That's good, because I would definitely need help."

We step out into the hallway, which is covered by a pale beige carpet. There's one door at the very end. I guess this lady has the whole floor to herself.

We walk to the end. The door has nothing on it. It's painted white like the rest of the hallway.

"Behold," Kara says, and flings open the door.

The place opens up. Sprawls, I mean. Don't all mansions sprawl?

The living room is huge. It has a bank of wide windows that overlook the park, plants hanging all around them. When it rains, I'll bet the water slides down and it's like standing in a tropical forest.

I linger by the window. Down below, there's a well-built man with a head of curly hair playing Frisbee with a black Labrador retriever. He's very muscular. The man, I mean.

Kara follows my gaze. "Knowing *you*," she says, "you're probably admiring the types of fauna in the pond."

This always happens, and it bothers me. I am pretty innocent, but it bothers me when people think I'm *that* innocent.

"I was," I say. "I was admiring the fauna in the pond."

"There's also the most beautiful guy I've ever seen," she says. "Boy, will I enjoy this view." She takes her coat off and throws it on the red sofa. "Lots of possibilities in this place. Come on. I want to show you the rest of the house."

I follow her down the hallway, thick with modern art, canvasses with various geometric shapes in white and brick-red and brown. Complementing them are white and brown sculptures. The whole house hugs you with its paintings and pillows and potted plants.

"Come," Kara says, gesturing with her right hand.

The main bedroom is huge, with a giant bed and twelve red, orange and brown throw pillows. Kara tells me that a maid from Jamaica comes in twice a week, so Kara doesn't even have to do much cleaning.

We head back out into the hall. Kara opens the bathroom, and with the mirrored walls, the pale pink glass over the shower, the skylight and dark rug, it's a bather's paradise. The tub is two feet deep. My kingdom for a deep tub.

Farther down the hall are two small bedrooms, one with a bed and one with a sofa and a desk.

"She could rent these rooms out while she's away," I say.

"Can you imagine how many wealthy second and third homes go to waste while there are homeless people nine stories below, but you can't let homeless people live in your house?"

I think of the people at the soup kitchen. But it's not like Judith can just let them live here for a few weeks.

"We'll make good use of these rooms ourselves," Kara says. "Don't worry. If one of us gets a man, we can entertain him here, and if not, we'll catch up here a few times a week and plot strategies."

A few times a week? "Maybe once a week," I say.

"Spoilsport."

Kara dashes into the living room and jumps onto the

brown sofa. I sit on the red couch across from her. In the basket are Mrs. Green's flat, oversized art books, including a photography book that's just fall leaves. The prettiest ones have raindrops on them. I suppose they sprayed them all with a squeeze bottle. I wish I could be more naive about it.

Kara reclines on the couch and puts her hands behind her head. "So when are you going to your next event?"

I position a brown throw pillow behind my head. "Never."

"Come on," Kara says. "Also, can I have Tim's phone number?"

"No."

"Seriously. When are you going back to the soup kitchen?"

"I'm going to wait until next month. I have a few other activities on my list."

"Like what? Mensa?"

"No." She doesn't have to know I'm considering joining. "On Tuesday I'm going to this panel on biases in the media." I figure that people who think about the media are actually reading, and that means they will be more smart than social. The problem with my last two events was that they weren't a surefire draw for smart people. The next one will be.

"Sounds boring," Kara says, reaching into the basket. "Why can't this woman subscribe to *Us*? Seems like our friend Judith Green needs to get a life."

I cringe.

"Oh, sorry," Kara says. "I forgot how you feel about 'Get a life.'"

"I hate that expression," I say. "It really means 'I am better than you' and 'Get *my* life.'"

Kara pulls a memo pad out of Judith's basket. It says Lexapro® on top.

I tell her, "Last year, Dr. Petrov made me write a list of things I love. We should write a list of things we hate."

She smiles. "Things like 'Get a life'?"

"Exactly."

We run to her desk and cobble together a list on the pad. Each time we come up with a new entry, it sets off bursts of laughter and commiseration. Inside of ten minutes we have:

THINGS WE HATE

1. "Get a life."
2. Taxi drivers who refer to their customers as "fares."
3. Stores that make you check your bags when you enter. (Who wants to entrust their $200 worth of new stuff to some teenager in exchange for half of a playing card?)
4. People who hold napkins over their faces on the subway—as if our germs aren't going to fit through their napkin.
5. When you call a company about a bill, and their system tells you to punch in your account number, and then a person gets on and asks you for your number anyway.
6. When you're really tired and you get on the E train without looking where it's going because you just want to get home but it turns out the train is actually going the other way and the next stop says "23" and you're all excited because you think it's 23rd street in Manhattan and you get out and then you realize it's that *dumb* "23rd/Ely" stop in Queens and now you're on Ely Avenue which no one's ever heard of and you have to pay a whole nother $2 to go across the street to the other platform.

7. That *nother* isn't a word.
8. When you get a haircut and the hair-cutter has big breasts and they're in your face and you don't want to seem like you're looking but you can't turn your head or she'll cut your eye.
9. People who smoke pot but brag that they don't drink.

"This is fun!" Kara says. "You should move in here. We can do stuff like this every night."

I don't say anything.

"Come on," Kara says. "It'll be like constant sleepovers. You could keep some of your stuff here 'til the end of the month."

The truth is, Kara kissed me once. Last year. She has dated women before, although she says she prefers men. So I always have to be a little careful around her. That's why I only want to hang around here once a week. Kara knows I'm not interested in her in that special way, but still.

"I'll think about it," I say.

"Okay," she says, resigned. "Don't worry about me sitting here with this lavish library and pool-deep tub while you're discussing newspaper biases."

"It's magazines, too."

"I'm sure there will be a *lot* of hot men there." She rolls her eyes.

But oddly enough, it is there that I meet my match—sort of.

Seven

My therapist, Dr. Petrov, grew up with my father in London. Even though my father travels a lot, he calls me when he can. And he insists that I see Petrov once every two weeks. It used to be every week, but that was a little much. This month, I only have to see Petrov once, because he's going on vacation next week.

"Volunteering is the perfect way to help you be more social," Petrov tells me, leaning back in his chair as clouds and gray fill the window behind him. Petrov has salt-and-pepper hair and is in his late forties.

"I didn't even have a conversation with anyone while I was volunteering," I say.

"You must have had a conversation with *some*one," he says.

"Oh, that's right, I forgot. 'Would you like an apple?' 'No, that's instant diarrhea.'"

"Well, the fact that you're more in tune with the struggles of the poor will help you in your daily interactions," Petrov says. "Rather than focusing on yourself, you will have a better perspective on what's in other people's minds. It helps you understand your problems aren't so big and gets you invested in society. Don't look at these opportunities as singles events. Look at them as ways to learn to relate to different kinds of people. Then you'll be more likely to get along with the single people you meet."

"Good, that's less selfish. Instead of using volunteer opportunities to meet men, I'll use them for free therapy."

"At least in this case, you're being selfish while helping others."

He's brilliant.

"The other thing is," Petrov says, "once you meet someone, your problems aren't going to end that instant. You seem to believe that once you find a person who's like you, you won't ever need to change, because now you fit in with someone. But we are always learning and changing and adapting, and there will always be a need to change and compromise, not just for your husband, but for other people you meet. The more opportunities you take to interact with other people, the more equipped you will be for a relationship."

"No one ever tells men to change," I say. "It's only women who are told to change. Tim was anal, and I'll bet he's not in therapy."

"How do you know?" Petrov asks.

"How many men do you have as guests—er, clients?"

"I would say that thirty percent of my clients are men."

I smile smugly. I feel bad for people who aren't smart enough to debate therapists and call them on all their B.S.

"I'm not saying you have to change everything about you," Petrov says. "Obviously you are a caring person who wants to do the right thing, and I appreciate your moral values. But you're only twenty. You need to learn more about the world before you come to easy conclusions. We both know you're smart and you know a lot about philosophy and literature and history. But I'm sure that you can admit there are plenty of things you don't know."

"I don't know why raucous and ruckus have to be two different words."

"Exactly."

I don't think he paid attention.

"I want you to realize that you are not the only person who has trouble fitting in. Look at the guy who mentioned the diarrhea. He said something inappropriate and didn't think about the fact that it wasn't socially acceptable. Lots of people have trouble fitting into this world. I think if you re-alize that, you'll feel a little more comfortable."

"Maybe I should have asked him out," I say. "We could go to Washington Square Park and play chess with Pepto-Bis-mol tablets."

"I'm not saying you have to date the homeless—"

Now he's getting exasperated with me. It's a fine line—and I walk it in this office often.

"I'm saying you have to keep opening yourself up to new experiences, not get angry because you didn't meet some-one who's just like you at the soup kitchen. Keep volun-teering once a week. Go to that newspaper bias meeting, and attend the next one and the next one. Once people see your face a lot, they'll become comfortable with you, and vice versa. Maybe Tim was distracted because he's running the show, but if he sees you there more than once, he'll warm to you. You can be a hard person to get to know at first."

"How would you know?" I ask. "It's your job to ask me questions. If you don't know me by now, that sounds like a professional failing on your part."

Don't worry. Petrov loves me. He should pay me because I make him feel so useful.

"What about Kara?" Petrov asks. "Why don't you want to spend more than one day a week with her at Judith's place? You told me she invited you to move in for a few weeks."

"You know why I don't want to do that."

"Kara hasn't kissed you in a year."

"I know," I say. "She's a good friend, but…it doesn't help me meet anyone if I'm stuck inside her house."

"But you enjoy being with her," Petrov says. "And when you feel better about yourself, other people can tell. When you're proud—like after you worked at the soup kitchen—people can tell that, too. Working on yourself is as important to dating as trying to find people to date. I think Kara brings a unique perspective to your life."

"That's one way to look at it."

Petrov sighs. "Just remember. Every new social interaction brings you closer to your goals, even if you don't realize it."

Eight

With my goals in mind and my future social interactions at stake, I head out to the FAIR event at Housing Works, a used bookstore in Soho. FAIR stands for Fairness and Accuracy in Reporting. It's a group in New York that holds panels once a month on unbalanced or unresearched news coverage.

The three panelists settle into a row of desks at the back of the store. Two of them are magazine editors and one is a newspaper editor. I look around. There are a lot of young people here with backpacks and glasses. I'm in my element! At last! I should have come here earlier. Maybe the trick is not to go to social events, but to go to intellectual events and be social *at* them.

They lead off by talking about whether American newspapers 1) lie about Israel, and 2) in which direction. I've been too self-centered to know much about foreign affairs, but I'm aware that my ignorance is dangerous and I need to learn more. Hence: FAIR.

The two magazine editors say they are "just disgusted"

with the handling of foreign news by most of the print media, who they say "want everything handed to them." They mention an essay by Noam Chomsky. I haven't read him yet, but I've *been meaning to,* which should count for half a point or something.

My mind wanders. So do my eyes. Everyone here has brought friends. There's a guy in a striped shirt whose right hand rests on his tall girlfriend's shoulder. On the other side of him is a girl with pigtails next to a guy with red hair. Behind them is a young man with dark straight hair and glasses with dark frames. He's raising his hand to ask a question.

Wait—stop the camera there.

He looks geeky and smart, and he appears to be alone.

Score!

His hand descends because he's been called on.

"I think there's a brilliance but a lack of practicality in Noam Chomsky," he says. "Most of the people who read *Manufacturing Consent* still have only a rudimentary understanding of the process by which news is gathered and reported. Which is not to say that the mainstream media—" he chuckles "—has done much to prove itself unworthy of the image...."

I've already stopped listening to what he's saying, because I'm stuck on the fact that he pronounced the name No-AM. He could be talking like Woodstock in the Charlie Brown cartoons right now and I wouldn't notice, because he started off by saying No-AM. Even the panelists pronounce it "Nome" instead of "No-AM." I don't know which pronunciation is correct, but the fact that this guy has made an effort to say No-AM shows that he's a person for whom attention to language is paramount.

And he doesn't stop there. He says "going to" instead of gonna. He says "Clinton" instead of Clin-in. He gesticulates.

I decide to inconspicuously edge toward him.

I have to stop when a girl in baggy army pants and a guy who's tall and gawky close the space between them. They're like human elevator doors. I wind around them.

There are more discussions and further questions, and I keep tabs on the nerdy guy out of the corner of my eye. He seems enthralled by the panel and doesn't take his eyes off it for a minute. Isn't anyone else here because they want to find a mate? There are three million unmarried people in New York. Then again, what the statisticians don't tell you is that 2.9 million of them are living with someone.

Okay, I admit I sound awful right now. But it's not just that I want a boyfriend. I want someone to talk to. It would be nice if he's a boy.

Suddenly, I notice people picking up their bags.

"I guess we have time for one last question," the moderator says.

One question?

"Anyone?"

It's about to be over!

"One more question," the moderator repeats.

I look at nerdy glasses-boy. He's turning to leave.

Think, Carrie.

My hand darts in the air.

"Yes?"

"I don't have a question, necessarily," I sputter, "but what I wanted to say was, first, I definitely second the comments about No-*AM* Chomsky made earlier by the brilliant gentleman over there. Secondly, I want to say that I've enjoyed everyone's comments so much, especially in a world where most people don't pay much attention to foreign affairs, so if anyone here wants to join me nearby in grabbing a bite to eat and discussing these topics further, they should come see me."

The moderator smiles. "That's great. Well, everyone, don't forget to sign our mailing list."

The nerdy guy has finished zipping up his backpack and is about to walk out. I have to do something. Someday, I'll be too old to get away with stuff based on inexperience and naiveté.

I walk up behind him. "So, do you want to come with us?" I ask. He looks back, startled. I hope he's not paying enough attention to ask who "us" is.

He says, "I can't stay out late."

A guy who doesn't stay out all night! "It won't be long," I say. "A friend of mine is meeting me at the restaurant. She was supposed to come to this, but she's late. I'll see if anyone else is interested."

I look behind me and in front of me. "Nope."

"Where are you going?" he asks.

"A Malaysian place." There's one a few blocks from here. I know this because Cy and I celebrated his birthday there last year. Damn. All those things about breaking up with someone are true. There's always stuff to remind you. But if I take this place and reuse it for good ends, that will replace its evil connotation.

"I've never had Malaysian," he says. "But I always wanted to try it."

Score!

We head down Crosby Street, a narrow alley dotted with Dumpsters full of construction debris, passing the backs of shops. Some of them have naked, unused mannequins pressed up to their windows, and they're mooning us.

"What's your name?" the guy asks me, trying to balance on the cobblestones as we walk. I almost trip over a pile of dirty cardboard boxes resting against a new BMW. Quite a juxtaposition.

"Carrie," I say. "What's yours?"

"Nolan," he says.

"Oh!" I say. "Like Nolan Bushnell."

He stops, then looks at me. "You're the only person who's ever said anything besides Nolan Ryan."

"Who's Nolan Ryan?" I ask.

And he grins the biggest grin in the world.

Penang is crowded. There's a slim bar at the front, but the key is the dining room in the back, which is decorated lavishly with tikis and coconuts and bamboo—and couples. Always couples.

The waitress asks how many we're waiting for. "I don't think my friend's coming," I say. "Just two."

Nolan gives me a strange look.

"She always calls on my cell if she's going to be late," I say, but I'm lying. I don't even have a cell phone. If I got one, that would only double the number of calls I'm not getting.

We sit at a table and read the menus. Nolan has the darkest hair I've ever seen. I think it's black. He's gazing intently at his menu. I look down the list of fruity drinks. Even though I hate the level of institutionalized peer pressure that comes with drinking, I've also found that alcohol does a good job of stopping me from thinking so hard.

I sneak another peek at Nolan. He has kind of a triangular nose. He's good-looking in a nerdy way. Thank God I took a chance. Sometimes it doesn't seem worth it to push myself out, but then when something good actually comes of it, I feel glad I never quite gave up.

When the waitress comes to take our orders, Nolan says, "We need another minute."

I watch him staring at the menu, hard.

"They have delicious piña coladas here," I say. "I still have a craving from the last time I had one."

"I don't drink," he says.

Oh.

"I don't drink that much, either," I sputter, "and I always resented all the pressure, but now I do it once in a while."

He smiles as if I made that up so he'd like me. Then he goes back to the menu. "They don't have too many vegetarian dishes here."

"Are you a vegetarian?"

"Yes," he says. "It's a much healthier lifestyle. And there are moral reasons to avoid eating dead animals. If you'd read the things that I have, you'd never even be able to *look* at meat."

"I do read a lot," I say.

"Obviously not what I have."

Oh.

The waitress returns. "Can I get you two a drink?"

"I don't drink," Nolan tells her.

She seems taken aback by his abruptness, and she looks at me almost sympathetically. My throat feels dry. "Just water," I croak.

She nods and leaves.

And now I understand.

For the first time in my life, I understand the peer pressure to drink. If you try to drink to lessen your inhibitions and the other person doesn't, you just feel dopey. You have to have someone else encouraging you, getting stupid with you, so you're not the only one.

Maybe getting older means learning the rationale for everyone else's idiocy. But is this what I want? To be just as stupid as everyone else?

Maybe Nolan has been sent here to remind me of the moral, straitlaced teetotaler I used to be.

Nolan puts down his menu. "Look at *them,*" he says, motioning with his head. In a corner of the room, under a canopy of bamboo and tiki, a young couple is making out.

"I hate public displays of affection," I tell him.

"Well, that would be repulsive enough," he says, "but it looks like they're on a first date." He pronounces the *T* harshly. "They shouldn't act like that on a first date."

I'm half amused and half horrified. I used to have rules like that, but I've spent the past year teaching myself not to be so black and white. The couple isn't hurting anyone, are they?

"How do you know they're on a first date?" I ask him.

"When the waitress brought us here, I heard them asking each other where they grew up and stuff," Nolan says. "Typical mindless patter."

I laugh. "Not like at FAIR."

"No, FAIR is different." He softens a bit. He has very dark eyebrows, and his face is pleasant. "Have you been to their discussions before?"

"No," I say. "I was tired of everyone in New York only caring about sex and wild parties, and I wanted to find something more important to do."

Nolan smiles. "Exactly!"

I'm getting through to him!

Then he asks me, "Which magazines do you read?"

I'm usually the one to judge people on unfair criteria. "The *Atlantic Monthly. Harper's. Utne Reader.*" I'm lying about the last one.

"Did you see the article in the *Utne* about the Bagram detention center in Afghanistan?"

"Yeah." I half expect him to respond, *"Okay, so what did you think?"* But then I could say, *"You asked if I saw it, not if I read it."* In any case, I'm spared the test because the waitress arrives to take our orders. He gets something that has no meat, of course, and feeling guilty, I stick to a noodle dish.

As she leaves, an Asian waiter with dyed blond hair passes with a tray of colorful drinks. Those piña coladas sure look creamy. My head turns as I watch them pass.

"If you want one, you can get one," Nolan says tiredly.

"When I was in college, I never drank," I explain. "But I realized that drinking isn't the worst thing you can do."

"That's how bad things have gotten," he says. "People justify every action by saying, 'Well, at least I'm not murdering someone.' We've got such an anything-goes mentality, we spend all our time *rationalizing*. Unless you do what everyone does, you don't fit in. Alcohol makes people behave recklessly. And physically, it isn't healthy, either."

He pronounces it *I*-ther.

"Wow," I say. "I need to meet more people like you. I'd stopped believing there were any."

Nolan nods. "Sometimes you lower your standards until you can barely remember what being a thinking human being really means."

And as he says this, I think my worst fear has come true.

Last year, when I was even more shy and socially awkward than I am now—if you can believe that—I always worried that when I finally learned to fit in with the world, I might meet someone who would have liked me the way I was. And now I'm sitting across from a voracious reader, a smart, one-of-a-kind guy who has strict standards and moral absolutes, and I've lowered my standards too much to be good enough for him.

"Well, I have to go use the lavatory," he says. "Notice that I didn't say bathroom. I never say *bathroom*. There's not even a bath *in* it."

He gets up and walks away.

I have met the enemy, and he is me.

Nine

"Who the fuck is Nolan Bushnell?"

I'm heading into Judith's building with Kara. I don't have a legal proofing assignment for the next few nights, so I've got time to waste.

"Nolan Bushnell is *only* the guy who designed the world's first video game," I explain, following Kara into the mailroom to pick up Judith's mail. "He also started the chain of Chuck E. Cheese's Pizza Time theaters."

"I can't figure out which one is less impressive."

"Chuck E. Cheese."

"That was a rhetorical question, fool."

Upstairs, she drops the mail onto the amorphous stack of papers on the dining room table. I glance at Judith's caller ID box to see if anyone has phoned. If Judith gets any really important calls, Kara is supposed to call her in Mexico.

"What does it say on the caller ID?" Kara asks.

"Unavailable," I say. "And Anonymous."

"Oh. It's my last two boyfriends."

We open the shelves to find plates so we'll be ready when dinner arrives. We're going to order sushi and watch an old movie.

"Is Nolan a real veggie?" she asks me.

"As opposed to what?"

"Some people claim they're vegetarians but they still eat hamburgers or fish."

"I think he's real."

"Really boring," Kara says, setting out the plates. "I think what he needs is a nice, juicy steak."

I laugh, and then I realize that isn't fair. It sounds like the vegetarian version of "She just needs to get laid." I'm sure Kara would say that about Nolan, as well.

"When are you seeing Nolan next?" Kara asks.

"Sunday," I say. "He asked if I've ever eaten at this veggie place on Eighth Street, and I never have, and he didn't ask me out, so I said it would be neat if he showed me around a menu there."

"Clever move," Kara says. "Why Sunday?"

"Nolan refuses to go out Fridays or Saturdays. He says he can't stand it when people make you feel like there's something wrong with you if you're not out on a Friday or Saturday night, so he only goes out on Sundays."

"Oh no!" she gasps, looking at me. "He's Carrie times three."

She didn't make that sound like a good thing.

Later that night, Kara and I are lying back on Judith's huge bed, looking up through her skylight. I'll go back to my room in a minute. I'm not tired yet. A plane flies overhead. A few stars are out.

I ask, "Where did Judith Sarakin Green get all this money?"

Kara stretches. "I think she invented green."

"She must get amazing residuals."

I realize something: I feel content right now. Almost…happy. I like being with my best friend. I like that we ate delicious sushi, I like that we watched the movie *Laura,* and I love that I'm not under an ounce of pressure to be anything other than who I am.

Why can't I feel this comfortable on a *date*?

Checking the mail and looking at the answering machine are the kind of mundane things that I mutter about in my internal dialogue. But I actually had someone to do them with. Maybe having a roommate a few times a week will help me learn to include other people in my daily thoughts. Maybe I should stay here more often after all.

"So what did your shrink have to say?" Kara asks.

"He says even if I get into a relationship with someone who's like me, I'll still have to struggle and compromise and change at times," I say. "Do you think it's pointless for me to search for someone who's like me?"

"Of course not," Kara says, yawning. "It's just that it might take a while. I think getting older is about realizing it won't be that easy. All the times when you're a teenager and you wish to God you could find one person who understands you, you think, 'someday.' You try things to get people to notice you, like piercing your face or starting an underground magazine or wrestling or trying out for the school play or, in your case, getting good grades, because you assume 'someday' someone will appreciate or 'get' you—and then you become an adult and realize all those things that make you most unique aren't necessarily going to be the things that attract other people."

"So you have little control over it?" I ask. "Maybe no one's ever going to get me. I've been looking for that person since freshman year, and it's getting tiring."

"We just have to be realistic about it," Kara says. "My new theory is that there is a subset of really interesting people in the world and a subset of really dull people. The interesting people, the ones who make art or climb mountains or build bridges, get depressed because other people disappoint them. The dull people are depressed because they don't want, or don't know how, to make art or climb mountains or build bridges. So the very interesting people are depressed and the very boring people are depressed and the normal, average, easygoing people in the middle have already found each other. The rest of us are bouncing around like bingo balls."

"So where am I?" I say. "I can't meet your definition of interesting, because I don't do anything artistic. I don't like parties, and I have no desire to go mountain-climbing."

"But you're interesting anyway," Kara says, turning to look at me.

She's wearing navy blue flannel pajamas. I used to think that all women except me wore nightgowns to bed, but apparently some of them wear pajamas.

"Most people would not find me interesting," I say. "If I asked them to describe me, they'd say, 'Well, you never want to leave your house. Your life is all in your head—'"

"Your *mind* is interesting," she says.

"People don't know that."

"Then maybe the problem isn't that there are a subset of dull people and a subset of interesting people," Kara says. "Maybe the problem is that we don't take the time to find what's interesting about each *other*."

"But on a date you don't get that kind of time," I say. "You finish your meal and you either kiss or don't kiss."

She laughs. "In college, we had time to get to know each other before going on dates. But Nolan's going to let you take your time, right? He doesn't seem pushy about that kind of thing."

"No, he's not," I say. "He doesn't seem pushy about getting to know me at *all,* and that's the problem. I wish I felt more excited about him. What's wrong with me?"

"Nothing's wrong with you," Kara says. "You opened yourself up to new possibilities, and now maybe Nolan isn't interesting enough to *you.*"

"But he's interesting in his own way," I say. "Just like you were saying."

"I'm sure Nolan is interesting in his own way," Kara says, "but what you might find, in the end, is that Nolan is not interesting to *you.* You can probably interest yourself more than Nolan can interest you."

"Is that what it's come to?" I ask. "That I don't love anyone as much as myself?"

"Who does?"

Ten

My dad calls me a few hours before my second date with Nolan. "I'm glad you met someone nice," he says. He sounds like he's walking around his hotel room. I can picture the posh amenities—minibar, immaculate king-size bed, portable fax machine on the desk.

"Yeah, Nolan's pretty nice." I try to sound brave whenever I talk to my dad. It's not like he can zip home from Luxembourg to counsel me. I have old Petrov for that.

"How are things otherwise?" Dad asks.

"I have an idea," I tell him.

"Yes?"

I hear noise in the background. He must be getting a fax or maybe the maid is in the room.

"You know how I missed out on enjoying the college experience with kids my age?" I ask.

"Uh-huh."

I always make him feel guilty about that.

"Well," I say, drumming my fingers on my desk, "I think

I'm ready to be an undergraduate now." I take a breath and launch into my speech. "Since I'm still young, and I only majored in philosophy, I'll bet some college could take me again as an undergrad. There are a lot of things I haven't learned. I'm only twenty years old, and I'm sure colleges would understand that I went to school too young and I want another chance. You'd only have to be willing to pay for another four years."

He's quiet for a minute.

"Just think about it," I add. "I'd be safer on a college campus than in New York City alone. And you and Dr. Petrov want me to make more friends, don't you?"

"What about going to graduate school?"

"People are antisocial in graduate school," I say. "I can be antisocial in New York for free. Being an undergrad would be better. What do you think is the value of getting lost on a campus with a thousand freshmen your age? What is the value of having discussions in your dorm about old TV shows at three a.m.?"

"You did that?"

"No. That's the point!"

"I've never heard of anyone being an undergrad twice," Dad says.

"Because it's so expensive that no one has tried it," I say. "But I don't see what would be so terrible about a school making an exception. There's plenty more for me to learn."

"I don't know if they'd allow it," Dad says. "Which schools would you want me to ask?"

"Any schools that have smart people in them," I say. "You know a few deans."

"I'll ask around. I'm not so sure of their policies."

I smile to myself. "All I want is for you to try."

"I'll do my best."

That evening I feel happier. I'm optimistic about my backup plan. I will meet smart kids! Kids who are inexperienced at socializing! Kids only a few years younger than I! Anticipation is the best antidepressant.

I feel energized as I head to the veggie place on Eighth Street. I arrive before Nolan does. I'm a little disappointed because the tables are touching one another in long rows, and they don't afford much privacy. How can I get to know Nolan better if we're squished next to other couples? As awkward as I am, I always manage to find people who are even more poorly schooled in dating than I am. Even *I* know you shouldn't take your date to a place with communal eating.

Nolan looks perturbed when he enters. He shakes his hair slightly, like he's a dog. As soon as we sit down, he tells me what's bothering him.

"Do you know that movie *Say Anything*?" he asks me.

"From the eighties?"

He nods, seeming angry. "Girls always talk about that movie. My sister was going on and on and on, on the phone today…"

That's a lot of ons.

"…about how she wants to find a man like Lloyd Dobler, and I've been hearing this from, like, every girl, and it's ridiculous."

The waitress brings us water in little glasses. They're small, like jam bottles. Maybe they *were* jam bottles.

"That movie's okay," I say. "It's not the best I've seen or anything." I can compromise on this.

"Girls are lying," he says.

"What?"

"Girls are lying about Lloyd Dobler."

"Okay…"

"First off—" Nolan looks at the ceiling "—we're supposed to love this guy. But he has no personality and no goals."

"He has a goal. It's kickboxing."

Nolan laughs as if I was being sarcastic. "There's no way a valedictorian would fall for a guy just because of kickboxing."

It's not necessarily that Nolan is more moral than I am. He's just more snobby. I wonder where he got this elitism?

"Where did you go to college?" I ask him.

"Tufts."

I almost laugh. Tufts is where people go if they can't get into Harvard. Wait a minute—now I'm being judgmental. There are other reasons to go to Tufts. Like if you can't get into Yale.

"Do you really think," I say, "that a valedictorian would never fall for a guy who's nice and sweet, just because he's not as smart as she is?"

"Well, he'd have to be somewhat smart," Nolan says, looking at the drink menu. "I mean, what could they talk about? This is why girls are lying. None of them would give Dobler the time of day if he didn't have goals."

Now I realize I have nothing to lose. I am going to share with Nolan the things I've learned over the past year. Because the truth is, Nolan is going to learn them soon enough, and five years from now, he's going to be a great catch. Why should some other girl be the early bird? Sometimes you have to stick around with a guy and wait for him to ripen.

The waitress takes our order, and I order a stir-fry with

something called seitan, which I figure is really soy, although Nolan tells me it's wheat gluten. I thought everything here was secretly soy.

"I used to judge people by where they went to college," I say, "or what they did for a living, but then I realized there are some really smart people who didn't go to a prestigious college, or people who are smart about different things than I am."

"Oh, the old 'street-smartness' argument?" He rolls his eyes.

"I know," I say. "You can't have an intellectual discussion with street smarts. But you can learn a lot of other valuable things."

"Like what?" He seems uncomfortable. Behind him, the kitchen has an inordinate amount of steam issuing from it, and it almost looks like it's coming from his ears.

"Well, I was just volunteering at a soup kitchen last weekend, and…do you know they almost never serve soup?"

He laughs. "Yes. I volunteered a few times while I was at Tufts."

He volunteered! He has a soft side! Kara is right—you really have to probe someone to get to know them better. "Well, I went to Harvard and I didn't even know that," I say. "Isn't that stupid?"

"Yes," he says.

Thank you very much.

He adds, "My sister works in social services in Boston, so I know all about that stuff. I don't know how she has the patience."

"See? And she's probably not smarter than you."

"She's definitely not."

"So your sister has a lot of patience and is great, even if she's not smarter than you. Maybe Lloyd Dobler has more patience than smart people."

He's staring down at the table, but he's listening.

I add, "I've just learned to try to judge people on whether they're nice, not just on whether they're smart."

"I guess you have a point. It's just that sometimes, people look at me like I'm crazy if I want to discuss anything intellectual, like at a party. When I told people at work that I was going to FAIR, they were like, 'That's how you spend your night?' Of course, they're assholes."

"So people make you feel like you don't fit in," I say. He's like me!

"Sort of," he says.

I give him a kind smile, but he looks toward the kitchen.

The waiter delivers our steaming plates. The vegetables in my stir-fry are so rich in color they're almost beautiful; I've never seen carrots that orange or beans that green. They're green beans, incidentally, because the string has been removed. I consider telling Nolan about my discovery, but I don't want to muddle the issue with legumes.

The dish is scrumptious. Nolan has good taste. Of course, there must be a lot of sugar in this. Anything that boasts of being "natural" and "fat-free" often has plenty of sugar, which is both natural and fat-free.

I ask Nolan a few questions about his sister in Boston. Turns out she's only a year younger than he is, and she's more social. She's getting married and she's only twenty-two.

I tell him about my father, and that my mother died of cancer when I was two. His eyes soften. He reveals that his sister had leukemia when she was little but is now free of it. She had to retake a year of elementary school. I can imagine what Nolan went through.

"She's the bravest person I've ever met," Nolan tells me. "I wish I could be as brave as she is."

I smile. "I'm sure you do brave things."

"I'm trying to learn from her," Nolan says. "I guess I've got time, right?"

"Sure," I say. "And you can teach her to be smarter."

Nolan looks down at the table. "I shouldn't have said that about her."

"It's okay. You're the older sibling. You *should* be smarter."

He nods. "That's right."

"Everything okay here?" The waitress smiles at us, her teeth white as paper.

"Good," I say, but the jury is still out on Nolan. I think he's got promise. He's a bit lacking in the sense of humor department, but there are signs of a thinking, feeling person in there. I just don't know how he feels about me. We're avoiding that kind of talk.

He might just be shy, though. In dating, you always have to allow for the possibility that the other person is even more inept than you, although with me it's a long shot.

We finish up and both say we had a nice time, but we don't mention meeting up again. I'm still not sure how I feel. Nolan is a unique person. And he clearly loves his sister. I definitely wouldn't mind taking the time to get to know him better. He's still more promising than the jerks I've met.

I'll have to see if he calls. Maybe I'll call him once more. Then I can ask him point-blank if he wants to be friends, or if there's a chance we could be more.

Eleven

Thank God for Kara.

The next night we're scheduled to eat sushi together, right before I go to my late-night legal proofing shift. We're also planning to go to a bar together the following evening. Knowing that I can catch up with her makes my struggles a bit more palatable.

Before I leave to meet Kara, I keep checking my voice-mail to see if Nolan has called. Does it make sense that I like him more when he's not around? He seems so good in principle.

That night, Kara and I relax across on Judith's couches with vodka cranberry juices in our hands, surrounded by the art deco pillows. She and I are trying to decide if there's hope for Nolan as a boyfriend.

Kara says, "Let me ask you an honest question."

I set down *Architectural Digest* on Judith's bale of magazines.

"Are you attracted to Nolan at all?" she asks.

I say, "He's decent-looking."

"That's not my question. Are you attracted to him?"

"I like the way he looks…"

"Do you feel. Like touching. His body."

"No, but it's not because—"

"I *know* he doesn't look like Frankenstein," Kara says. "I'm talking about *attraction*. It's okay to admit you're not attracted to someone. It's not an insult to him." She leans forward. "If you don't have it for him, you don't have it for him."

"But I *should* like him," I say. "On New Year's Eve I was making out with Kurt, who was totally wrong for me. Maybe I'm like those horrible women who only want to date jerks."

"Don't ever make the mistake of feeling like you have to choose between a guy who's boring and a guy who's a jerk," Kara says. "You want to date someone who's nice *and* has a personality. There's nothing wrong with that. You didn't call that guy Kurt from New Year's Eve, right? So you don't like jerks. Find someone who's nice and smart *and* interesting."

"But Nolan is…"

"Perfect?" Kara rolls her eyes. "Maybe you need someone a little less perfect." She grabs a pillow. "And he needs to find a big fat hamburger."

"He has rational explanations for why he's a vegetarian. I should admire him."

Our sushi arrives at that moment, speaking of vegetarians. Kara likes to have peaches with it. "My brother gave me this idea," she says, dumping a can into the bowl.

"How come you hardly talk to him?" I ask, as she wiggles the can to get the last bits. This is the kind of thing I'd never ask someone who wasn't a good friend. Kara is sensitive about her family. Her parents split up right as she started college, and they kept using her against each other. Eventually she stopped talking to both of them. She still talks to her brother a few times a year, but that's about it.

"I don't know," Kara says, sitting down and sighing. "I got a call yesterday."

"From your brother?"

"From my mom."

Wow—that's important. I turn to her on the couch, lifting my chopsticks. "What did she say?"

"She didn't leave a message. If I'm not around, she won't leave a message. I saw her number on my caller ID."

"Maybe she's sorry she never speaks to you," I say. I have trouble comprehending relatives not talking to each other. Probably because I hardly have any myself.

"My mother only cares about how things *look,*" Kara says. "She's done that her whole life. According to her, I'm just a big failure. Last year I told my brother, Eric, to tell Mom I was dating a woman. Guess what happened? She stopped even mentioning my name to him."

"But she just called you," I point out.

"True," Kara says. "She's done that a few times lately. She just broke up with her boyfriend. Suddenly she wants me for a best friend."

"You don't know that that's the reason."

Kara shrugs. "She knows where I am. She can do better than ringing a few times and hanging up."

I ask her what her life was like growing up.

"Do you know anything about Great Neck, New York?" she asks.

I shake my head.

"It's on Long Island."

"I know that…."

"It's extremely wealthy, and everyone's in everyone else's

business," Kara says. "People's kids are like contest entries. See who can do better. No one's happy with their lives—houses, cars, vacuum cleaners, kids—unless they have better ones than their neighbors."

"Oh." My childhood wasn't like that at all. Most of the kids in my school in New York, which was a private school, had the same things I did and lived in expensive apartments. But I rarely got the chance to make friends, since everyone was a few years ahead of me, anyway. I had friends in first and second grade, when kids only cared about whether you played with blocks and computer games. After they started caring how you looked and whether you talked about the same TV shows, it went downhill.

"You know what I miss about Great Neck, though?" Kara says.

I shrug.

"Best Bagels," she says. "We had a tradition on Sundays. Before any of us woke up, my dad would slip out and head to the main street, Middle Neck Road, and pick up these huge, flat sunflower-seed bagels from Best. They're so flat that you can spread cream cheese *on* them instead of inside. He bought chocolate milk, too, and Eric and I would put away three bagels each while Mom and Dad read the *Times*. I haven't had those flat bagels in ages."

I can tell she misses the tradition as much as the bagels.

"Ah, well," she says. "Sushi'll have to do." She sets her bowl aside and gets up to put *The Godfather* in the DVD. I reach for some Philadelphia rolls. I think they have to do with Philadelphia cream cheese and not the city.

During the movie, I feel relaxed and renewed. I'm spending quality time with my best friend. It's much less stressful than eating with Nolan.

★ ★ ★

As I sit on the subway heading to my assignment that night, the lights shining in and out and reflecting on the ads, I realize that I really do want to move in with Kara for the last two weeks of her house-sitting assignment. It won't replace a romantic relationship, but it's wonderful to have mundane conversations with someone without being on a date. It's like we both have a stake in each other's day-to-day affairs of life.

I don't really want to head to a bar with Kara tomorrow. I just want to hang out with her at Judith Sarakin Green's, among DVDs and rows of books and windows on the park.

Why do I deny my true feelings all the time? I *enjoy* hanging out with Kara. She's a great friend. I can still work on my resolution, but I want a place to come back to, with someone who understands me.

Whenever I'm at a proofreading assignment after midnight, most of the other people have just come from day jobs and are dead tired. They bring snacks to keep themselves awake—Ho-Hos and Kandy Kakes and nuts and brownies—and continually refill their cups from the coffee station, sometimes just with hot water so they don't have to pay. The whole place at night smells of chocolate and coffee beans.

As the munching and brewing and refilling goes on around me, I sit with my white legal pad and consider my progress. It's the middle of January. So far, I've gone to one bar, attended FAIR once, volunteered at a soup kitchen and gone on two dates with Nolan. That's promising.

I don't know if Nolan will ultimately help me fulfill my goal of finding a man who is like me. First, he actually has to call again. Or I have to call him and use my feminine wiles to get him into a compromising position. I'll ask Kara about that tomorrow night at the bar. She's an expert.

Tall Al, the supervisor, comes into the proofing office to give me an assignment. I read the brief painstakingly, managing to find two missing periods and three inverted quotation marks. It takes about forty-five minutes and I hand it back to Al.

There is nothing to do for the next hour. The typists are inputting the corrections, but they're slow. I use the extra time to think.

I think about which living war veterans would not be included in the category of "Veterans of Foreign Wars."

I think about what the difference is between a hunchback and a humpback.

I think about how someone can "draw" a blank.

I think about why it took until 2001 for someone to invent those fake torch things with orange crepe paper that blows and looks like fire.

I think about how stores can sell more than one mug that says "#1 DAD."

I think about whether you say "I went to a Yankee game" or "I went to a Yankees game."

My assignment ends at four a.m.

I tiredly remind my supervisor to order a car and then I walk to the bank of elevators in the hall.

Downstairs, it's freezing out. My breath hovers in midair. A black sedan is supposed to come soon with a number in the window—667. I have narrowly escaped evil. Two marble statues of lions stand guard outside the building, and the only sound is a high-pitched ringing in the distance. I always stand just beyond the doorway, between the lions, so the security guards can see me.

When the car shows up, I get an idea.

"Where are you heading?" the driver asks as I duck into the back seat.

"Great Neck," I say. "Long Island."

His eyes narrow. "You're sure?"

"Sure," I say cheerfully. "That's exactly where I'm going."

The big prize for working the overnight shift, besides the two dollars an hour extra, is the view of late-night Manhattan in the hired car. Most nights, the car first veers west toward the Hudson River so we can take the West Side Highway down to the Village. As we go, we usually pass the *New York Times* workers in their noisy orange-lit garage on 43rd Street, tossing bales of fresh newspapers onto the delivery trucks. They're really loud at four in the morning. Sometimes I almost forget that Times Square is named for the *Times*.

But tonight I have requested Long Island instead. We head north toward the 59th Street Bridge, which will take us east to Queens. The streets are nearly empty, except for homeless people who haven't found a safe spot and have chosen to wander all night and sleep during the day—the kind whom we might assume are hookers or drug pushers because we're not equipped to handle the horror of a person who is out there because he has no choice.

We pass the Manhattan side of the East River with its glittering high-rises, and then we are over the bridge to Queens. This borough is full of neighborhoods that I hear about on the news but have never seen. If I haven't heard about your town on the New York news, it's a good sign, because it means it hasn't had many murders and fires.

The neighborhoods in Queens change quickly from poor

to middle-class to poor to middle-class, one ethnicity to another, with no clear warning. Latino groceries suddenly give way to shops with signs in Chinese. It would be interesting to chart how the different ethnic groups came to spread out. The types of homes change suddenly, too; there are blocks full of projects—brick facades with identical protruding Friedrich air conditioners—and then there is an invisible line and we hit tall individual working-class homes that must go back to the eighteen-hundreds.

In Bayside we pass 220th Street, the highest numbered street I've ever seen in New York—and suddenly everything changes.

It's like when the Wizard of Oz goes from black-and-white to color. We coast on a low bridge over marshes and meadows, cattails poking up and hay piles on the side, and ahead of us, a green ball field glows in front of tall, barren winter trees.

Signs announce a Long Island town I've never heard of—Douglaston. There must not be many murders and fires in Douglaston. Businesses like Long Island Physical Therapy and a "saloon" belly up to the street; nothing is a simple clinic or bar anymore. The homes don't look wealthy, but they have their own yards, and I imagine the location accounts for the price tag—if you can be in Manhattan by train in twenty minutes and have grass, you're going to pay.

We pass through the town of Little Neck (what's with all these Necks?) and into Great Neck. The bagel store is on Middle Neck Road, near the train station. The driver lets me out and I observe the trappings of restored history—new-old lanterns, a sign welcoming me to the "village" of Great Neck, an intricate bulletin board advertising town functions.

I know Kara hated this place, but to an outsider, it's quaint. Not to mention trendy. As I stroll up Middle Neck Road I take inventory of the Yuppie shops—the Handbag Gallery, an upscale children's clothier, fine candies, Linda Silver Designs, Maret Gifts, Bruce's Bakery.

Then I see it—Best Bagels. It's got a line out the door. Everyone must love their flat bagels.

The train ride back to Penn Station in Manhattan takes less than a half-hour. As the sun comes up, I hail a cab to the Upper West Side and leave a bag of flat sunflower-seed bagels with the doorman. I scrawl a note for Kara: *To Kara. Love, the Bagel Fairy.*

I venture back into the brisk morning air to return to my apartment. I realize that it's not just that I want someone to do things for me—I miss having someone to do things *for*. I'm glad I fetched Kara's favorite bagels. I can't wait to hear later what her reaction was when she woke up and got them.

Twelve

At home I lapse into satisfied slumber, and I don't reawaken until one p.m. It bothers me that Kara and I have to go to a bar tonight, but we'll probably stay for an hour and then return to Judith's.

Tonight, I'm going to tell Kara that I want to move in for the last two weeks. We'll have some great adventures together.

At seven, I take a shower and dress so I look half decent. I even put on some makeup. I take the subway uptown. We're having a pre-bar drink at Judith's apartment and then we're going to head out. She said it saves you money to have a drink first—you can get to the bar and sip seltzers, and you still get buzzed.

In Kara's elevator, I notice a little sign next to a speaker that says, "Press here for lobby or emergency service." Something bugs me about it. Then I realize it's written in dactylic meter. I wonder if they did that on purpose.

I get out of the elevator on the ninth floor and stroll to

Kara's door, whistling a tune. It'll be fun to stay here for two weeks. I knock on the door.

When she opens it, I see, on the coffee table, the biggest pair of work boots I ever could have imagined.

The male specimen behind the boots is about six feet tall, something I can tell even though he's stretched languidly across Judith's couch. His hair is high and purposely messy, and he has a lazy squint. He's wearing a woven blue and brown bracelet around his left wrist. There's an open suitcase resting against the short side of the couch and a pile of pressed shirts on the table.

"Hey," the guy says.

"Carrie!" Kara says. "This is Jackson."

Jackson raises his hand, palm flat toward me.

"He's a friend from college," she tells me.

"You went to Smith," I say. "It's a girls' school."

"He was my roommate's friend from Fordham," she says. "He just moved to New York with his band. They're really good!"

And you're letting him hang out in our house? I think. But of course, it's not mine.

"Come into my room," Kara says to me, heading down the hall. "I have to show you something."

As soon as she enters Judith's bedroom, she shuts the door and backs up to it. "Isn't he the most gorgeous thing you've ever seen?"

"Oh, sure," I say, "if you like people who spend over an hour moussing their hair to make it look random."

"I knew you'd understand," Kara says, hugging me. "He called me a few weeks ago and said he needs a place to crash, and I said instead of sleeping on the floor with his band-mates, he could stay with me until he finds a place. Didn't I tell you about that?"

I shake my head.

"At the time, I didn't even realize I'd get this assignment at Judith's. Now he can stay in her extra room."

There goes my plan for the next two weeks. There's still a second extra room, but it wouldn't be the same.

Kara flashes me an evil grin. "I've had a crush on him since I met him. Now he's in my clutches. If you have extra space in New York, you can get anyone. Do you feel okay? You look worried."

"I'm not," I say. "I just…I've heard of people crashing at someone's place in New York for 'a few weeks' and then they end up staying six months."

Kara smiles. "With any luck," she says. "Don't worry. I can look out for myself. You're such a good friend. Oh, I loved the bagels! How on earth did you get them?"

I'll bet Jackson never would have gotten those bagels for Kara.

"I have my ways," I say, not feeling very excited anymore.

"You'll tell me in time," Kara says. "Oh, one more thing."

"What?"

"Is it okay if Jackson comes to the bar with us?"

I'm glum as I sit on one side of Kara on the subway that evening. Jackson sits on the other. He keeps wincing and pinching the bridge of his nose as if to press out his headache. Since he just got in from Chicago this afternoon, I'm sure he's tired. I mean, those two hours on the plane can really kill you.

"Don't you think so, Jack?" Kara asks Jackson.

"What?" Jackson asks tiredly.

"Shouldn't Carrie cook dinner for Nolan sometime?"

"Yeh," Jackson says.

Kara says, "Next Sunday, Jackson has band practice until late and I'm subbing for someone at work. Judith's place will be free if you want to invite Nolan over for a meal and really impress him. Guys always find it romantic if you cook for them. All I ask is that you give me the disgusting details afterward."

"I don't even know if he'll come," I say.

"Call him," Kara says. "Third dates are crucial. You might as well find out once and for all if he wants you, instead of going back and forth on whether you want him, like you keep doing."

Now I need Nolan more than ever, actually. If Kara starts dating Jackson, she'll never have time for me.

"I'll make Nolan dinner at Judith's," I say. "And I'll see if he tries to kiss me or something."

"Good," Kara says. "If he doesn't kiss you, there's nothing wrong with having a new male friend. Maybe you'll meet his cute friends, and one of them *will* want you."

Jackson suddenly takes interest. "What's this?" he says. "You're going to give a guy the 'friends' speech?"

"Only if he doesn't like her," Kara says.

Jackson seems to accept this, and goes back to rubbing the bridge of his nose.

The bar in Tribeca has no sign outside. If you're hip, you're supposed to just know it exists. I like the way it's set up inside, because basically, it's one long room—no tables, no chairs, nothing but a bar on one side and space on the other. This establishment seems to specialize in two things: really low lighting, and name brands. A bevy of neon signs for beers, flavored brandies and even fruit juices line the walls. The backlighting behind the bar makes the bottles of vodka glow, along with something blue called Hpnotiq. A lot of the guys are dressed the same way as Jackson: loose, button-down shirts, open at the top, and jeans. If I'd chosen a bar myself, I wouldn't have picked this place. It's the Great Neck of bars—the site of a competition to see who's better.

But I remind myself that part of the plan is to do what normal people do. So I will try to fit in.

Both Kara and Jackson have invited friends to our little fete, and they're already there when we arrive. There's Kara's tall friend Nicole, who has long lashes, thinks she's sophisticated, and won't date any guy with chest hair unless he agrees to shave it. Kara told me about this once, explaining that Nicole "skeeves hair." Nicole has lately met with resistance asking hairy guys to shave theirs, so now she tries to date only non-hairies. I guess we all have our hang-ups.

Jackson's two band-mates are here, too. Their names are Aaron and Neil. Aaron has a crewcut and two earrings in his left ear. Well, it's not actually a crewcut—it's more of an I'm-balding-anyway-so-I-took-matters-into-my-own-hands cut. Neil is more conventional looking but has a set jaw and looks angry. His head is sort of square.

"So, what does everyone want to drink?" Jackson asks, wagging his finger at each of us.

He gets to me and I ask for a margarita, and he nods. "With salt," I add. The other girls get cosmos and the guys order beers. I tell myself to keep my mouth shut for the rest of the night and just observe. No pressure…no pressure. I only have to stay for an hour.

I look around the room for prospects, but most of the guys are dressed slickly like Jackson and seem to have girls already. Of course, maybe they'd look at my group and think the same of us, so I try to remain hopeful.

One thing I can tell for sure is how badly Kara wants Jackson. She stares at him as he heads to the bar. She exchanges glances with Nicole and giggles. Meanwhile, Aaron and Neil both talk to Kara and Nicole, and they ignore me. I don't know how they can tell already what a misfit I am. I've barely said anything. Maybe it's that I'm not wearing high heels. Or a low-cut, tight blouse. Or maybe it's because I've barely said anything—but it's not like I can butt in.

Did you know that I was on an elevator today with instructions in dactylic meter? I think of saying, but I don't.

Kara and Nicole ask the guys about their band, and Neil tells them they have a gig in two weeks. They'll be the first of three bands that night, and they go on at nine, which means they won't have a big crowd yet, but at least it's a gig at a decent place.

"Will you get paid?" I ask.

All four of them stop talking and look at me. I feel like I've made a major gaffe. Wasn't it a reasonable question?

"We'll split the pot," Neil says boredly.

I never know what to say to keep a conversation going. The guys return to talking to Nicole and she knows just what to say to them. I notice that Jackson is trying to find a safe way to carry all our drinks. There are six drinks, so I dart to the bar to help him retrieve the rest. At least I feel useful. Unlike at the soup kitchen.

"You got these?" he asks me, as I balance someone's cosmo on my palm. He touches my hand slightly.

"Got 'em," I say.

"So how did you and Kara meet?" he asks, as we return to the group.

"Legal proofreading," I say.

When we get there Aaron announces, "I'll buy next

round." Hey, this isn't so bad, boys feeling they have to pay for us just because we're girls.

I scan the bar stools. No one is there alone. Certainly no guys who look normal and brainy like Nolan.

At least I didn't feel intimidated by Nolan. We can grow together, discover the world together. Avoid bars together.

"So Kara's house-sitting for this rich widow," Jackson announces.

"Sweet," Neil says.

"The master bedroom has, like, a skylight," Jackson adds.

"And a library, too," I say, but they give me weird looks.

Jackson continues, nudging Kara, "And what are they paying you?"

"Two hundred a week."

"Two hundred a week," Jackson repeats, "to pick up some woman's mail and watch DVDs."

"And to drive her car around the block," I put in.

Jackson gives me a friendly smile, but no one else does. The guys start talking about various jobs they had where they really didn't have to do anything, punctuated by "awesome"s from the girls and "sweet"s from the guys. Soon they slide into a discussion of things they've stolen from their jobs. Neil once took a plastic life-size Ronald McDonald from outside McDonald's. He filched it for a girlfriend, but she didn't want it, so he tossed it over a fence into a school playground. Aaron did one better. He took home a laptop from a two-day temp job and never got caught.

That actually sounds felonious.

Then they start talking about how they shoplifted when they were in junior high. Apparently, every single one of them did it. Kara and Jackson swiped cigarettes. Nicole took a lipstick.

I didn't realize shoplifting in middle school was such a universal experience. Not on my planet, but of course, I'm the only person *on* my planet.

While they share more shoplifting stories, I try to think of something funny I can contribute—maybe there was a kid in my class who got arrested. Maybe I took extra lined paper for my spelling test. But I don't remember anything. So I stand there stupidly, holding my Mexican medicine.

Suddenly I notice Aaron looking at me. "You don't look happy," he says.

Then they're all staring at me.

Here we go. They were talking about stealing computers and I'm the one who's out of place.

"I'm fine," I say. Now Nicole is looking from me to Aaron and smiling at him, as if he did me a big favor by acknowledging me.

"I'm going to the bathroom," I say. I'm sure they'll feel relieved. As will I. But before I leave, suddenly I'm the center of conversation.

"You can't go," Neil says. "You'll break the seal."

"What seal?" I ask.

They're all smiling. "You've never heard of that?" Jackson says.

For a smart person, I sure feel dumb.

"It's an expression," Kara says kindly. "It's a known fact that if you go to the bathroom near the beginning of your night at a bar, you'll have to keep going all night. But if you hold it in, you forget about it."

"Did they do studies?"

The guys laugh and look at each other. Neil guffaws. "Yeah. They did a Gallup poll."

"A Gallup poll," Aaron echoes, and elbows him in the ribs.

I'm humiliated. "I'll risk it," I say, and I slink toward the bathroom.

Once there, I avoid looking at myself in the mirror and run into one of the two stalls. I shut the door, pull down my pants and sit on the toilet, thus breaking the seal.

I look at my watch. My watch is too big for a girl's watch. It has a little square with the date in it, which I need to know, because without school, it's hard to keep track of it. It keeps changing every twenty-four hours.

My watch says I've killed only a half-hour. That's bad. I want to go home and sleep off this nightmare of a night. It's hard to believe that early this same morning, I was heading to Great Neck to get bagels for Kara.

When I return to the room, the guys and dolls are in the throes of vapid conversation. Instead of joining them again, I stroll to the front window to look outside. There's a string of shops across the street, one of which is just a paper store selling all colors of stationery. It seems a risky thing to sell when you've got to pay New York rents. Hopefully there are corporations that need reams of lavender card stock.

Cabs roll by. Girls with no jackets walk quickly on a frosty night. I will definitely call Nolan and invite him to dinner. My resolution was to find someone like me, and I have. I'm not sure why I've been so wishy-washy. It will just take more time to get to know him.

Suddenly I hear someone behind me.

"Hey."

I turn around to find Jackson staring at me.

"Hey," I say.

His hair is still expertly moussed, but other than that, he looks more relaxed than before, maybe a little drunk. "Do you like Charles Bukowski?" he asks.

"The writer?"

He laughs. "No, my cousin Charles Bukowski. Yeah, the writer. Kara said you like to read." He looks back at Kara, who winks at him.

"I've read a few of the poems, but not his fiction," I say. So Kara sent him over to be nice to me. Like I'm a little kid.

"Are you uncomfortable?" he asks me.

Trying to imply how I feel again—there must be a male handbook full of ways to condescend to women. "Did Kara send you to talk to me?"

"No," he says. "I mean, I told her I was going to come talk to you."

Just then, Aaron comes up, too, and hits Jackson on the back. "Hey, bud," he says.

"Now, don't be cock blocking," Jackson tells him, and they both laugh.

"I resent that," Aaron says. "I'm the best wingman you'll ever see."

"What?" I say.

"What what?" Jackson says.

"What's 'cock blocking'?" I ask.

They look at each other. Aaron says, "You don't get out much, do you."

I shake my head.

"And she's damn proud of it," Jackson says, smiling and patting me on the shoulder. "That's okay. 'Cock blocking' is when a guy is trying to talk to a girl, and his buddy keeps getting in the way, instead of disappearing like he's supposed to."

"And a wingman," Aaron explains, "is the opposite of a cock blocker. He helps you talk to a girl, and then—" he makes his fingers fly like an eagle "—he quietly flies away."

I stare at them blankly. Do people really say these things?

I can't imagine *Nolan* ever saying "cock block." And it's rude. If you stop a guy from talking to a girl, you're stopping the whole guy, not just his "cock." Who came up with such a cruel term?

"Aaron's an awesome wingman," Jackson says, slapping his buddy on the back.

"In college I got him laid twice in one night," Aaron brags.

"How nice for you," I say. "Time to break the seal again." I take off for the bathroom. Once inside, I pace in front of the scratched mirror. I don't want to be in conversation with Aaron and Jackson, talking about cocks and wings. Is this what I have to do to fit in? Should I come up with a list of fake stories about shoplifting for next time? And ways to entertain cocks? Hanging out in bars is worse than I thought if it's all an elaborate production to get a cock in front of a girl and then let the cock follow its will.

I pace over the blue and white tiles. Finally, I realize this isn't doing me any good. My watch says I have ten minutes left.

I come out. Kara and Aaron and Nicole and Neil and Jackson and some girl I don't recognize are engrossed in conversation. Kara doesn't look concerned about my disappearance. I catch Kara's attention and wave goodbye. She mouths, *You're leaving?* I nod.

She tells Jackson to hold on and then runs over to me. She says, "I'm going to get him so drunk." I smile. "Be safe," Kara says, and runs back to Jackson's side.

I tiptoe toward the door and then I'm out of there.

But I don't make for the subway right away. I walk under the streetlights, listening to the few remaining leaves on the trees fluttering in the January wind. I try to accept the term *cock block.* I have to think about things that shock me over and over until they're palatable. It's not that I'm afraid of sex or men or their penises; I just don't want a "cock" to be the only thing that matters.

Next time I'm at Judith's, *if* I ever get to go there again, I am going to take our hate list and write in big letters:

COCK. BLOCK.

The next day, every time I pass a man on the street, I imagine him as a giant walking cock. The city is full of cocks. They're not thinking human beings; they have no goal other than to be big, unblocked cocks. I see Walk/Don't Walk signs flashing COCK/DON'T COCK BLOCK. I peer in a store window and it says, "Kenneth Cole Erection."

Any drop of hope I had in the world, any possibility that anyone is at all like me, is gone. They're all cocks.

I call Nolan after lunch. He's not in, and I don't leave a message. I'll call him later. I am going to see him next weekend no matter what it takes, and he will shelter me from this crazy, cruel world.

The phone doesn't ring for most of the next afternoon. I keep thinking maybe Kara will call, apologize for ignoring me most of the night, and explain that she had to seduce Jackson. Or maybe Nolan will call and say he's been visiting his sister in Boston and he spent time thinking about what I said and he can't wait to see me again. Wouldn't that be great? He'd be a more reliable partner-in-confusion than Kara.

At three p.m., I finally get a call: my father. Sometimes it's disappointing to hear his voice when I'm waiting for someone else to call, even though I love him. But he has news—

he's made tentative inquiries to colleges about the idea of a graduate going back.

"Dean Nymczik at Harvard hasn't returned my call yet," Dad says. "I spoke to my friends at Boston College and Iowa. I wish I knew more people at other schools."

"I know," I say. "I can make calls, too."

"There's a school with a special program for underage geniuses," Dad says. "Simon's Rock of Bard College in Massachusetts. They understand your plight and they might be able to have you there as an adviser. You could help kids who are like you used to be."

I like the idea, but I don't know if I want to be the oldest person at a school any more than I wanted to be the youngest. For a change, I think I should try to fit in.

We talk a little more and I tell Dad about making dinner for Nolan. Might as well let him think I'm doing just fine. In fact, I plan to call Nolan again later. I'll try him until I get him.

Thirteen

Nolan, believe it or not, takes me up on my offer to cook him dinner Sunday night. I lied and said that Judith's place is my aunt's apartment. After I make him dinner, Kara will have four more days at Judith's, and then she's out of there.

I tell Kara over the phone that Nolan has accepted my offer. She sounds happy. Of course she does. If we both have boyfriends, our social status is "even." Or maybe that's in my head. Kara has never completely dismissed me when she had a boyfriend, just became less needy. Can I blame her?

She lowers her voice as she talks, because Jackson is walking around the apartment. She tells me that nothing happened with him yet, but she's still working on it.

When Sunday evening comes, I move from pot to pan in Judith's apartment, letting the warm aromas fill the kitchen. I'm not actually cooking—just reheating the stuff I bought at the gourmet food store around the corner. I fill an Evian bottle with vodka so I can get myself drunk without Nolan knowing I'm drinking. Smart, right?

I have everything ready within an hour—stuffed mushrooms, potato gnocchi, Caesar salad (not soggy), soda and a pint of frozen gelato. I set up plates on the long table in the dining room. Now, all I have to do is sit on the living room couch, waiting for Nolan to buzz.

He shows up right on time with a bottle of mineral water in his arm as a gift. I don't know whether to kiss him on the cheek, and he doesn't seem to know what to do, either, so I just say, "Have a seat."

"Nice place," Nolan says, setting his water on the table and sitting on the red sofa.

Good response. Maybe it was these dinners out that intimidated him. Maybe he prefers relaxing atmospheres.

"I like it," I say. "Come take a tour."

He gets up and wanders over to the window. "Look at that pond," he says. "I'll bet there's all kinds of fauna in it."

We wend our way through the halls, and he recognizes a few of the paintings. Now I'm impressed. The guy is probably too smart or knowledgeable for most of the people he dates, if he finds women to date at all. It took someone like me to meet him. He's mine! We'll learn how to socialize together.

And once I have a little vodka in me, I might even be able to get him to want me.

I put a classical station on Judith's old stereo system. Unfortunately, they're playing Beethoven's Seventh. Thanks a lot, guys—music to bury someone by. But I leave on the station and lay the food out while Nolan approaches the table. "This is a salad, and this is gnocchi—"

"Are there nuts in it?" He stops dead in his tracks.

"What?"

"I don't eat nuts."

"Oh," I say. "Does that have to do with vegetarianism?"

"No," he says. "I just don't like nuts."

"Good," I chuckle, "because you are what you eat."

He doesn't respond. He probably doesn't realize how close nut is to nurd.

I bring out the first appetizer—black olive spread and bruschetta and toast squares.

"Are there nuts in that?" he asks.

This is pointless. "It's just tomatoes and onions," I say. "There are no nuts."

"I appreciate your going to the trouble," he says, and I think that this might turn out okay.

So what if he says things that are awkward? That only means we're made for each other.

He sits at the table and takes off his glasses. There are small red ridges in his nose where they were pinching him. He looks cute without his glasses. Some people just look lost without their specs. He opens his red napkin in his lap and I pour him some mineral water. Then I pour myself some faux Evian and splash it with cranberry.

"Juice in water?" he asks.

"It's good. Want some?"

He shrugs, so I give him just a speck. I watch the pink dot tumble down his glass.

I sit and we talk about classical music and college, and stuff ourselves with bruschetta. I tell him I wish I could go back to college.

He disagrees, saying everyone there was "juvenile."

I respond by saying, "I agree, and for me to consider everyone else at school juvenile is pretty bad, because I was sixteen!"

He actually smiles. I've gotten him to smile!

The conversation is alternately fun and awkward. I keep drinking vodka. Wouldn't you know it, Nolan gets handsomer and handsomer. I manage to inject a few comments into the conversation that are seductive, but they only make him act uncomfortable.

Fall in love with me, I think. *Lean across the table and tell me you've been waiting for me all your life, that you were scared you'd never find someone like me.*

"Well," I say once we've polished off our entrees. "We did a good job on this."

He has spent a lot of the time poking through his food, maybe to ensure he wouldn't eat a nut, but suddenly he notices me. "That was the best meal I've had in a long time," he says. "My mother is going to be happy."

He's going to tell his mother about me! How cute.

"I can help you clean up," he says.

Yes! That could be frisky. Maybe the alcohol worked on him. Then I realize he hasn't had any. The only thing it could mean is, he likes me! It's nice to have it be me and not alcohol.

He follows me into the kitchen with his plate, and we scrape them into the trash basket and do the same with the other dishes. I fill the sink with water and lather the dishwashing liquid. Then I dip my hand into a pile of soapsuds and flick them at him. He merely flinches. I flick more suds at him, but he steps away.

I sigh quietly and rinse and dry, and we are alongside each other again, but he doesn't try anything.

I stare at him as he dries the last dish. I can see my reflection in it. I don't look half bad today. *Kiss me,* I think. But he turns away—it almost seems purposeful.

We stack the dry plates on the counter, head into the living room and drop onto the couches.

"These couches are great, aren't they?" I ask.

"Yeah," he says. "I like the pillows."

"There are more on the bed."

He gets up and goes to the window. "Your aunt must love the view."

"My what? Oh, yeah." I get up and join him there. "So do I."

He walks away and sits on the couch again. This is almost painful.

"Do you want to watch a movie?" I say. "We were going to watch a movie, right?"

"Oh, yeah," he says. "What do you have?"

"Have you seen *Bull Durham*?"

He looks skeptical. "I've heard of it, but what's it about?"

"Baseball…"

"I don't like sports."

"Or nuts," I say. "So you must really hate sports nuts."

He winces, but not at the joke. (Which definitely would have been appropriate.) "I don't 'hate' anything," he announces. "I only 'dislike' stuff."

"I agree with you," I say quickly. "I've always hated the word *hate*. Oops, I mean, disliked it. But *Bull Durham* isn't just about sports. It has philosophy and literary references and things."

"Okay."

We sit on the couch to watch.

At first, Nolan seems bored. Then, he becomes visibly uncomfortable. Maybe it's the part when Jenny Robertson and Tim Robbins have heated sex. Or when Tim Robbins asks if he and Susan Sarandon are "gonna fuck." Or when Susan

ties Tim Robbins up on her bed. Even if the movie is really
about sex more than sports, I think it's clever. And highly rec-
ommended for seducing someone.

Someone normal, that is.

I move closer to Nolan on the couch. The fact that he
told me he hates the word *hate* clues me in that there's still
a chance I could really like him. Even if he's easily irritated,
he's also literate and full of quirks. Hating the word *hate* is
an intriguing one.

But as I move closer, he seems to stiffen up. He's purposely
keeping his eyes on the movie.

Finally, there's a lurid sex scene between Susan Sarandon
and Kevin Costner. Then, the film ends. I get up to press the
power button.

Behind me, Nolan says, "Well, this was fun." There's no
emotion in his voice.

I turn around and he's getting up from the couch. *No!
Don't do that!*

"Is there anything else you want to do before you go?" I
say. Between the movie and the alcohol, I've been driven practically crazy. It's partly Nolan and partly just random desire.

He almost smiles. "It's late," he says. "I'll see you at the
next FAIR."

"I'll be there." I watch his fingers clench the doorknob,
but I want him to come back. We were both on the couch,
and it's late, and he just ate a full dinner and watched a sexy
movie—and he's leaving?

The door closes.

How did that happen?

I hear his footsteps fading down the hall.

Wait a minute! Come back here! What should I have done
instead? I have zero skills in this area. He was sitting next to

me watching the movie for two hours and he didn't make a move, but I didn't know what to do, either. And he acted uncomfortable when I closed in.

Kara and Jackson won't be back until midnight. It's only ten p.m. I'm dying to be kissed. I haven't felt like this in ages. I'm not usually like this. You believe me, right? Well, during my senior year of college I went through periods of just wanting to smooch someone, whoever it might be, but I never acted on it. Not that I could, anyway.

I'm all revved up with no place to go.

I head over to my purse and pull almost everything out until I find it—the glossy sliver of paper with Kurt's phone number on it.

It only takes me five minutes of apologizing, saying I was busy for the past three weeks, and telling Kurt I'm about to watch *Bull Durham,* to get him to agree to take a subway and a taxi from Brooklyn up to Judith's place.

See? Some guys are easy.

Now I'll have to watch *Bull Durham* again, but it shouldn't take very long to get Kurt in the mood. He'll have some of my vodka, too. I'll be with a guy—a guy who isn't afraid to kiss me.

Screw Kara, screw Jackson, screw Nolan, screw Donner and Blitzen. I'm going to get some action.

I make sure the pillows are arranged neatly on the couch.

When Kurt arrives, he's even better looking than I remembered. He's grown a soul patch, but I can still see his shaving scars.

"How are you?" I ask, taking his winter coat and hanging it by the door. He stares at me the whole time. I ask if he wants a drink. He does.

Ten minutes into *Bull Durham,* we're on the couch groping each other. He really is cute, and a good kisser. He smells manly. I can detect his sexual desire, something I never felt coming from Nolan.

He sucks on my neck and kisses his way under my shirt. Then he reaches up and starts unbuttoning it. I'm not going to go much further than that, but I feel like fooling around, and so I am. I have needs, okay?

My shirt is off and I lift Kurt's. Wouldn't you know it, the goofy hipster has a nice body. Almost completely hairless— smooth as a baby. Take *that,* Nicole!

I move his chain necklace and kiss the nape of his neck. He slides his palms around my breasts, all perky and sensitive. Wow, he's good at this.

I hear a key in the front door.

I look up from the couch. Kurt does, too.

Kurt's eyes widen.

It's Jackson, standing in the doorway. He's an hour early.

"Fuck!" Kurt yells. He grabs for his shirt and stands up. "Don't kill me! Don't kill me!"

"Huh?" Jackson says.

"That's not my boyfriend—" I try to tell Kurt, but he's running around.

"Don't kill me!" Kurt yells at Jackson. "I didn't know, dude. I'm leaving. I'm leaving!"

Jackson stares at him, then me. The breeze from the doorway reminds me that I'm half naked. I look down for my bra and shirt.

Before I can say anything else to Kurt, he's out the door. Jackson stomps into his room and slams his own door.

I have nothing more to say about this.

Fourteen

One time, I took a class pass–fail and got an A anyway.

What does that have to do with anything? Nothing. I just wanted you to know it.

Fifteen

Kara needs to talk to me.

Three days are left in January and I've pretty much failed on my resolution. Plus, there are several additional accomplishments: I scared off Nolan and Kurt, permanently scarred Jackson and added delightful new terms to my lexicon like "wingman" and "cock block." And the month isn't even over yet.

When Kara comes to my apartment, I let her in and she sits in my living room and looks around. "Something's different from last time I was here," she says.

"I moved the unabridged dictionary to the kitchen."

"Oh. So can you tell me exactly what happened on Sunday?"

I sit across from her. "Well," I say, "Nolan came over, as we planned. I made him a big dinner. He seemed to enjoy it."

"You didn't make meat, did you?"

"Absolutely not. It was gnocchi. Oh, apparently he won't eat nuts, either. Anyway, I drank two cranberry vodkas and

I decided I wanted to kiss him. And there were times when I thought it was going to happen, like when we were doing the dishes together or standing near the window, but he moved away. We were *this* close, and nothing."

"Did you put *Bull Durham* on?"

"It didn't work."

"And that's when…"

"That's when I called Kurt."

Kara looks at me. "You…you…dog."

I think for a second. "Am I a man? I've turned into a man. I acted like a man. It's…the end."

"The end of what?"

"The end of feminism." I stand up. "We're not just jealous of men—we're turning into them."

"Hold on," Kara says, putting her hands up. "Hold on. Just because you wanted a guy to kiss you doesn't make you a man."

"We're men!" I say, pacing. "We're men!"

"No, we're not. You had a perfectly logical reaction. You tried to get a nice guy to kiss you, he wouldn't, so you called up a hunk. It doesn't mean you've turned into a man. It means you wanted love and sex, but since you couldn't get either, you took sex."

"But you just called me a dog…"

"I was joking. Carrie, you are the least doglike person I know. Now tell me the truth. If you could have spent last night doing anything, what would it have been?"

"Having dinner and watching a movie with someone like Nolan," I say, "but someone who liked me a little more."

"Right," Kara said. "You still wanted to be with someone nice. Is that doggish, anti-feminist or misanthropic? Everyone wants to be happy, and I'm so sick of hearing that we don't have the right or that we want too much."

Right now, I like Kara better than Kurt, Nolan and Jackson put together.

"Well, anyway," Kara says, "that's not what I came here to talk to you about."

"Oh." I sit down.

Kara lets out a breath. "Jackson likes you."

"Jackson? *Your* Jackson?"

Kara looks upset. "He was never my Jackson," she says. "He's only there because of the room. I thought I could get him to like me. Then I thought he was after Nicole, but he's not. He's attracted to you."

"He said that? He doesn't even know me."

"It doesn't matter. He thought you were cute at the beginning, and I guess he got an impression of you from listening to my stories. But now that he's seen you half-naked, he says he can't get you out of his mind."

All I had to do was take my top off? Wowee.

"You don't like Jackson, do you?" Kara says. "Because if *you* were into someone, and he liked me, I wouldn't pursue it…"

"No," I say. "He's your type, not mine." Actually, if Jackson reads books and cares about the right things, I might like him. He hasn't been mean to me or anything. But I'm not going to tell Kara that. Jackson probably wouldn't like me if he knew the real me, anyway. And if he does, he'll find a way to pursue it without offending Kara.

"Anyway, he moved out. His buddies found a new place for him to live. He knows how I feel, and he doesn't feel the same way. So we agreed it's too uncomfortable."

"I'm sorry," I say resignedly. "I didn't mean for that to happen. I know it was your house-sitting job, and I haven't really helped out."

"It's all right." She still seems upset.

"I didn't do anything to—"

"I know, I know." Kara waves me off. "You can't help it. Apparently Jackson dislikes aggressive girls. How am I supposed to figure out what boys want? I would have been quiet and shy if I knew that's what he liked. I *am* quiet and shy."

What, in months without *R*s and *U*s?

"Maybe we should forget this month ever happened," I say.

Kara looks at me. "No way. It's been a great month. I made money at Judith's, we ate delicious sushi and we saw some excellent movies. It doesn't have to depend on men."

"What if we're still telling ourselves that when we're fifty?"

"Then shoot me. But not yet." Kara looks at me seriously. "If you randomly met a guy like Jackson, would you be into him?"

I consider it for a half second. "I...I don't know. But I've been so confused lately."

"What do you mean?"

"I feel lost."

"How?"

"I used to know what I wanted. Now I have these shades of gray, and I'm supposed to consider everything before passing judgment, but it just makes me more confused. Maybe I've become less of a person by broadening my horizons."

"You were judgmental before," Kara says. "Now you're not. That's a *good* thing."

"But now I have no standards for anything, and I have no clear path," I say. "What am I supposed to do?"

"How about just be twenty years old?"

"But what *is* twenty? It's not even old enough to legally drink, but I can't claim the blissful ignorance of a teenager."

"All our twenties are like that," Kara says. "We don't have

scripts and schedules anymore. See it as an opportunity, not a burden."

"Sometimes I don't get to decide which it is."

She smiles and puts her hands over mine. "You'll figure it out," she says. "At least we're both giving our lives a little kick-start, right? I want to go to your next soup kitchen thing. Carrie, you are full of adventures, and you don't give yourself enough credit."

That's probably the nicest thing anyone's said to me since I was dating Cy.

"My mom called again this morning," Kara says, sighing. "I was asleep and I missed the call."

"You should talk to her," I tell her. "She *is* your mom."

"I know. But she always makes me feel bad about myself."

My dad always makes me feel *better* about myself, not worse. That's rough. I think I need to pay more attention to where other people are coming from. For every problem I had in my childhood, I guess I had some lucky experiences, too.

"Well, don't let her get you down," I say, for lack of more original advice. "You're a good person."

Kara nods silently, then gets up to go. "I know."

Sixteen

Kara has been away visiting her mom in Great Neck for the past two days. Tonight is the last night at Judith's, so I'm staying over and watching the house for her. I check my messages at home frequently, but Nolan hasn't called. In a way I'm relieved. Maybe I've failed in my goal to find someone like me, but I've learned that I'm not necessarily looking for someone who's *exactly* like me. There are certain behaviors and perspectives that matter, but there are more subtle things that factor into it, too.

I've also learned that if I meet a guy who has things in common with me, like Nolan, I don't always have to assume it will turn into true love. But in Nolan's case, I'm not sure he even wants to bother being a friend.

I think the most important thing I learned this month is that giving new situations a chance is the only way to figure out what I want. And it's an evolving process—a process that didn't end when I left college.

I get a phone message at home around five p.m., and as usual, it's my dad. I call him back.

"There are a few schools that are willing to meet with you," he says. "You have to talk to them, though. Besides Simon's Rock of Bard, there's Iowa."

"What else?"

"The dean of Harvard, Nymczik—he said he's willing to hear you out, but he won't make any guarantees."

"You know what you might have to do, Dad."

He sighs. "You're not going to make me buy a building, are you?"

I don't say anything.

"I will if I have to," he says. "But first you have to decide what you really want."

I don't *know* what I really want.

I like this city. Do I really want to give it up for four years?

Kara lives here, and I'd like to return to the soup kitchen. And then there's Petrov. For all his nonsense, he has helped me.

And then there's the walk I take after I hang up the phone, another walk like the one I took on my block on New Year's Day.

Only this time, I don't see kids fighting. Instead, I see an average-looking older couple coming my way. She has straight hair and no makeup, she's smiling ear to ear, and she looks to be in her forties. The man is telling her a story, and he's smiling, too. They're holding hands and laughing, and for some reason I don't resent them. They just seem cool and down-to-earth and fun, and this feeling of *purity* moves through my body. It seems so easy, easy to find someone to get along with.

Neither the man nor the woman seems to be pushing or

trying to figure out a balance or trying to get away. They simply look happy to be together.

And I still think this could happen to me. I have a surge of hope—an inexplicable, rare burst of optimism.

Every time I think I'm ready to leave New York, it pulls me back in.

Seventeen

I spend the evening at Judith's pondering my options. It wouldn't hurt to head to New England and the Midwest to check out a few colleges. But a road trip could be a big undertaking. I've never done anything like that before. Especially by myself.

As I'm thinking about this, there's a key in Judith's door: Kara.

"Kara!" I say. "How was your mom?"

But she doesn't answer me. Instead, she tells me she just got a call on her cell phone.

We both need to go down to the law office right away.

On the subway, Kara tells me about her mom. She said she went to see her and they had a long talk. Kara told her mom off. Her mom apologized for how she treated Kara in college—not an easy thing for her to do. Things aren't perfect, Kara says, but she's going to try to see her mom more often.

She's also going to visit her brother soon. Her brother's getting married next year.

"You should see him," I say. "I wish I had more relatives."

"I know," Kara says. "I told my mom what a great friend you've been to me. She wants to meet you, too. She always used to meet my friends."

I feel honored.

"Plus, you went to Harvard, so naturally, you'd be welcomed."

I laugh. "If only she knew how boring I am."

Kara looks at me. "Don't ever change," she says. "I mean it. I don't want everyone to be the same—can you imagine if I knew more than one Nicole? I'd kill myself. You really are one of the most interesting people I've ever met, Carrie. And the most repressed."

"You mean *one* of the most repressed?"

"No, the *most* repressed. It's okay. It's part of what's cool."

Kara doesn't seem worried as we ride the elevator to the tenth floor of the law firm. Neither of us knows what this is about.

Mr. DeKuyper is in the room. A younger attorney is sitting at the desk, but he's not the one talking.

"Sit down," Mr. DeKuyper says to both of us.

Kara and I do.

Then he spreads out some paperwork. The younger lawyer looks at it.

"Carrie was your recommendation for this job, correct?"

"Uh, yes," Kara says.

"Then this concerns *both* of you," Mr. DeKuyper says.

The younger attorney speaks up. "Let's get to the point."

"Tom, take it easy…" Mr. DeKuyper says. "Basically, it

seems that one of our clients had an unusually high bill. We only wrote her a three-page lawyer letter, but it ended up costing two hundred dollars for a car trip to Great Neck. Do you know anything about this?"

I open my mouth to comment, but before I can—

"We're sorry," Kara says. "Carrie thought she was doing me a favor and running an errand. I guess it went too far."

"Well," Mr. DeKuyper says, looking at me, "we're heading into a season for temps that's going to be a little bit slow—"

"Can we talk about this tomorrow?" Kara says. "I just got back from a long trip."

Mr. DeKuyper is shocked.

Maybe the stress of dealing with her mother has gotten to Kara. She basically just told her boss to shove it.

I follow her out and we head down to the subway.

On the train, Kara says, "They keep me on as a temp even though I'm working regular hours. They were supposed to hire me full time two months ago, and they won't. They don't want to pay me benefits."

"But you need your job," I say.

"Eh." She shrugs. "I have to start auditioning for commercials again. I got too lazy. This is the shot in the arm I need. Besides, I needed time off, and they hate giving time off." She looks at me. "But I guess you won't get any more temp assignments from them, either."

"They were right," I say. "February is slow for temping. I need a shot in the arm, too. I need to consider my options."

Kara's eyes soften. "I'm sorry if I dissed you in the bar that night when Jackson was there, by the way."

I say, "I'm sorry I acted resentful when he showed up."

"I'm sorry I used to give you the impression you should change."

"I'm sorry that I said if you slept with Jackson you'd probably get an STD."

"I don't remember you saying that."

"Oh. I guess I only thought it."

"I forgive you. Let's get some sushi and enjoy our last night at Judith's."

We're plowing through some California rolls when the cleaning woman from Jamaica knocks on our door.

What now?

"I have some unfortunate news," she tells both of us, coming in. "Judith won't be back for a few days. She's in the hospital because she got stung by a Mexican bark scorpion. I've been so busy making arrangements that I didn't have a chance to tell you."

I look at Kara. Mexican bark scorpion?

"Anyway," the maid says. "If you can work a few more days, I can pay you the extra money she left for emergencies, until she gets back."

"Sounds fine by me," Kara says.

The maid peels off a few bills. I look at them. They're hundreds.

"Judith also wants to remind you to move the Oldsmobile," she says. "I'm sorry I can't do it myself. I never learned to drive. Where I grew up, I only took subways."

"In Jamaica?" I ask.

She looks at me strangely.

Kara says, "She's from Jamaica, *Queens*."

"Oh." No wonder she doesn't have a Jamaican accent.

Kara raises an eyebrow. "Do *you* know how to drive?" she asks after the maid leaves.

"Yeah," I say. "Why?"

Kara sits down. "We're both jobless. You have colleges to visit. I have a brother in the Midwest. All this talk of driving... We should rent a car for a week!"

I get up and walk over to the window to gaze at Central Park.

"Come on," Kara says. "How many times are you jobless and free of entanglements? New York will still be here when we get back."

I look out over the city. A road trip? Why not? I can always get back to the bars and soup kitchens and social events when I return. There are eight million ways to meet people in the city, and you don't have to be naked.

I might as well see the country, touring colleges and working on self-improvement and figuring out what I really want to do. Then, when I return, I can draw up a brand-new schedule for socializing and meeting boys—and for once, I'll know how to handle all of it.

I really, really mean it this time.

EMMA TOWNSEND
SAVES CHRISTMAS
Melanie Murray

One

When I was growing up, my parents, my brother Jeff and I would spend every December twenty-third in our den, caught in the glow of flashing, garland-bound lights, stringing popcorn and watching Christmas movies: *Miracle on 34th Street, The Quiet Man, It's a Wonderful Life.* My favorite was *White Christmas,* but not for the reason you'd think. You may assume I loved that movie because I grew up in Vermont, and because my family makes their living off Christmas. But actually what I loved was the middle part, where Rosemary Clooney ditches the inn and Bing Crosby and hightails it for New York City. In New York City she wears a fabulous dress and sings at a nightclub with tuxedoed gentlemen. When she goes back to Vermont, she's promptly stuffed into a gaudy red ball gown, forced to perform in the freezing cold, and gets only a crappy plastic toy for a present. Not to mention having to make out with Bing Crosby. This ending always disappointed me.

Now that I'm older and have made my own escape to

New York, I've learned to appreciate the month of December, which I used to detest, since it always meant grueling work and occasional humiliation. In December, this city becomes crowded with giant, trimmed trees, daintily painted with white lights and fenced in with smart wire borders. The decorations are tasteful, and used in moderation: red bows and poinsettias and elegant angels blowing golden horns. Window displays come alive with scenes from novels, songs, fables. Even the citizens get into the spirit. Acts of kindness happen all the time. Just the other day, as I was struggling under the weight of three large Saks packages, a very nice elderly man gave up his subway seat to me. Now there's the Christmas spirit for you! Right in the middle of a commute!

Yup. Nothing can beat the holiday season in New York. It's actually relaxing, not like home in Vermont, where all you do is worry about which family will complain if the apple cider supply runs low and whether or not the townspeople will like the decorations your mother chooses for the annual town Christmas Faire. In New York, there's nobody in your business. No responsibilities or obligations to your neighbors. If you don't want to decorate, you don't have to. If you want to spend your Christmas bonus on twelve pairs of shoes, go right ahead. If you want to while away December twenty-fifth in front of the television, watching old *ER* episodes and eating pretzels, be my guest. You can do whatever you want for Christmas.

When you're in New York. Which I won't be.

"Emma, darling, can't you bring something, um, *nicer?*" My brother's girlfriend, Jenny Shaw, gestures limply to the designer clothes that rim my cranberry-tinted cedar closet like obedient color-coded soldiers. Lit from above by very expensive recessed lighting, she holds a small, pumpkin-

colored Pomeranian in one hand and one of my old button-down flannel shirts in the other. "Are the people in
your hometown blind?"

Now, normally I'd be right by her side, ridiculing this
pending fashion tragedy with a hearty "yuck" and a pity-
ing head-shake. In fact, Jenny's fashion snobbery is my favorite thing about her. But instead of voicing disgust, I
take the shirt from her as a small feeling of dread spins like
a top in my stomach. "Well, it's cold there, you know.
Colder than here." I am trying not to care that sweet, im-
maculately put-together Jenny is glimpsing the flannel
skeletons in my closet. I crumple the shirt into a ball and
add it to the growing pile of poorly made, cotton button-
downs that sit on the closet floor, waiting patiently for their
yearly trip to Vermont. These shirts mock me with their
plaidness and Jenny's smart winter-white pants and black
cowl-neck sweater aren't helping. Even my own clothes
aren't cheering me up—I had purposely worn my brand-
new baby-blue Ralph Lauren cashmere sweater so that the
packing of the flannel couldn't get me down. It's not
working.

Jenny stoops to let Ilsa jump free, and carefully eyes the
rest of my Vermont attire, which spills out of a corner cupboard in my closet. I'm fortunate to have a clothes closet
roughly the same size as my childhood bedroom. Affording
this apartment is a badge of my ascension up the career ladder: Upper West Side, great views, a closet that can accommodate two chairs and one small end table and still have
plenty of room for hiding dirty little secrets like wool pajamas and thermal underwear. But now Jenny makes a sound
like a drum cymbal as she shakes her head at my Christmas
clothing options. Her brows are knitting together in confu-

sion. Poor thing—frontier clothing can be quite troubling, especially the first time you confront it.

"Hey, Emma!" Jeff calls out to me from my bedroom. "I've got a little something for you—it'll put you in the mood!"

Jenny and I turn toward the door, and get blasted by the sound of Burl Ives singing *"Here comes Santa Claus, here comes Santa Claus..."* This is followed by the velvet peal of my brother's giggles.

"Jeffrey! Where'd you get that?" I charge out of the closet like a pent-up bull, getting away with a tone that only a sister who's been suffering a full day of an older brother's torture can. Jeff runs around to the other side of the bed, holding his sides as his short, stocky body shakes with laughter. This is the *last* straw—he's been giddily bouncing around in my apartment all morning, fiddling with my thermostat, putting my CDs and DVDs out of alphabetical order, opening my mail. He's drunk on freedom, and it's driving me *crazy*. It's bad enough that his girlfriend has to know about my Vermont wardrobe. But Burl Ives? That's low, even for Jeff.

"What, did you smuggle that thing in here?"

"It's just *Christmas* music, Emma. What's the problem?" Jenny scolds as she follows me out of the closet holding a stack of Diesel jeans. They lighten in color as they rise from the platform of her open palms.

I sink down onto my bed and stare at the jeans, and then glance at my shoes—faux-croc blue Versaces. I guess I should be patient with Jeff. He's cracking under the pressure of his own liberty. Can you imagine? Not having to go home for Christmas? It's my dream! And this was supposed to be *my* year. Since first moving away from home for college, Jeff and I have slowly shaved a holiday a year from the Visiting

Vermont calendar. Not that it's been easy. The first time we missed Halloween, three years ago, my mother overnighted each of us a jack-o'-lantern with cut-out tears dripping down their pumpkiny cheeks. Last Thanksgiving, after my boss made me stay in my office the whole weekend to handle an emergency deposition, she mailed me a paper turkey with a hole where the heart should be.

But a little mail-order guilt is a small price to pay for not having to go home. And so this year, I was going for the big kahuna: Christmas. A tricky undertaking to be sure, because, while those other holidays are just family gatherings, Christmas is my parents' bread and butter. I knew there was no way they'd let the two of us not come home, so I purposely didn't tell Jeff my plans. Unfortunately, we're cut from the same cloth, and were each plotting to stick the other with the family for the holidays. His fast one was faster than mine, though, and now I'm going home for Christmas without him.

So here I stand, sadly taking the stack of Diesel jeans from Jenny's perfectly manicured hands and walking it back into the closet, knowing I'm headed to the land of Levi's.

"You know, actually, you guys could use some Christmas cheer," Jenny says, looking around my white and china-blue room. "Both of your apartments are completely undecorated. It's sad." She stands over my bed and picks Ilsa up out of a pile of socks.

Jeff and I groan in simultaneous disgust as he aims the remote control at my stereo, bringing down the volume on Burl. Neither of us finds the Christmas season very cheery, reminding us as it does of long, cold hours of tree-chopping and light-hanging. But we've both escaped Bethlehem, Vermont, where Christmas is a business—and that business breaks your back. And we both count it a triumph over our humble upbringing that we're living in a state far away from our parents, in our own apartments, and that we have earned the right to *not* decorate.

"Well," Jenny asks, her tone betraying a touch of impatience at my sour mood, "explain to me again why Eric can't go home with you?" She begins to fold and pack my clothes into my open luggage, three great gaping holes of empty promise.

"Well, I mean, he *could*," I say at the same time as Jeff responds, "He can't go." Jenny looks at Jeff like he's a delusional wino. "He'd drop Em like a dirty habit if he went to Bethlehem," he says.

"I don't think that's true, Jeff. He might like it there," I say, totally dejected at his assessment of my boyfriend situation.

"Wanna bet? I'd dump you if you dragged me there for Christmas."

"Well, the point is moot, anyway. He's got his family Aspen thing."

"And you have crazy Nana and the Bethlehem Christmas Faire." Suddenly, he jumps up and makes a whooping sound of delight. "I'm free! *Free!*" He grabs Jenny, picks her up and swings her in a circle.

I collapse back onto my bed and stare at my ceiling, thoughts of Eric in skiwear dancing in my head and torturing my heart.

Eric Wesson is my boyfriend, and, metaphorically speaking, he's from a different part of town than I am. He grew up on the Upper East Side and has a trust fund. His parents serve on charity boards and give money to colleges and get their outings cited in society pages. He's the kind of man I could never have been with if I had stayed in Vermont. But in New York, fairy tales come true every day. In New York it's perfectly possible for a climbing-up-the-mountain girl like me to end up with a standing-at-the-peak guy like him.

Eric and I met just under a year ago, around the same time I was beginning to realize all the pitfalls of being a working woman. I mean, when I was a girl, my father always preached the importance of education, and of being self-sufficient, and of having my own stuff. Growing up, it seemed a simple enough formula: working hard equals getting out of Vermont. And I worked harder than anyone (except for maybe Jeff). Dartmouth, Harvard Law, one of the most prestigious law firms in New York City—all designed to save me from a life of farm toil.

But the thing is, and maybe this seems like common sense to you, but being a lawyer is *hard work.* And the lifestyle is decidedly un-glamorous! Now, I'm not a lazy person and, sure, I like the moola and the car services and the flattering cut of those smart lawyer-y suits, but long hours on a Christmas-tree farm and long hours in a law firm have something in common: *long hours.* And who wants to be married to books on torts and case law and court decisions from 1935? Not me. Who wants to spend Friday nights half-asleep in a musty old law office with only a gallon of caffeine and a wrinkled suit for company? Not me.

Granted, the Rosemary Clooney image of tuxedoed gentlemen, shimmying around me with lusty expressions on their faces is a bit much to ask for. I'd started to think that it wouldn't be such a bad idea to settle for a nice guy who had a healthy hairline and an open wallet. To live out my life as a *society wife.* And then I met Eric. He went to school with Jenny's sister, and I knew immediately that he was the one. No. 1, he's really good-looking. No. 2, he's got a lot of money. No. 3, he owns a home in the Hamptons, No. 4…he didn't flinch when I told him about me growing up on a Christmas-tree farm, and seemed to really enjoy his mother's discomfort when we told *her* about me growing up on a Christmas-tree farm.

From my experience, it takes strong character and nobility of heart to make a rich kid accept No. 4.

I immediately rerouted all my energy from being my boss's lacky and focused it on becoming a *society fiancée*. Our relationship has progressed at the proper pace, just in accordance with my "Eric to-do" list: get phone number, go out on date, get first kiss, have first sleepover, receive expensive yet sentimental first gift, etcetera. And now, after meeting his parents and getting Jeff's approval, there's nothing left to do but snag that engagement. But here's the kicker: Eric can only ask me to marry him the day *after* Christmas, because it's Wesson tradition. Both Eric's father and grandfather got down on one knee on December twenty-sixth, and both, by all accounts, have had long, prosperous, happy marriages.

And on December twenty-sixth, I'll be in Vermont.

"I'm sure Eric would love Bethlehem. It sounds like a lovely place. Idyllic, even," Jenny says.

"Yes, yes. Idyllic. And quaint." Jeff sits next to me. "And all that other crap that Molly and David love about it." Jeff has referred to our parents by their first names since he was seven. "But if Eric gets a load of Molly's outfits and the town Christmas Faire and Nana's carol-singing—"

"Jeff, don't be mean."

"—my little Emma here will be single faster than you can say *local yokels.*" He slings an arm around my shoulders. "Listen, kiddo. I'm really sorry. But next year—next year, I'll go and you can stay home. I promise."

He kisses my forehead and I rest my head on his shoulder, the thought of waiting another entire year before getting engaged making it impossible for me to even lift up my head on my own.

But what am I supposed to do? Leave my parents without *two* pairs of hands on their busiest day of the year?

Jenny looks at us—two grown lawyers commiserating like one of us is headed off to Sing Sing. Her expression is one of polite confusion, and, not knowing quite how to handle us, she continues to pack my clothes. Jeff and I sit there, pathetically watching Jenny do all my work. She picks up flannel after thermal after flannel, the clothes looking like dirty dishrags under the exquisite perfection of her French manicure. And it is at this moment that my future flashes across my mind: The thermal underwear. The light-up lawn ornaments. The scratchy, brown cotton shift I'll be forced to wear during the Christmas Faire nativity scene. I fling Jeff's arm from my shoulder. Why should he get to have a civilized holiday, dressed in nice clothes and not cutting down trees and not spending all of Christmas day outside in a drafty craft booth teaching senior citizens how to make ornaments using old paper-towel rolls and dried cherries? Why can't it be my turn to have a normal, refined holiday?

"Stop!" I lunge at Jenny and rip the flannel out of her hands.

She squeaks in fright. "What are you do—"

"You know what? I am not spending one more holiday season dressed like a farm girl!" I jump up and pick up all the boots and ratty jeans and flannel and LL Bean socks and run them back into my closet. "I am boycotting all farm clothes!"

Jeff jumps off my bed and follows me into the closet, his voice full of panic. "Whoa, whoa, whoa, Emma. You're not backing out, are you? Jenny's family's already expecting me! Her father's going to let me drive his Alfa Romeo!" He picks up the clothes that I just tried to cram back into my closet and starts to walk them back into my room.

"No!" I throw my arms around his back and try to poke the clothes out of his hold, just like the football players do on Eric's favorite football team. A flurry of cotton lands on the floor. Ilsa dashes in and runs around Jeff's feet while barking at him, and Jenny stands in the doorway watching us tug-of-war over a pair of corduroys from Old Navy.

"Jeff! Give them to me!" I yank them, hard, out of his hand.

"You've lost your mind," Jeff mutters through deep, heaving breaths. "Please don't do this. If you don't go home, then I'll have to, and I think one more Christmas in Vermont will cause my brain to spontaneously combust right in the middle of the Christmas Faire. I'm older! I've had to endure three more of these than you have!"

My hands are on the tops of my knees, and I peer up at him. "Oh, shut up, Jeff. I'm going home for Christmas. And I'll string the popcorn, and assemble Christmas Faire booths and listen to Mom chatter on and on about me inheriting the farm, but I will *not* wear flannel!"

Two

A lone car passes me on route I-91, the road to that big nowhere up north, Bethlehem, Vermont. I can't believe that after all my careful plotting, after all the imaginary conversations I had with my mother where I asserted my independence and cut the shackles of Christmases past from my ankles, that I'm stuck going home, just like always. My little outburst with Jeff this morning made it painfully clear that my fragile brain can't take an extended stay. But after this visit, I'm done. If I have to personally carry air conditioners down to hell to freeze it over, so help me God this will be my last Vermont Christmas.

I tap my fingers on the steering wheel and glance down at my driving clothes—a silk shell and Donna Karan pantsuit, covered in my new purple coat with the rabbit-fur front that Eric bought for my very first ski trip, the ski trip that will never be (until next year, that is). It's flashy, which is why I told Eric I had to have it—his mother thinks that I'm a country mouse, and I wanted to have a city-mouse wardrobe for my visit with them. It will definitely stand out in Bethlehem, though, and for a split moment I wonder whether I should have brought it.

"No!" I exclaim to the car. "No Vermont clothes!"

A couple of hours on the road and Bethlehem's already seeping into my consciousness.

The feeling of dread that's been brewing since I found out Jeff beat me to the Christmas punch intensifies. I don't mean to be an ungrateful child, but I *hate* going home. First of all, there's nothing to do there but work, work and more work. Second, since moving to New York, Jeff and I have become the recipients of some *attitude* from the good people of Bethlehem. Most of this stems from the fact that we are practically the only two people who have ever left the town. My parents, outside of the two months my father could get away from the farm to try college, have never even gone on a vacation. Every year, Jeff and I offer to foot the bill for a cruise or a week at a beach somewhere, but they'll never take us up on it. Bethlehem has some kind of voodoo, cosmic pull on their souls, just like on all the other townsfolk. And since Jeff and I figured out how to break the spell, we've become the target of some nastiness.

In the past, I've tried to minimize the comments and stares from my parents' neighbors by covering myself in flannel, pulling my blond hair back in a ponytail and performing all Christmas-related tasks with a modest smile. But this year, I'm just going to have to take it, because there will be no woodsman clothes for me: during the next few days it'll be Missoni sweaters and Ferragamo heels. Through my fashion choices, I will be subtly communicating to my mother and father that just because I'm home, doesn't mean that I'm on twenty-four-hour Christmas tree delivery duty.

Not that there'll be any deliveries to make. I've succeeded in pushing back my Christmas arrival date to the twenty-third, so there will be very few farm chores. All I'll be responsible for are the last-minute Faire tasks.

Ah. The annual Bethlehem Christmas Faire. Another big reason I hate going home. Jeff's right. The thought of spending one more Christmas day outside, in the middle of a boring old Christmas Faire that hasn't changed in the one-hundred-plus years it's been mounted, is enough to give me a migraine headache. The good citizens of Bethlehem take this event very seriously, too, which makes it even worse. There's a strict code of which family does what. (Townsends have decorated, run the ornament-making station and mounted the closing Nativity Scene since the late 1800s.) And only members of the six original founding families of Bethlehem can serve on the Faire's planning committee. So, as you can imagine, nothing ever changes: every year it's the same booths, the same music, the same food, the same people attending. The only thing that does change is the decorations, because that's my mother's department and she's constantly being "creative" with her theme. If only she could do something about the nativity scene costumes, which I suspect have been in existence since the very first Faire.

My lip curls at the thought of that cheap, scratchy, burlap touching my skin, so I try to imagine what it'll be like when I'm married. No more law firm! No more Vermont Christmases! It'll be me and Eric's credit cards and his beautiful homes and his snooty mother and his three cars.

Even these thoughts can't drive the disappointment out of my heart, though. And now the drive's gotten down-right creepy. Mine is the only car on the road. There are no homes or buildings or even street lamps lining the highway once you get this far north, and the trees are all capped with snow. I twist the radio dial and run through the stations. The only one that comes through is playing the travesty of a holiday song "Rockin' Around the Christmas Tree." When this nightmare is followed by "The Twelve Days of Christmas," I moan in frustration and mock-hit the front of the radio. It's been hijacked by Christmas. I plug in my iPod transmitter just in time to miss a rousing rendition of "Grandma Got Run Over By A Reindeer" and let out a relaxed sigh as my Eagles playlist starts. I have a soft spot for the Eagles ever since high school at Allendale Academy, when Tim Latch (the dreamiest, richest kid in my class) and his band played "Take It Easy" at the freshman talent show.

Once the Eagles have sufficiently chilled me out, I grab my cell and punch in Eric's number. We haven't talked in three days. He's been giving me the silent treatment, because I had to drop out of the ski trip. In a way, it's quite cute. I mean, he was obviously planning on taking advantage of the Wesson Family Proposal day. My family has ruined things for both of us.

The phone rings three spotty, staticky times before he picks up.

"Emma?"

"Eric!" I am so relieved to hear his voice, even if it is flickering in and out of earshot. "Hey. How are you?"

"Hold on, sweetheart." I can hear him talking to somebody over his shoulder. He called me "sweetheart"—that must be a sign that he's getting over the disappointment of not being with me.

"Hello?" I shout into the phone.

"Hey."

"Why hadn't you called me?" I say this in the most pouty, childlike voice I can muster.

"I'm sorry, sweetie, just— Oh. Hold on."

I wait for about three more seconds while these odd people-talking-under-water sounds drift into my ear.

"Sorry, Em. I'm at the club."

"The club?"

"Yeah. You knew this would happen. My mother's driving me crazy, parading me around town, introducing me to all these plastic society girls. I really wish you were here. It'd be so much more fun."

Since the day Eric's mother found out I was from a Christmas-tree farm in Vermont, she's been desperate to break us up. I haven't even come clean about all the details, either! Imagine what she'll think when she finds out about the burlap Christmas Faire costumes. And I don't get it. Jenny's family is just as well off as Eric's and they *love* Jeff.

"Don't talk to those girls, Eric. I'm the only one for you!" I shout confidently into the phone.

"Em, I gotta run. My mom's coming, with a—oh God. It's this girl I know from high school. She's got a lisp. I've got to hide."

I try to tell him I love him but the phone cuts out on me. This state! You'd think they'd figure out how to accommodate technology from at least the latter half of the last century. It's not Canada, for crying out loud!

I come into St. Johnsbury, Vermont, and get off the interstate. This is the worst part of the drive, from the highway to my town, because you have to pass through the town of Allendale. I tuck a strand of hair behind my ear as the huge, towering mansions come into view, one after the other, like one of those miniature picture books that you flick to make the images blur into a movie. Tim Latch's home comes up on my left—it's an English-Tudor-style monstrosity of a house. I press down on the gas pedal and speed my way past it.

Tim Latch. The cutest boy at Allendale Academy, and the love of my high-school life. Our romance fizzled shortly after it began. We hit it off, he asked me to go with him to the tenth grade winter semiformal. The morning of the dance, Jeff and I were helping my dad deliver trees, and wouldn't you know that the first delivery was to Tim's family. I was in flannel and dirty corduroys and scuffed-up boots—I looked like a grubby boy. I panicked when I realized where we were, and tried to hide myself on the floor of Dad's truck. But it was too late. Tim and a bunch of his friends saw me, and the look on Tim's face when he realized I was a *local,* well, it wasn't pretty.

One of his friends pointed at me and shouted, "Hey, isn't that your date?" and then they all started laughing. Tim just made a face like they were all crazy, and said, "That's not my date!" and they all laughed and laughed while I burrowed down into the floor of the truck. I cried the whole way home and pretty much for the rest of the night, while I sat wrapped in a blanket on the couch, thinking about who Tim was dancing with and listening to my mother tell my father that he never should've sent us to that school anyway, because it put ideas in our heads.

I hate that this memory still bothers me. I glance in the rearview mirror to remind myself that I'm not the same little flannel-wrapped farm girl I used to be. If only Tim Latch could see me now!

I continue down the road, the Eagles playing softly as I pass the official state marker of the little town of Bethlehem. There's a small silhouette of a manger on the sign, and a printed banner saying "Incorporated in 1802. Population 226." What the sign doesn't tell you is that half the town's related by blood or marriage (or *both* in some disturbing cases) and that it's Christmas year round here. As I turn onto Route 16, the main road that takes you through the center of town, I am shocked and pleased to hear the sound of my ringing cell phone.

"Hullo?"

"Hey, little pumpkin."

"Are we speaking?"

Jeff's warm laugh silences me. "Em, I just called to say I'm sorry, and that I know what you're giving up here."

I turn the steering wheel with my left hand, and see Mrs. Henry coming down the sidewalk. She's on the Christmas Faire committee with my mom; they went to elementary and high school together, and she's got about the biggest nose you ever saw. It's unfortunate. My brother used to try to shoot it with his BB gun when we were growing up. I say into the phone, "Well, here's Mrs. Henry. My first townie sighting of the holiday season. She looks old."

"Aw, that old bat'll be alive and kicking for the next hundred years."

"Jeff, let me go—"

"Okay, kiddo. I just wanted to say good luck, and that you're the one thing I'll miss this year. Love you."

The first thing anyone notices about my hometown is the town square—yep, a town square, just like in any TV show or movie you see that takes place in a small New England town. Bethlehem sits under the shadow of the White Mountains, and looks like Frank Capra laid it out. The square's in the middle, lined on each side by a handful of buildings and a white clapboard church that has a steeple the folks of Bethlehem think scrapes the basement of heaven, though in reality it's about as tall as a four-story New York City brownstone.

Around the white-washed entryway to the square hangs the banner, made every year by the Henry family, that proudly proclaims, "Welcome to Bethlehem. Home of Christmas." Through the archway, I can see a grove of about fifty trees my dad has set up for the Faire. My mom makes sure these are up and decorated the Saturday after Thanksgiving. Tantrums were thrown last year when Jeff and I didn't come home to help. This year, apparently my mother has chosen a citrus theme, because the trees are covered in orange lights, orange bows, and what appear to be actual oranges. There are also a few limes and lemons thrown in for what I imagine is my mother's idea of citrus balance. It's a Florida Christmas, ladies and gentlemen! I wonder what the mayor makes of this. Mayor Reilly has always expressed displeasure at my mother's more eccentric decorating ideas. Last year they had a fight right on the steps of the General Store over whether or not poodles had any place in the nativity scene—she had a Noah's Ark theme going.

Just then, as I'm waiting for a light to turn green, a long, bony finger taps my window, and I jump in my seat. Mrs. Henry and her nose peer through my driver side window, fogging it up with her hot, nosy breath.

"Hey, Mrs. Henry," I say as I roll down the window. "How are you today?"

"Emma Jane." Mrs. Henry's birdlike head pokes into the interior of my car while I cringe at the sound of my full name. "Well, this is some car."

"Uh, thanks, Mrs. Henry. It's a Lexus." The whole town

will know the color and exact make of this vehicle by noon tomorrow. "So, how's everything? All set for the big Faire?"

Mrs. Henry retracts her head like a turtle retreating into its shell, and purses her lips. "I'm not saying anything, Emma Jane. I'm not saying anything." And then she runs away from the car, crosses the street and heads up the stairs that lead to the entrance of the General Store.

Unbelievable. In town for about two seconds, and I'm already the topic of gossip. People go into that store for more than supplies, that's for sure.

I slowly pull onto the road that leads to the Townsend farm. The drive has worn me out, and I long for my bathtub—the one with the massage jets and huge basin. I long to sink down into it and have Eric knead away the knots in my shoulders. Alas, there will be no relaxation for me. Mom will put me straight to work stringing popcorn and then Dad and I will have to add it to all the orange trees in the center of town. My mother strings popcorn every December twenty-third, all day long, for the Faire. (She says the popcorn can't be strung earlier than the twenty-third, because strung popcorn looks limp after three days, and it would be an insult to the town and to the baby Jesus if the popcorn looked limp.)

Our long windy driveway is marked by a medium-size plastic banner stretched between two wooden stakes, "Townsend Tree Farm." I park behind my father's dusty pickup truck and two other pickups that I haven't seen before—they probably belong to my dad's farmhands du jour. The yard looks mostly as it always does. There's a table to the right of the driveway, with stacks of wreaths on it, and three miniature versions of the different-size trees we sell. Beside that table is the cider-selling stand—Nana's station.

Usually she mans this table wearing a peppermint-striped Santa hat, and doles out both apple cider and maple syrup with a saucy Depression-era wit that customers seem to find atmospheric but that always made me and Jeff shudder in embarrassment. But not only isn't she here, but there aren't any jugs of cider or tins of syrup to be seen, either.

The rest of the house is decorated to the nines, as is my mother's standard M.O. A train of white wicker reindeer litters the top of the garage, headed off by a light-up Rudolph. A collection of plastic, three-foot-high candy canes stands on either side of the driveway. The house is outlined in Christmas lights. The surrounding bushes are covered in garish, huge colored light bulbs. Is it any wonder that Jeff and I choose *not* to decorate?

But perched right in the middle of the yard is a new addition to the decor: a giant, what must be a ten-foot, block of ice. *Ice.*

Now that's interesting.

I zip up my purple rabbit-fur-front jacket, cover my chin-length blond hair in a matching purple coyote-skin hat, grab my stuff from the trunk, and turn off my cell phone. I take a step toward the yard and slide about fifteen feet. It's my shoes. I had wanted to make a statement by wearing classy shoes (this pair, $300 Christian LaCroix pumps) but Christian LaCroix obviously knows nothing about navigating patches of snow and ice. I struggle against the poor conditions, cross the yard, and upon a brief examination of the bizarro ice slab—it's so frickin' cold in Vermont, it's not even steaming or melting—discover several marks on the surface, like somebody's trying to build an ice sculpture. God, I hope this isn't my mother's handiwork—that'd be all the town gossips would need. One more reason to chitchat about that eccentric Molly Townsend and her crazy artistic notions. But I remind myself that this is the last year I'm going to have to deal with it.

When I get to the front door, I kick my shoes against the cement steps to loosen the caked-on layer of snow, and also to get some circulation back into my feet. Then I ring the doorbell before letting myself in. The front door gets stuck on two small, tweed suitcases that I remember from when I was a kid and would play "Leaving Bethlehem," a game that Jeff, my cousin Liza and I created.

"Hey, I'm home!" My shout echoes into the house and then disappears. I scoot inside and check the place out. Christmas Central, as expected. It's a gift, really. To be able to maintain the same level of hokeyness from year to year is my mother's gift. First of all, the whole place has the sickly sweet stench of sugar cookies—thanks to the, oh, I don't know, dozen or so scented candles that are burning. It's a miracle she hasn't burned this place down yet. Especially with all the mistletoe, dancing just above the candle flames. Every year, my mother hangs mistletoe wherever she can. Something about Christmas turns Mom and Dad into a pair of randy teenagers. When Jeff and I were kids, we'd organize special ops to get them to quit with the making out. We'd get our walkie-talkies working and grab fistfuls of pine needles, then ambush them, showering them with the ammo. This rarely slowed them down.

I take a step toward the kitchen and get thwacked upside the head by a hanging forest of paper snowflakes. I take another step and hear the crackle of breaking pine needles beneath my feet. It's a Christmas-tree farm job hazard—there are always pine needles *everywhere*. They get in your clothes, your hair, your food. There were pine needles in my *bed,* even in July. Not something the Latches or the Wessons had to worry about, I'd bet the farm on it.

Our kitchen, with its wooden beams and dark gray slate tile mined in nearby New Hampshire, is another vision of Christmas delights. Jenny Shaw wants quaint? Decorations? Well, she would love it in here. As a matter of fact, Santa Claus should move his whole operation to the kitchen. From the advent calendar hanging on the refrigerator to my mother's nutcracker collection to the string lights hanging from ceiling to floor, the place looks like the North Pole's prop closet. The only non-Christmas-related items in here are a part of my mother's ceramic cow collection, the focal point of which is a cow-shaped teapot my mother refers to as the tea *cattle*. I am sure you can see why it was so important for me to escape this fate.

But something's off, because there are only a handful of cookies sitting on the countertop. And only four pies. And then I realize the oddest thing of all.

Silence.

No crooning Bing Crosby wishing for a white Christmas.

"Hello?" I start to walk back toward the hallway, when a huge swelling scream, made up of small, high-pitched voices, comes thundering from behind the cellar door. In one *swoosh,* three blond children, shirtless, crowned with construction-paper headdresses and masked in Crayola red, white and yellow slash marks, come tumbling into the kitchen, battle poses at the ready. "A pilgrim!" shouts the middle-size child, Jake Jr., who has the same pageboy haircut and pug nose that my cousin Liza had when she was young. The toddler, Kimmy, who could barely take a few steps last year when I saw her, freezes in fear at a stranger. The oldest, a platinum blonde named Elizabeth, screeches,

"It's Emmy from New York!" Then they all three rush at me. I step and jump and tell my little second cousins to get their hands off my outfit. It's Donna Karan, for crying out loud! They circle me, JJ pretending he's hunting and Lizzie peppering me with questions about the Rockettes and the Empire State Building and the Statue of Liberty. I'm trapped in *Lord of the Flies.*

"Hello?" My voice sounds wobbly as I call for adult assistance. Let me just say it right now: I'm bad with kids. Like, preternaturally bad. They confuse me and tire me out and often our interactions end with one of us screaming bloody murder, and I always feel like I'm the butt of their jokes. If children under the age of ten even know how to make jokes, that is. So I am desperate in my pleas for help, but the only response I get is the shuffling sound of footsteps coming from behind the door of the basement.

A deep voice yells, "Wait'll I get you, Injuns!"

Good Lord. Now I'm trapped in *Peter Pan.* The kids shrink back in on me, screeching in delighted fright at the approaching danger, as I hear Liza coming down the front stairs. "Emma Jane, is that you?"

"Yes, yes. Help me."

Liza enters the kitchen with a laundry basket in her hands. At the same time, the door to the basement swings wide open and a dirty-looking guy whom I assume is my father's newest farmhand pops out in front of the children, causing them to emit a round of high-pitched squeals that are sure to bring dogs running to our yard. Something about the farmhand starts bells clanging in my head. As he scoops one of the screaming-banshee children into his arms, I'm suddenly struck by the fact that this dirty tree-farmer is none other than Tim Latch, my high school crush. But that's just silly. I was thinking about him before—that's why my brain is making this association.

Wait a minute. He has the same brown eyes, and that freckle just beneath his left eyebrow, and the little scar by his upper lip from when Jake Reilly (who happens to be married to Liza) hit him in the face with a baseball during our senior-year baseball tournament. Oh, my God. This is Tim Latch. In my kitchen. A scruffy, weather-beaten version of Tim Latch, a version with a tool belt around his waist and wearing brown, paint-splattered cargo pants and a white T-shirt. He has stubble and light brown, cropped hair that creates a skinhead look I am shocked to see suits him rather well. I tilt my head in horrified confusion.

"Tim?"

He shakes his head, and does a double-take when he sees me standing there. "Oh, Emma! It's, uh, hi there." He takes a step away from me and blows some air out of his mouth. He looks as uncomfortable as I feel.

Before I can respond, Liza takes my hand and gives me a perfunctory kiss on the cheek, followed by a flat smile. Then she quickly checks me out, no doubt filling up her gossip arsenal with tidbits about my clothes.

"Well, Emma Jane! It's good to have you home." Lizzie and JJ form a ring-around-the-rosy circle with Liza trapped in the middle. "God, you're so thin."

I ignore this. "Well, it's good to be home." I sound much less sincere than I meant to. It's just that I was expecting to see at least one friendly face here. I didn't expect to have to see my cousin until Faire day, never mind the shocking sight of Tim Latch standing in my mother's provincial kitchen— right next to her tea cattle!

I run my hands down the front of my suit and take a deep

breath. It's okay. No big deal. So it's Tim Latch. In my house. So what? I am no longer the plaid-wearing girl of our youth. I mean, are these designer clothes? Yes. Is this a hundred-and-fifty-dollar haircut? Sure is. So, eat your heart out, Tim Latch. This is what could have been yours!

"We were actually worried that you wouldn't get here in time." Liza batters her way through her children's circle, goes to the sink and washes her hands.

"Well, I don't know how much I'll be able to help. I mean, I forgot to bring all my work clothes." Man, that wasn't subtle at all.

Liza rolls her eyes. "Of course you didn't."

"Is that my little EJT?" My mother's voice follows the slam of the front door.

The first thing I notice as she comes into the kitchen carrying a basket of pinecones is that she's blond, which she wasn't last year. Then I notice her navy blue knit sweater with the silk-screened Christmas village scene on the front that looks suspiciously like the Bethlehem Town Square. I can't believe she'd wear this in front of Tim, and shoot a glance his way to see if he's horrified or not. My mother lunges forward to envelop me in a Shalimar cloud of hugs.

"Look at her, look at her," she says as she holds me at arm's length and looks me up and down. "No snacking, I see."

I tug at the edges of my clothes, trying to smooth out the wrinkles from the journey.

My mother turns to Liza and asks, "Did you tell Emma Jane the news, dear?"

The smile on my mother's face is one I've seen before. It's the one she gets just before springing some wacko Christmas scheme on me. Like last year when she made me wear a Rudolph the Red-Nosed Reindeer costume while hawking our apple cider on the side of Route 16.

I look behind me desperately, searching for someone to stop my mother from telling me whatever it is she's going to tell me. "Where's Dad?"

"Oh, yeah, yeah, he—he'll be up," Tim Latch answers, as my mother starts giggling like a monkey on helium.

"You won't believe it, Emma Jane! We're doing just like you and Jeff always said we should—we're going to Jamaica! For Christmas!"

Three

Standing in my mother's decorated kitchen next to Tim Latch and wearing a Donna Karan suit, I feel the way Wile E. Coyote must, after he's chased the Road Runner too far and finds himself suspended in midair over a deep ravine.

"J-Jamaica? What are you talking about?"

"There's no use trying to talk her out of it," says Liza, a resigned look in her eye. It's no secret that Liza, my dad's niece, has always sided with her parents in thinking my mom's a loon.

"Mom, what do you mean you're going to Jamaica?" I ask again. My parents have never, *never* missed a Bethlehem Christmas. I didn't think it was within my mother's DNA to even consider stepping over the county line. God knows, Jeff and I have tried to get her to come visit us, but, again, the woman has *never* left Vermont.

"Is that my Emma cakes?" My father comes bounding into the room.

"Emma Cakes?" Tim makes a face.

"Daddy—" He slugs his arm around me, pulls the hat off my head and kisses my hair.

My dad is huge. We're talking Paul Bunyan huge. He's six-five, with blond curly hair and a beard to match. Though year after year, gray overtakes the blond, and the crow's feet around his blue eyes get deeper and deeper. Jeff says that he ages exponentially according to how many trees he has to cut down every year. And it's too bad that my father has spent almost his whole life on this farm, too, because he's something of a genius. He reads like some people breathe—always has a book or two strewn about the house—and when Jeff and me were kids, he'd lull us to sleep at bedtime with articles from the *Wall Street Journal*. Jeff calls him Professor Farmer.

"Okay, Uncle Dave and Aunt Molly, Jake and I will be back in an hour to take you to the airport. Lizzie! JJ! Kimmy! Let's go. It's good to see you, Emma Jane." Liza looks at me for a beat, then emits a deep sigh and waddles out the door. I mentally note her Northern Lights outfit, the eyes darting from child to child, the back weighed down by two full bags of kid supplies. Her movements are slow, deliberate, and there's a general air of exhaustion about her. One more checkmark in the plus column for society wife: Eric will be able to afford us a battery of nannies.

"So, sweetheart, are you thirsty? We've got a new batch of apple cider, ready to go." My mother corrals me toward the kitchen table and pulls a jug from the fridge.

Tim says something to my father about "finishing the sculpting" while grabbing a fork out of my mother's silverware drawer and pulling a pie out of the refrigerator. He looks awfully comfortable around here, and I have the horrible realization that he's probably living in the farmer's cabin out behind our house. Wow, has my mother been keeping secrets from me. But before I can grill her about Tim's presence here, I have to get to the bottom of this Jamaican Christmas mystery.

"Mom, stop. Just tell me what's going on, okay?"

My parents hold hands on the other side of the table and my dad says, "Well, angel, your mother and I are going to take a little trip to the beach."

"Okay. I get that part. But, why? How? Why?" Looking from my mother to father to my mother again, it soon becomes clear that neither one of them is looking me in the eye. "Why didn't you tell me and Jeff about this before I drove all the way up here?"

My mother pours herself a mug full of cider and stirs it with a cinnamon stick. "Sweetheart, yes, well, we didn't think you'd come if you knew."

I'm missing something. And I start to squint like I'm trying to work out an algebra problem or figure out a phrase in a foreign language. Then it knocks me on the head like Jeff used to do. "Wait a minute." I snap my fingers. "The Faire! You tricked me into coming up here to run our part of the Faire!"

My mother puts her papery hand on top of mine and assumes her best empathy face. It really irritates me, that face.

"Dear, *trick* is a strong word, no?"

My father tugs at his beard. "The Townsends have obligations to the town. We have to set up the booths and run the ornament-making station, and your grandmother can't do it all alone. Obviously we'd prefer that Jeff was here, but Tim will help you." He playfully reaches out to tousle my hair one more time.

I look at Tim, who sheepishly grins through a mouthful of pie, then raises his shoulders at me apologetically.

"But, but…Mom, you're on the Faire committee! You can't leave for Christmas!"

"Have some pie."

My mother has a way of being deliberately obtuse and cheery when things are crashing down around you. She reaches for the pie Tim's attacking, but he wraps a protective arm around it.

"There's another apple over there." He points to the top of the refrigerator.

I'm starting to get a headache.

"I don't want pie. I want you to level with me." I put on my lawyer voice, the one my boss uses on hostile witnesses. "Tell me exactly what happened."

My parents look at each other guiltily. I'm still squinting at them. It's going to wreak havoc on the skin around my eyes.

"Well, Emma Cakes." My father pulls on his beard. "As you know, there are several Faire committee meetings, and—"

"We just felt that it was time—"

"That is to say that the committee decided—"

"—to take a year off—"

"—it was time for a change—"

"—and since you and Jeff clearly aren't interested in the holidays—"

"Stop!" I shout, and stand. "One at a time. What happened?"

My mother sips her cider and my father's mouth clamps shut. I look back and forth between them.

"Mrs. Scanlon decided that instead of the nativity scene ending the Faire this year they should let her son sing 'O, Holy Night.' There was a big fight and your mother quit the committee." Tim says all this calmly through mouthfuls of pie, then turns to my dad and asks, "Did I get that right?"

"That about sums it up."

"You *quit*?" My mother keeps her nose in her cider mug and doesn't answer me. "You quit the committee? But haven't Townsends been on the committee since, like, I don't know——"

"1898," my father prompts.

"Yeah. Since 1898?"

"Yes, well, that Mary Ellen Scanlon has had it in for me since your father took me to prom. And now, with my maple syrup winning best of region three years in a row, the poor thing's acting out."

In all the years I have known my mother, Mary Ellen Scanlon has always been one of her best friends. And my nana and Mary Ellen's mother *are* best friends. They were born a day apart and had a double wedding.

Now, I'm not gonna lie—I'm no Jeff when it comes to smarts. So it takes me a minute to work all this out.

My parents not in Bethlehem for Christmas. No end-of-the-Faire nativity scene. It's conceivable that I could stay here and make sure all the craft booths get set up, ask Tim Latch (Lord help me) to assist my nana with the ornament-making station during the actual Faire, and then actually *fly to Colorado* in time to get proposed to. I'd get everything I wanted—and look like a really good daughter to boot.

It's my very own Christmas miracle. An orchestra of heavenly angels begins to sing in my head, *"I'm free! Free at last! Thank the Lord I'm free at last!"* My heart pounds—this is such a heady sensation: I am dizzy with happiness.

"Jamaica, huh? Jamaica. Imagine that?" My voice sounds

breathy, full of excitement. "We sure will miss you!" And a little too relieved.

My mother mercifully misses the joy in my voice, and her eyes get teary. "Your father and I have wanted to take a trip to a beach since we first got married, and we've never been able to, because of the farm and the Faire—and you kids, of course." My father nods in assent, though this is the first time I've ever heard about them wanting to go on a vacation. "And if the Faire committee wants 'O, Holy Night' instead of our beautifully poignant Christmas scene, then *we* don't want *them*."

Well, I'm so beside myself that I jump up and hug each of my parents. "Christmas in Jamaica! Jamaica!" Jeff is never going to believe this. My parents. Ditching their responsibilities. It's amazing. And long overdue. My mother could use some sun.

"Is she here?" The slam of the back screen door interrupts our hugging session—and in walks a gaggle of octogenarians. It's Nana and her old-person posse: Mrs. Scanlon, her childhood friend; Barney Downing, the town sheep farmer (whose livestock were the unfortunate recipients of several mohawks from Jeff and me) and Norm Bray, a retired teacher who was my grandpa's best friend for more than sixty years.

"The gang's here to see you off," Nana barks to my parents, her voice sounding as bossy as a Marine colonel's.

God. She's the incredible shrinking woman of Bethlehem! Each time I see her, she's smaller than she was before. She looks like an extra from *Lord of the Rings,* especially with that Santa hat on her head.

While Mr. Bray and Mr. Downing join Tim Latch at the apple pie, old Mrs. Scanlon takes my mother by the hand and says, "I don't know what to do with my Mary Ellen. That Joe Jr. can't hit a note with a five-pound weight."

"Well, my Emma Jane is here and that'll make for a good Faire for me!" Nana's eyes are huge behind her glasses. Like two milk saucers, with giant blue eyeballs floating in the middle of them, they ricochet around as she grabs my hands and looks me up and down.

I try to hug her, but she slips out of my grasp like a wisp of air.

She has an immense amount of energy, as if she's on speed. She goes running to the sewing closet, and comes back with this very chintzy looking red faux-velvet material, which she holds up to me. "Em, you and I are going to man the Townsend ornament station in elf costumes! That'll set tongues off!"

"Oh, no—an elf?" I want somebody to shoot me dead. The last thing I need is for Tim Latch to be witnessing this humiliating display. I try to step away from my grandmother. "Actually, Nana, I just got here. Can we do this later?"

She completely ignores me, takes some pins out of her pocket and begins to *pin* the costume right onto my *Donna Karan* ensemble. This is now officially a nightmare. I cringe at each thrust, my heart hurting at the sound of quality fibers being ripped to shreds. Old Mrs. Scanlon joins in, she and Nana perfectly synchronized in their work as if they've been doing this together for years.

"And Normie said he'd dress up like Santa! Ooh, Emma!"

I sneak a glance at Tim Latch, but thankfully, he's not even looking at me. He's really enjoying that pie.

The next thirty minutes or so are a blur. My mother produces four garbage bags full of strung popcorn, and proceeds to drill all kinds of Faire details into my head. My father runs back and forth from his study, trying to decide which books to bring to Jamaica. Nana and Mrs. Scanlon continue to pin me into this one-hundred-percent polyester costume at the expense of my poor suit, and Tim Latch eats that entire apple pie from the counter, just standing there dipping into the center of it with a fork. Finally, Liza and her husband Jake come back to the house and usher my parents into their old pickup truck. (Liza's children sit in the bed of the truck with my mother, singing Christmas carols as they pull away.)

The minute the truck pulls out of the driveway, this massive Kafkaesque transformation takes over my nana. Her entire posture changes, creeping upward from her toes. "Thank God they're gone!" she shouts, raising a curled fist at the door. "Ingrates!"

"Oh, here we go," Mr. Downing grumbles.

"They think they get to have fun and poor old Helen will do all the work? Well, I've logged my Faire time." Nana proceeds to whiz around the kitchen like a dervish, flinging open cupboard doors, pulling out an assortment of bottles and cups and saucers.

"We know, Helen," says Mr. Bray.

"Miss Emma, it's up to your generation now. I'm retired. Make the pension checks out to Helen Townsend."

She's babbling like a lunatic, and all I can do is stand there, covered in cheap red velvet, sputtering in confusion.

"Don't get all riled, Helen. Your blood pressure, now." Mrs. Scanlon's attempts at soothing fall on deaf ears.

"Think again, sister!"

"They didn't mean anything by it, Helen." Tim tries to sound comforting but is unsuccessful, probably because of his constant mouthful of pie (he's now moved on to pumpkin). "Emma and I'll take care of everything. All you'll have to do is show up."

Tim takes a can of whipped cream and squirts a large dollop onto his fork before taking another bite. Where'd he learn these manners?

My nana shows no sign of ceasing her bottle-hunting expedition. I spy a Bailey's Irish Cream in the collection strewn about the counter and hand it to her. "Is this what you're looking for, Nana?"

Her eyes light up and she snatches it from my hand. "Oh, you always were a firecracker, Emma. You and Jeff had the right idea, getting away from all this nonsense." She pours two teacups full of the brown, creamy liquid, and hands one to Mrs. Scanlon. They throw them back like pirates. Nana rips the Santa hat off her head, barks, "Come on fellas," to the gentlemen at the counter, and dashes out the door, as fast as a seventy-six-year-old woman with a fake hip and cataracts can. Mrs. Scanlon, Mr. Downing and Mr. Bray follow her out with a few waves and hearty chuckles.

And just like that, I find myself in my mother's kitchen in Bethlehem, Vermont, on December twenty-third, with nobody but Tim Latch, son of the richest man in northeastern Vermont.

"She's upset that they didn't invite her," he says to me.

"Uh. I can see that," I reply and nervously smile at him.

Tim stares at me for a minute and we descend into a very uncomfortable silence. The fink. He's probably desperate to plot his escape from me, unaware of how close I am to infiltrating his ranks. The fiend! He rocks onto his toes for a moment, then walks to the counter and starts putting away all the bottles that Nana left on the counter. When that's done, he goes to the sink, washes his fork, dries it and puts it in the drawer.

As I watch him avoid me, all my Nancy Drew instincts come bubbling up from out of nowhere. I mean, why? Instead of spending the days before the holiday in his own mansion, sipping sherry and chatting with his family about all the money they have, why is he dressed like an artist bum from the East Village and hanging out at the Townsend tree farm? I look around for clues, but see only the string lights and nutcracker collection. Then I look down and see the half-hemmed elf costume still clinging to the threads of my Donna Karan.

"I don't believe this." This is *so* not how I would've planned our reunion.

"Want some help?" He steps toward me and tries to remove some of the pins.

I tuck into a deep recess of my brain the factoid that neither of his hands sports a wedding band.

"No. No, no, no, no, no, no, no." It's like I'm a rapper. I furiously start trying to remove myself from the dress. How can a grown woman, a woman with degrees from two Ivy League schools and wearing three-hundred-dollar shoes be so insecure? This is awful. So I avoid my discomfort by attempting to satiate my immense curiosity.

"So, what are *you* doing here?"

He smiles sheepishly, and merely says, "Your parents have been really looking forward to this trip."

The cagey type, eh? Well, fine. What does it matter to me anyway? Why should I care if he's throwing his life away to moonlight as a townie? All I know is, Eric would never, never eat standing up. Or mix his fruit pies. Oh hell, I don't even know what I'm saying anymore. It's been a trying day.

I rip the last pin out of my clothes, throw the ensemble onto the counter and wander into the living room, so I can get a few moments to process the fact that my parents have *left the country* for Christmas.

Unfortunately, my family living room has been devoured by a Lilliputian-size ceramic Christmas village. Oh, my poor mother and her decorating zeal. The miniature village, which she regularly adds to by compulsively shopping online, is comprised of tiny, painted facsimiles of homes and town buildings and trees and even a skating pond with miniature, magnetic skaters wheeling around in a circle. A Matchbox-sized train trudges around the whole scene, making a tinny chugging sound. There's barely room in here for the Christmas tree, which I notice has zero presents underneath it. (I hope Eric will have time to get more than just a ring for me—I love presents.)

I collapse onto the sofa that's crammed into a corner. Out of the glare of Tim's judgy gaze, I begin to remember the gloriousness of what's just happened. All I have to do is hang some popcorn, set up some booths, and then I'm home free. Really, how could I have asked for anything more? I get to have my cake and *eat it, too!* I'm the good daughter for coming all the way up here, and still I get to go to Colorado. Hurrah! Without my parents here to guilt me into staying, and without that silly Mary and Joseph scene to keep me here late on Christmas Day, I am as good as gone. I might even find a flight that leaves on Christmas Eve! This is better than I could have planned myself.

Tim appears in the doorway, holding two pieces of my luggage, and swerves his head to avoid getting conked by a bushy bundle of mistletoe. "I'll take these up to your room. Is that all right?"

"Um, oh, okay." I jump off the couch and step toward him, hoping to block his view of the living room. It's not right that my mother keeps this tacky Christmas village out in plain view when there's someone like Tim in our midst.

He doesn't move. He just stands in the doorway, holding my bags, staring me down.

And I realize that I haven't looked in a mirror since I got here, and my suit's been maimed and my makeup's probably worn off and my hair's most likely flat as a sheet. And even though it looks like Tim hasn't showered in a while, he still knows a well-put-together woman when he sees it.

"What?"

"Nothing." He nods three times, then carries my bags up to my room.

"It's at the top of the stairs, to your right!" I call.

His voice floats down the stairs. "I know."

Enough. Enough thinking about Tim Latch and what he must think of our house and the decorations. It's none of my business, anyway. From here on in, I am going to focus on getting the Townsend Faire tasks taken care of, so that I can get to Colorado and bag the title of society wife. I head into the kitchen. The four garbage bags full of popcorn sit silently waiting by the door. I pour myself a glass of water, grab the phone and leave Jeff a message. He's going to faint dead away when he hears what happened.

Tim comes into the kitchen, opens the cellar door and grabs one of my father's chainsaws. "So, I'll be out front— just come get me when you're ready to go downtown to hang the popcorn."

"Okay. Give me a few minutes."

The sound of the front door slamming follows Tim out the door, and I'm left alone in my house.

For perhaps the first time ever.

I head on up to my room, the room where I spent count-less hours hiding from my mother's embarrassing behavior, to change out of my pierced clothes. The banister is cov-ered in garland, and, sure enough, there's mistletoe at the top of the stairs and hanging from my doorway, too. Silver gar-land is strung from the four corners of the bedroom, meet-ing in the center of the ceiling and topped off with a big, lusty bouquet of holly and mistletoe that hangs right over my four-poster bed. I really hope my parents didn't do it in here.

Tim has placed the largest of my luggage pieces on the dresser. I open it and grab a Missoni sweater and a pair of Lucky jeans that Jenny and I agreed, at the last minute, should make the trip. When I kick off my pumps, my feet crunch down on pine needles. Unbelievable. There isn't even a tree in here. I moan in frustration, grab the Dustbuster I installed by my bed when I was eleven, and attempt to clean up my floor. Man, these suckers are everywhere. I end up contorting myself to fit beneath the bed, busting the dust out of every corner of my room until every last pine nee-dle has been sucked up.

It's sweaty work.

By the time I actually change, unpack and hang all my clothes (I may not be staying long, but these precious gar-ments need to breath the sweet air of freedom), and color-code my shoes and boots (I suppose five pairs of pumps and three pairs of boots were a bit too much for a three-day trip), the sun has started to disappear behind the mountains and a chill has set in. I always forget how cold it is here. I try three times to leave Eric a message before getting through to his voice-mail, then call my travel agent in New York and leave her a message, telling her to book me on a flight out of anywhere within a two-hundred-mile radius of where I am, to Aspen for Christmas Eve night. Then, I go downstairs, grab one of the hefty popcorn bags and make my way outside.

Who knew popcorn could be so heavy? Well, it is. When I'm a society wife, I'll have more time to tone. But lawyer- ing has made me flabby, and I have to drag the bag outside, which isn't easy to do in high-heeled boots and a furry win- ter coat. When I finally lug it onto the front porch, I notice the buzzing of a chainsaw and the disturbing smell of some- thing burning. And sure enough, because my day can't get any weirder, there's ol' Tim Latch wielding a chainsaw on the block of ice that stands in my yard.

I stand up straight and wipe my hand across my brow as I set off toward him. "Hey!" I shout as I walk, but Tim doesn't hear me and apparently has no peripheral vision through the goggles he's wearing. So I walk up to his turned back and poke him in the ribs. I ignore the little thrill I feel at actually touching him.

He shakes me off like a dog that just came out of a bath, shuts off the chainsaw and turns. "Emma."

"Hey. I've been screaming your name." Then a goofy smile crawls onto my face and sits there. This is ridiculous. We're not in high school anymore! Not to mention the fact that I am *spoken* for.

"I couldn't hear you. Chainsaw's going."

"What are you doing?"

"Isn't it obvious?" Tim gestures to the block of ice with one swooping motion of his arm. "It's a tree." His voice sounds quiet and thoughtful, like a Buddhist monk's. All I see is a slab of ice with dents in it.

"Um, right." Man, this is really not the Tim Latch of my fantasies. This Tim Latch is like the types you see in New

York, clinging to the shadows of buildings in Red Hook and Williamsburg. It's got me hooked: I have to know the story lurking behind Tim's transformation to yard boy. Maybe hanging popcorn at dusk with a fashion-conscious farm girl will make him spill the beans.

"So, are you ready?"

Tim smiles at me, and for a split second I remember how he used to look in school. Filled out. Muscular. Rich.

"Um." I clear my throat. "Uh, yeah. Popcorn time."

He nods and chuckles a bit. "All right, then. Let's go."

"Great." My cheeks are so cold they feel like they are going to crack if I smile again, but I smile anyway. "I appreciate it."

Tim lugs the bags of popcorn from my porch to his truck, and as I watch him, I start to feel like I'm fourteen all over again. Even though he's now a chainsaw-wielding ice-sculptor and clearly not my type. To me, he'll always be that fifteen-year-old kid singing "Take It Easy" and strutting through the halls of Allendale Academy. Hopefully I can remember that a lot's changed since the day I delivered him a tree and he delivered me a broken heart.

Four

An hour later, I am standing on a ladder in the middle of the Town Square, in the iridescent path of a generator's light, tossing strings of popcorn onto the branches of Townsend Farm pine trees.

This orange motif my mother went with is truly bizarre. Before I started the popcorn bonanza, I took a picture with my cell and e-mailed it to Jeff, who keeps a Christmas scrapbook, a living record of my mom's worst decorating faux pas. He keeps it in the library in his apartment, right next to a copy of his senior thesis.

"Do you think my mother's lost her mind?" I ask Tim, who is standing on the ground handing me the popcorn. Tim, my knight in shining armor, is apparently deathly afraid of heights.

"She was telling the town to fuck off. That's what I think."

The combination of Tim's soft voice and the harshness of his words are too incongruous, and despite myself, I start to giggle.

"Emma, please don't fall down!" His voice has a trace of nerves in it.

I peer down at him from my position on the ladder, take the string of popcorn from his outreached hand and continue dressing my mother's orange tree. I work my way down the ladder, until finally I'm on the ground standing on one side of the tree, passing the strand of popcorn back and forth to Tim, who stands on the other side. It's really weird how patient he is with this. In high school, he was always so brash, and energetic, and now he's calm and quiet and centered. Like a really hot monk.

"So, those heels aren't the best work shoes, you know," Tim says, handing me the thread of popcorn.

I look down at my Anne Klein boots. "They'll have to do. They're the shoes I brought." I smile a little, for after an hour of almost no conversation, the time to pry is almost at hand.

"I get the feeling you don't like decorating very much."

I might be wrong, but I think he's teasing me!

"You get the right feeling, then."

"How can you not like this? It's Christmas!"

His enthusiasm is so genuine and sweet it takes me by surprise.

"You sound like my brother's girlfriend. She loves Christmas decorations." I stuff the tail end of this string into the belly of the tree, then walk to a garbage bag to get another strand. "How about you? You don't really seem to mind this."

"It's all good." He evens out the layers of popcorn, adjusts the placement of a few pieces of fruit and checks one of the light bulbs, all the while humming "We Wish You a Merry Christmas" softly under his breath.

I decide to cut right to the chase. It's like cross-examining a witness. You have nice, friendly chitchat, then go in for the kill. "So, Tim, how long have you worked with my father?"

"Um, a couple of months now."

I stare straight ahead, pretending to be absorbed in my work, and casually say, "I thought you were supposed to take over the Latch dealerships. What happened?"

Tim peers around the side of the tree, forcing me to look up at him. He sure isn't wanting for height.

"Want some coffee?" he asks.

Want some coffee? What, did he go to Molly Townsend's Avoid-the-Question Seminar or something?

"Actually, that's a great idea, I'll be right back." I drop my handful of popcorn to the ground and head off to the General Store. That'll teach him to avoid my questions. Let him stand outside in the cold while *I* take a break.

I cut through the rest of the square, past the coterie of wicker angels that my mother always plants by the swings, and by the large copper statue of Ethan Allen that is wearing a Santa jacket and a halo of holly. When I get to the white wooden arch that looms over the entrance to the square, I happen to notice that Mrs. Henry, Mary Ellen Scanlon, and Mrs. Tate are gathered in a corner of the green, near the park benches. They're pointing back toward the grove of citrus Christmas trees, and when I wave at them, they quickly huddle up and walk toward Mrs. Scanlon's Christmas Shoppe.

I continue across the street to the General Store, hub of town politics, town groceries and town gossip. Randy Reilly, the proprietor of this one-stop shopper's paradise and Bethlehem's mayor, stands in the doorway surrounded by a group of plaid-clad extras straight out of central casting: Mayor Reilly's cousin, the one-eared tomato grower, plus the principal of the Bethlehem high school and the coach of the track team. They stop their conversation as I step up to them, but not before I hear their angry tone and several mentions of *Townsend*.

The mayor clears his throat. "Emma Jane Townsend! Well, now aren't you just a vision this fine Christmas season. That's uh…that's some jacket you got on there." I fold my arms across the purple-fur front of my coat as Mayor Reilly pulls up the waist of his pants and audibly sniffles. He's always given me the creeps. He's big and barrel-chested, and has worn the same flannel shirt since I was ten. He has a greasy comb-over and sun-ruddied cheeks. He's the kind of man you can easily picture sitting in a rocker on a porch somewhere with a shotgun across his lap.

"Hi, Mayor. It's the twenty-third. Popcorn time, you know. I just thought I'd get some coffee, to keep the chill away." Unmoved by my polite tone, the mob doesn't part for me until the mayor lets out a frighteningly piggish-sounding grunt.

"Coffee. I think we can take care of that for you."

I follow him into the store.

"Bingo tonight, Mayor?" I ask as he pours two coffees. There's no creamer—just that powdered kind. I've never understood why the General Store doesn't have real milk for the coffee. It's Vermont! Land of cows and ice cream! How can they not have real creamer? I remember the first time I saw a hermetically sealed creamer serving, at a coffee stand at Dartmouth. It was my freshman year. I started to cry—I had no idea the real world had such treasures in it.

"Nope, no Bingo tonight or tomorrow. On account of Jesus about to be born and all."

"Right, right." I take out my money and place it on the counter.

The mayor picks it up gingerly and counts it at least three times, then, without looking at me, says, "Now listen, Emma Jane, I don't mean to be an alarmist, but some of us noticed your parents pulling out of town today, in the back of Liza's truck."

Mayor Reilly's tone of voice, this obnoxious, stern, scolding tone of voice, pisses me off to no end.

"That's right, Mayor. Just a little vacation. Nothing to worry about."

It's like I punched him in his big fat gut—his entire being recoils at my evasive answer. "Emma Jane, it's Christmas! What business do your parents have leaving town? It's Faire time. Townsends set up the booths! They decorate! They put on the pageant!"

Dealing with this situation isn't exactly at the top of my list for Santa.

"Well, Mayor, I'm a Townsend, and this Faire will have booths. I'm sure you've noticed the lovely, citrusy Christmas trees we have this year—"

"Your mother's idea, I suppose."

"—so there's nothing to worry about."

He slams his hand down on the counter as his buddies enter the store—I can tell from the jangling of the entryway bells and the shuffling of feet. "But what about the pageant, Emma Jane? Who will be playing Mary and Joseph if your parents aren't here?"

Okay. This is bad, because obviously Mrs. Reilly is too scared of the mayor to let him know about the goings-on at the Faire Committee meetings. But there's no way out of it. I have to come clean. A cup of coffee in each hand, I slowly back away from the counter and wait to speak until I'm in the doorway. "Well, it was my understanding that the committee voted to cancel the nativity scene, Mayor."

His faces blows up and turns seven kinds of red, like a strawberry version of the blueberry girl in *Willy Wonka*. "No pageant!" he bellows. "Did you know about this?" he shouts to his gang of cronies.

They mutter in response. "No." "Nope." "Not at all, Randy."

I bolt out the door and run for Tim as the mayor shouts at my back, "Well, we'll just see about this!"

Five

Tim and I finish hanging all the popcorn in record time, and because of his tight-lipped responses to my attempts at unlocking the secrets of his current state of scruffiness, I pass the time in a frosty fantasy of Aspen skiing. But because I have never been skiing (my mother wouldn't let us go when we were young, because there was too much to be done around the farm), my fantasies are like an incomplete montage in a really low-budget, late-night movie. I can picture the ski lift, and the clothes, and the snow. But not the actual skiing. This is another demarcation between my kind and Tim's kind.

"Do you ski?" I ask him as we slide into the mottled vinyl seats of his truck.

"Huh? Yes. I ski."

His short, choppy sentences are beginning to grate on my nerves, and the fact that his truck has no heat *really* irritates me. There's nothing worse than rich kids who slum it for kicks. Eric would never run around town in a truck like this, with holes in the seats and a window that won't close all the way and only a radio in the dash. I rub my hands together maniacally and huddle my shoulders over my knees.

"I'm guessing you could afford to put a heater in this baby."

He looks at me and smiles that enigmatic grin that I'm becoming accustomed to hating. No wonder I was such a puddle of infatuation during high school. Tim's something. So mysterious, and quiet—it's like he's keeping a million secrets, which, of course, is a red flag to a curious bull like me. But it's okay. He may be impervious to my digging, but Bethlehem runs on two things, and two things only: Christmas and gossip. I bet I can get the scoop from Liza in record time. Of course, I will be discreet, because without Tim's help I could be the only person setting up the dumb Faire booths.

"Hey, what's going on?" I'm so wrapped up in my own thoughts that I didn't pay attention to where Tim was heading, and am unpleasantly surprised when the car stops in front of The Inn, the local bar of Bethlehem. It's the Cheers of Vermont, because everybody really does know your name, and only the regulars can stand the rickety rundown decor.

"We can warm up here."

I hate to tell him that we could also warm up in front of my parents' wood stove, but no matter. I could use a small drink, and Liza's husband, Jake Reilly, will no doubt be perched on a stool, nursing a beer and watching the Boston Bruins hockey game, so at least I'll find out if my parents made their flight okay.

"You want to go in there like that? I have an old coat back there, I think." He reaches back into the bed of the truck.

"Tim, there is no good reason in the world to make this jacket wait in the car," I say, knowing full well that my beautiful purple coat is going to stick out like a bad batch of apple cider amid The Inn crowd. "Look at it. Doesn't it make you feel good?"

He says nothing.

"You want to touch it?"

He shrugs and gets out of the truck.

I fumble through my bag, checking to see if my travel agent or Eric called (they didn't) and looking for lipstick and a mirror. By the time I feel presentable, Tim has come round to my side and opened the door for me. I step into the pitch black of a Vermont night and stumble my way over the snowy ground.

"Be careful. It's icy. Your shoes aren't built for icy," he says as he walks off toward the bar.

He's right. And they're definitely not made for walking in leftover snow. Somehow, despite the ingenuity of high-tech shoemakers, ice makes its way inside the shoes, soaking my toes and making me generally miserable. Then, just after Tim disappears inside the bar, I slip and almost *fall*. I grab a branch of a looming pine tree for balance, but do so with such fierceness that a hole rips in the middle of my left glove. My heart doesn't slow down for a good three seconds and there is a definite twinge in my ankle when I teeter up to the front door. I try to look at the bright side. I am so far removed from these pioneer conditions that I can't even walk a straight line in the snow anymore.

I give myself a final brush-off, take off my hat, run my fingers through my hair for a little volume, and push open the door into the land that time forgot. The only thing that ever changes at The Inn is the occasional keg. Mayor Reilly's brother Ben is behind the bar, Mr. Scanlon and Mr. Henry are playing pool, and the twenty-two-year-old Joe Scanlon, of "O, Holy Night" infamy, sits at the bar eating peanuts and staring at the television behind Ben Reilly's shoulder. Of course the whole place is decked out for the holidays—garland, lights, Motown carols blasting out of the jukebox, a shabby-looking tree that makes the Peanuts' Christmas branch look full, and a life-size Santa standing up by a rickety old popcorn maker. The worst part is that these decorations stay up year round and nobody says anything.

I step up to where Tim stands, ordering drinks for the two of us and asking Ben if he's seen my grandmother. Ben shakes his head and pours two amber-colored beers, then looks at me for a good, hard second.

Ah, yes, a good dose of the Bethlehem attitude. For the briefest of moments, I regret not taking Tim up on his offer of a less conspicuous coat. It must be obvious to all these pairs of eyes landing on me that this coat cost a fortune and has never been rubbed up against a pine tree. And here I am with Tim Latch, of all people! I'm just rubbing their noses in my good fortune, is what I'm doing! In a coat of opulence and with a man who could buy this joint in a matter of minutes.

To prevent too much of a gossip whirlwind, I place one hand on the bar and cover my chest (and coat) with the other. Ben hands us our beers and Tim stops me from reaching for my purse by pulling out his wallet, which is bursting with crisp bills. "Thanks, Ben."

"Hot date, you two?" Ben snickers. "Heard you were popcorning up the square."

"Just the finishing touches on the trees," Tim says as he lays down a ten-dollar bill.

I shift my weight and grip the handle of my beer mug. Just think about Aspen: that is all I can do. Think about how nice it'll be, hanging out in pubs jam-packed with vibrantly colored ski coats like mine, worn by tanned ladies and classy boys like my Eric, who will be thrilled to be seen with me.

I'm startled out of my reverie by a rhythmic tapping on my shoulder, and a mouthful of beer drips down my chin.

"Whoops!" My cousin Liza chortles, reaching behind Ben's bar for a towel. "I guess you can take the girl out of New York, but can't take the farm out of the girl."

I rub the back of my hand against my chin, trying to figure out what Liza's talking about. She dabs at my chest with a dirty dishrag, and I disappointedly look down to see a beer stain the size of the Louisiana Purchase matting down the fur and staining the fabric of my coat. "Son of a—" I unzip my coat, yank it off, spread it out on the bar, and desperately try to soak up the beer with the dirty dishrag, disappointed and annoyed and saddened that my jacket is totally ruined.

"You can probably dry-clean it, Em." Liza places her hand over mine, stopping my frantic cleaning attempts. "She always did care about her things," she says over the top of my head to Tim.

She takes the dishrag out of my hands and looks at Tim and me for a beat. I start chewing the inside of my lip, and put the coat back on, stain and all.

"I didn't get the time before to chat with you, Em, so why don't you two come on over." She takes my elbow and steers me over to a booth in the corner, where her husband, Jake, waits with three empty beer mugs and two full ones in front of him.

He's wearing overalls and a backward-turned Red Sox hat. He stands and kisses me on the cheek, appraising me with his eyes. I never thought I would think this, but I really wish I were wearing a flannel and some jeans.

"So!" Tim starts as he sits down and slumps into the far corner of the booth. "David and Molly make it okay?"

Jake responds, "Yup. I took the back roads to Burlington. You'll always make good time with me behind the wheel."

All Vermont has are back roads, but I think better of telling him and instead, slosh my beer around in the glass. Jake has always rubbed me the wrong way—well, ever since he married Liza. Before that, in high school, he and I had kind of a thing. A doomed, using-each-other-to-pass-the-time, farm kind of a thing.

Jake starts in with "Emma Jane, you look like you stepped out of a fashion magazine. Bet you're cold in that getup."

"I'm perfectly warm, Jake." I'm totally lying. I'm freezing.

"I think you look pretty, Emma." Despite her words, I can tell that Liza loves that I just ruined my coat. "So, I just can't believe that Jeff didn't come home this year. I never thought I'd see the day…" Liza *tsk-tsk*s while shaking her head in consternation and Jake pipes in with a resounding "uh-hmm."

"Well, he's busy, you know? And he had plans, with his girlfriend."

"Too busy to come home for Christmas?" Jake snorts, and Liza juts her head out from her neck as though she is choking down something hard to swallow.

I nervously pick up a handful of trail mix, sort out the pretzels from the Cheezits and start nibbling. I'm not usually a snacker, really. But Liza and Jake are staring at me right now, and Liza, well, it's really disturbing how much older than me she looks. And how tired. Maybe she'd be nicer to me if I sent her to a colorist. Or took her shopping.

"Where are the kids tonight, Jake?" Tim says, mercifully changing the subject, and the two of them begin talking about Jake Jr.'s hockey team.

"So, Emma Jane," Liza says sweetly, and sips her beer. "Is there anybody special for you yet?" She none-too-subtly gestures her head and flits her flat gray eyes toward Tim while threading a protective hand around Jake's elbow.

Jake shifts uncomfortably in his seat. I eat a mouthful of caramelized peanuts. Tim doesn't notice a thing.

"Um, yes, actually. There is somebody. He's pretty special."

"So what are you waiting for?" Her eyes disappear beneath folds of graying, pockish skin, and I exhale through my nose. The subtext here is as subtle as a revivalist minister's sermon. Instead of answering her I take another drink of beer and try to remember that she's been overexposed to this town, and that it's not her fault that she doesn't understand New York City rules, where it's perfectly acceptable for a woman in her late twenties to *not* be married. Though honestly, I agree with her. I don't want to be dating anymore. *Society wife.* And remembering my goal, I stand up to say my goodbyes.

"Listen, guys, I hate to drink and run, but I want to head back."

Tim looks up at me.

"But you just sat down!" Liza says.

"Yeah, well, I've got a long day tomorrow, you know, setting up the booths, and then I'll probably be leaving tomorrow night." I attempt to lean over the table and kiss Liza goodbye, but their faces, full of alarm, stop me dead.

"What do you mean?" Liza rises. "What about the Faire?"

"Well, Tim will be here for the actual Faire. He'll help Nana run the Townsend booth." Liza and Jake look at me in silence, shaking their heads slightly. The quietness is un-nerving, and words spill out of my mouth as I try to stifle the silence and get the grimaces on their faces to go away. "I think Eric might prop—"

"Emma Jane Townsend! How can you even think about spending Christmas away from Bethlehem?"

"Well—"

"And Tim helping your grandmother run the entire ornament-making station? But he's—no offense, Tim—he's not a *Townsend*." Her hands are on her hips.

Jake leans forward and calls out to Ben, "You owe me ten, Ben. I told you she'd bale on the Faire!"

Okay. You wouldn't believe the scene this comment causes. The music actually *stops* and Ben freezes momen-tarily, the tap beneath his fingers emptying beer into the waiting mug, over the rim and onto the floor. People stop talking. Mr. Scanlon's pool cue rests in mid-shot. Everybody looks at me. I smile weakly. Ben realizes the mess he's mak-ing and shuts off the beer tap, wipes his hand on the corner of his shirt and walks over to our booth, followed by a hand-ful of townspeople.

"What's going on with your family, Emma Jane? Don't make me call my brother."

I open my mouth but no sound comes out, and so I turn to Tim for help. All he does is finish his beer in one large, rather fratty gulp. He then reaches over for mine, and pro-ceeds to drink that one down. I turn back to Ben and the others, shove my hair behind my ears and mentally curse out Jeff and Mom and Dad for leaving me to deal with this.

"Bethlehem has been looking forward to this Faire since last year's Faire!" says Mr. Sullivan, the husband of the Beth-lehem pie-baking champion.

Ben nods in agreement. "No Faire, no Christmas!"

"Ben, Ben," I plead, my arms out in supplication. "Who said anything about canceling the Faire?"

"First, your parents sneak on out of town, and now you?" Jim Reilly, the mayor's second cousin on his father's side and manager of the Latch car dealership in Allendale, has a face like a blowfish. The hair coming out of his ears vibrates from the force of his wrath. "You Townsends think you can hang the town out to dry?"

"What are you talking about? Why do I—?"

"You and Jeff think you're too good for us. That's the problem," Jake says, swerving to avoid Liza's shushing swat. She shoots him a look and reaches across the throng to take the hand of Mrs. Weinsley, the school crossing guard.

"Don't cry, Beverly."

"But the nativity scene! If Emma's not here and Molly's not here, who'll play Mary?" Mrs. Weinsley has actual tears in her eyes.

Liza's mouth opens, and she and I exchange puzzled looks from across the table. It's clear that the Faire committee didn't exactly publicize this year's change of events, and though I am loath to be the bearer of even more bad news— twice in one day, at that—I can't let Liza take the heat on this one.

"Well, Mrs. Weinsley, the nativity scene was canceled anyway."

The four of them peer down at me in angry silence. Then they erupt in overlapping chatter, Ben the loudest of all.

"No nativity! What kind of mockery is this?"

"Well, it's his fault!" I shout and point toward the pool table, where Joe Scanlon stands with his father, lining up a shot. "He's the one who wants to sing 'O, Holy Night' instead!" This was a low blow, but it seemed like my only option.

Everyone in the bar collectively whirls around and stares accusingly at poor Joe, whose hundred-and-forty-pound frame shrinks an inch, if that's possible. He looks like a pimply, skinny scarecrow, and as he puts the pool cue in front of his body and tries to hide behind it, I feel a little sorry for him. But only a little. Mostly I'm just pleased to be out of the line of fire for a moment.

Ben, Mrs. Weinsley, Jim Reilly and Mr. Sullivan all walk toward him, and I follow, hearing Tim's soft chuckle behind me as I go.

"Don't blame me! It was Mom's fault, sir!" Joe whimpers as big Mr. Scanlon lashes him across the shoulder with his dirty baseball cap.

This whole situation is almost comical. Almost. Mostly it's just scary how militant these people are about a mere Christmas Faire. But even scarier is the fact that I am beginning to forget that I have a whole other life, that Eric is waiting for me, that I am a New York City–based lawyer whose days and nights turn without the input of these townsfolk. It's like the Twilight Zone in Bethlehem. You're here for a few hours, and your whole identity gets erased from your memory. It's like a blast of round-the-clock junk food, you get fuzzy-headed, and you can't remember what you meant to say, and all of a sudden you find yourself playing this role, the role of good little girl.

"Quiet! Everybody, be quiet!" I hold up my hands and shush them. "Just calm down. There's going to be a Faire. Okay?" They all turn to look at me, Joe Scanlon shaking like a leaf. Liza steps up behind me. "And why don't we just talk to the Faire Committee, and settle the 'O, Holy Night' issue once and for all, okay?"

Mr. Scanlon mutters something about Mrs. Scanlon being the death of him.

"Well, only the mayor has the power to interfere in committee affairs," Mrs. Weinsley says.

I swear this town gets more and more backward by the minute.

I take a deep breath and summon all my poise, remembering that I shouldn't laugh at all this ridiculousness. "Ben, call your brother. Tell him to convene a meeting for first thing in the morning. I'm going to fix this, everybody. I promise."

After the patrons of The Inn are lulled to a modicum of calm with promises of a committee meeting, Tim and I make our escape. As I wrap my scarf around my neck three times, I am disappointed to see that it is snowing. Snowing!

"Oh, crap!" I mutter, and try to pick my way over to Tim's truck without slipping on any icy patches. "It can't get any worse."

"Sure it can," he replies, looking toasty warm in his corduroy coat.

The coat's fleecy liner puffs around Tim's neck like sheep's clothing. I yank my own beery coat closer to my neck and blow on my hands to get some circulation going in my fingers.

Once the truck roars to life and begins to rumble down the road, I say to Tim, "Thanks for the help back there."

"I imagine you deal with a lot worse during the year." He winks at me.

He's right, but no defendant or plaintiff, impudent judge

or privileged senior partner can reduce my nerves to jelly the way a few angry New England locals can. I rest my head against the seat, stare out into the vast, barren Vermont night, and think about what a weak-willed loser I am. I totally caved! Was Eric even a thought in my head back there? Nope. All I cared about was saving my parents' good name and not being run out of town. Aren't I supposed to be *over* all these town politics? I am so disappointed in myself. And the creepy, barren view out the windshield does nothing but amplify how low I feel. No streetlights or other cars, and the lurking possibility that a deer will jump out in front of us at any time.

When we get back to the house, Tim immediately sets to work on his ice sculpture. He flicks on the huge outdoor floodlights my father hooked up so that we could sell our cider and trees late at night, and starts chiseling, while I go inside to check my cell for messages. Still no calls from Eric or the travel agent, which really pisses me off.

I wander from room to room, turning on all the Christmas tree lights and the dozens of electric candles that sit in all the windows of the house, trying to figure out what to say to convince the townspeople that Joe Scanlon should sing. I'll have to come up with something. If they reinstate the nativity scene, I'm totally screwed—I would have no idea how to organize such a thing in so little time. Not to mention that I'd be really pressed for time in getting to Colorado. (And who wants to look traveled when they get proposed to?) But I've always been a good extemporaneous arguer. And Mrs. Scanlon will likely do most of my job for me. Maybe I worry too much. I mean, the committee's already *decided*. All I have to do is reinforce how wonderful it will be to close with a song.

How do I get into these messes?

I head into the kitchen to rummage around for some food. Cookies, cakes, pies, sure. Candy canes? Yup. I could make myself a salad, but this day has been so trying, I just rip the head off a gingerbread man and go to town.

After dining on a lovely meal of apple cider and gingerbread cookies, I go into the living room and watch the model train go round and round the track. The faint buzzy sound of Tim's chainsaw massacre provides a suitable soundtrack to my mood, and I look out the window at him. He's circling the block of ice, kind of staring at it for seconds at a time and then attacking it with precision and a sure hand. He moves like a boxer, dancing around, weaving in and out, his focus absolute. I try to remember if he had any artistic leanings back in high school. I specifically remember that he was not a joiner. He wasn't in any clubs and he definitely wasn't in the honor society or on the yearbook committee, both things I did to help bolster my college applications. He played baseball. But he definitely was not one of the arty people. I look at the sculpture he's working on, and for the first time, I can make out the tree he's creating: the angle of the branches, the roundness of the ornaments, the sharp lines of the lights.

I release the curtain and step back into the space of my mother's house. Time passes by like a tortoise, and the chill in the air penetrates my sweater. I'm cold and bored and without anyone to talk to, and my mood is steadily dipping into a pit of melancholy. It is a strange feeling, being in this house alone. December twenty-third was always movie night in our house, Mom and Dad snuggling on the couch, my father eating the extra popcorn as fast as Mom could bring it out. The sound of my mother playfully slapping Dad's hands away from her would float down to where Jeff and I would be sitting on the floor, wrapping presents, or twisting macramé into little twine Rudolphs or cutting snowflakes out of silver paper.

But here I am, abandoned in Vermont. I can't believe my parents would leave me here like this. My father's cell number is pinned to the fridge underneath an old "My son is on the Honor Roll" magnet from Jeff's seventh grade, but they didn't even write down the name of the resort they're staying at or give me a phone number. And Jeff is probably at some hoity-toity party on Madison Avenue, surrounded by men in nice suits and women decorated with shiny gemstones and not giving poor old Emma a second thought. He hasn't even tried to check in with me today. My seventy-six-year-old nana can't be bothered to make time for me!

This could very well be the lowest moment of my life.

Self-pity doesn't visit me often, but when it does, I go whole hog. I totter up the stairs to my parents' bedroom, dig through my mother's drawer and choose the ugliest, most worn pair of pajama bottoms I can find. Then I put one of my father's ratty old sweatshirts on over a T-shirt, throwing over Missoni and Lucky in favor of pathetic comfort.

Trudging back down the stairs, crunching on pine needles and pouting, I slowly become aware that I can hear the opening credit music of *White Christmas*. I stand in the doorway of the den, looking totally unattractive in my parents' clothes, wrapped in an old afghan my grandmother made, and terrified to see Tim Latch sitting on my sofa. He has a mug full of what smells like hot chocolate and a big teeming bowl of popcorn. His shoes are off and his head is sweaty. He looks kind of sexy, I have to admit, though it's hard for me to have any kind of sexy thoughts dressed as I am.

"Done for the night?" I ask, walking into the room.

"Naw. Just taking a break." He puts his feet on the floor and sits up a little straighter.

"But it's almost eleven o'clock."

"Sculpting's not a nine-to-five job, Emma."

"So you're watching a movie?" I sit down on my dad's worn La-Z-Boy, tuck my feet under me and curl up in a ball. I'm feeling too sorry for myself to even think about changing, and the more terse Tim is, the less I care about what he thinks of me.

"Your mother told me I had to watch *White Christmas* with you tonight."

"What?"

"She said you'd be upset if you didn't watch this movie." He raises the remote control and turns up the volume.

I shake my head and laugh to myself. My poor mother— she really doesn't know me at all, sometimes. "I hate this movie."

"You do?" He looks at me in surprise.

"Yup. Jeff and I always hated the ending."

"Well, we're watching it tonight. Boss's orders." Tim stretches his legs out and places his socked feet on an ottoman, then passes me the popcorn. I look at him quickly and take a handful, and, before Bing Crosby pushes Danny Kaye out from that tumbling-down wall, say, "Thanks, Tim."

Six

The next morning at eight, I am awoken by the ringing telephone, and just as I'm drifting back on a barge of sleep, Nana comes charging into my room.

"Wake up, buttercup." She sets two cups of coffee down on the nightstand by my bed, then walks to the windows and snaps up all the blinds. I pull a pillow over my head.

"None of that now, missy. You've gone and started some trouble. Town meeting at ten sharp."

I groan from underneath the pillow, toss it from my head and sit up. The dim morning light barely brightens my room, and my small, brittle nana sits on my bed, her feet not touching the floor, sipping her coffee. She looks quite spry, actually, dressed in a smart white jogging suit with a pretty yellow collar, coiffed in full beauty-salon style, and bright-eyed as a crisp winter morning. This is amazing, seeing as how when I went to bed, at about one-thirty, she still was nowhere to be seen.

"What time did you get home last night, Nana?" I ask suspiciously as I take the second mug and indulge in a large, body-shocking sip of her rocket-fuel coffee.

"I expect it doesn't much matter what time an old woman comes home." She stares ahead of her and takes small sips from her mug.

It's awfully early in the morning to play this fishing-for-info game with her. And anyway, my nana is too tough a cookie to fall prey to my espionage tactics. "Well, I'd like to spend at least a little time with you."

She cackles and raises an eyebrow. "Was I born this century, Emma Jane?"

"What does *that* mean?"

"You have about as much interest in spending time with the family as Jeff does." She slaps the top of her thigh, reaches out to push a strand of hair off my face and gets up. "It's not so bad here, you know."

"If you like chopping down trees and milking sap at four-thirty a.m.," I grumble as I launch myself out of the bed and pad over to the bathroom.

"Well, darlin', you're in for a real treat this morning—that's money in the tin," she calls as she single-steps her way down the stairs.

To fortify myself for the town meeting, I take a long, soaking shower with the water as hot as Vermont heaters can get it. I blow my hair out while staring in the mirror and picturing myself in Aspen, Colorado, staring down at Eric on one knee and saying to him, "Yes, yes, yes." The reflection in the mirror can attest to the fact I don't look my best on no sleep. I've got to have time to spare in getting there, or my proposal memories will be filled with things like "had bags under my eyes" and "smelled like eau de airplane."

I pour myself into a power suit of D&G woolen pants

and black silk Nanette Lepore gypsy top. My aim here is to look modern and classy, but, if I learned anything from my trip to The Inn, it was to keep my color palette neutral. The last thing I want is the committee giving me the evil eye because I look too flashy. Good Lord, why did I leave all my button-downs in the city?

When I get downstairs, Nana has set a place at the breakfast table for me. Pancakes and syrup—no big surprise. You can't stay in Vermont and not have at least one pancake breakfast. I wouldn't be surprised if there's a "one pancake breakfast per three-day stay" provision in the state constitution. Tucking a paper napkin into the collar of my shirt I nibble at one fluffy cake, declining the syrup in atonement for my gingerbread-cookie dinner and buttered popcorn dessert. Tim sits right next to me devouring stack after stack, dipping berries into syrup, floating marshmallows into a giant mug of hot chocolate, and following all the sugar down with impressive swigs of cider.

"Kind of a lot of sugar for first thing in the morning, isn't it?" I say without lifting my eyes from the *Caledonian Record,* the local paper.

"It's all good."

Seriously, he didn't learn this hippie-dippie language at Allendale Academy. And I doubt they taught it at Harvard, either. The mystery deepens.

"Are you coming with me to the meeting?" I pull the milk pitcher over and lighten my coffee, which, according to Nana's recipe, could clean the pipes of a New York City apartment.

"Thought I'd set up the booths for you. That cool?" Tim leans back as my nana refills his coffee mug.

"Such a good boy, Timothy." She pinches his cheek.

"Watch your hands, Nana," I grumble, my eyes on my plate.

"Unless you'd rather I wait so you can help." He continues to lean back until he's balanced on the two back legs of the chair.

"No, no. It's okay. I hate setting up the booths."

"Then it'll be your lucky day." He slides out of his chair, walks over to my nana and kisses her cheek. "Lovely breakfast, Helen. Lovely." Then he grabs the chainsaw from behind the closet door and returns to the yard.

Nana springs into housekeeper mode, swooping down on his empty dishes and tossing everything in the sink. "That's a nice tall glass of water, right there," she says.

"Oh brother. Nana, you shouldn't be cleaning up after him."

"It's an old woman's pleasure."

I get up and walk to where my nana stands on a stool in front of the sink, elbow-deep in Tim's dirty dishes, and stare out the window at him.

"He's a handsome man, Emma."

I look down to see her staring at me, all thick lenses and giant googly eyes and a teasing grin.

"Nana, what's his story, anyway? Why is he here?"

She snorts. "It's his business."

"Well, I'm curious. He's a Latch. I just don't get why anybody would—"

"Choose this?" My nana lets all the water out of the sink, wipes her hand on sparkly Frosty the Snow Man towel and pats my cheek. "Ask him yourself, dear."

I am pulling into the parking lot across from the town square, running totally late after spending half an hour trying to track down my travel agent, when my cell phone rings. It's Jeff.

"It's about time. There's shit going down here. Mom and Dad have left the country. The town's up in arms. Tim Latch is a townie. What do you have to say about this?" I bark into the phone as soon as I pick it up.

"Hey, Emma. How are you?"

I can barely make out his voice over the cacophony coming through the line: carols and revelry and crowds of laughter. "What's going on over there?" I say as I pick my way across the street delicately, watching the steam come out of my own mouth and praying that the cold doesn't take all the volume out of my hair. "It's not even ten-thirty in the morning yet!"

"I never thought I'd hear myself say this, but I wish I was home."

I drop the phone into a snowbank.

"Jeff! Don't hang up! I dropped the phone!" I shout. I rip off my glove and dig into the icy slush; the phone slips through my fingers three times until I finally get a hold of it.

"*You wish you here?* You have a lot of nerve, Jeffrey Townsend. Are you about to head into a meeting with Randy Reilly and a town full of angry Christmas-lovers?"

"That doesn't sound so bad, actually. I can't take this. They're gathered around Jenny's mother's piano and singing! Jenny's *singing*. I don't think I can be with her anymore." I haven't heard Jeff sound this disappointed since my freshman year of law school, when his student rival for first in their class got a better grade.

Let me just say for the record, I hate when Jeff is upset. It gives me a sickly feeling in my stomach, mostly because

Jeff is usually so in control of any situation. When he's off his game, you know something's really wrong. "I'm sorry, Jeff. It can't be as bad as all that."

He doesn't answer right away, and I can hear a male voice bellowing "Away in a Manger" in what I can only assume is an annual solo performance. "Jeff? Are you there?"

"Unfortunately." His is the answer of a pouty child.

"Well, is Jenny happy to have you there?"

"Who can tell? She's too busy eating cookies to notice me."

"Um, well, I don't know what to say. Think of it this way. You could be here. In Bethlehem, having to convince the town to let Joe Scanlon sing a solo at the end of the Faire."

Jeff laughs at that, and a warm feeling wells in me. "I miss you, Jeffrey. A lot. This has been the most surreal eighteen hours of my life, and I just wish you were here."

"Well, if Jenny's mother keeps trying to kiss me under the mistletoe, I could be."

I click off and climb the stairs to the General Store. It's locked and a paper sign Scotch-taped to the glass pane on the front door says Closed Due To Town Business. Underneath that, in smaller print, it says Key In Mailbox.

Christmas bells ring as I open the old wooden door and step into the darkened, dusty General Store. I follow the drone of the mayor's voice back to a set of double doors that open into the yellowing Bingo room. It's boxy and smells like old rubber and stale milk. About four dozen people are seated around dining tables. Liza is near the front, Kimmy on her lap, JJ on the floor playing with Lego and Lizzie sitting next to her. When Lizzie sees me, she shouts, "Cousin Emmie's here!" jumps off her chair and runs over to where I stand. The entire room turns to look at me, and the mayor shoots me a critical look as Liza mouths, *Where have you been?*

Lizzie takes my hand with her sticky one and leads me from the doorway. "You'll need some coffee first, Emmie," she stage-whispers. "My mommy says you're in bunches of trouble." She's like a little old lady trapped in a five-year-old's body. She leads me over to a snack table. I pour myself some coffee, sprinkle it with condensed faux-creamer and take in the scene, while little Lizzie proceeds to eat a bunch of grapes.

Mayor Reilly stands at the head of the room in front of a huge Bingo board and seven Faire Committee chairs. My mother's name is still etched into one of the chair's backboards, though the chair is sadly empty. Mrs. Reilly, a short, round, black-haired lady who resembles a big fat beetle, and the rest of the committee sit quietly as Mayor Reilly talks on and on about the history of the town and the importance of the Faire and how tradition is the cornerstone of a Bethlehem Christmas. This isn't anything I haven't heard before from my father.

As I pour myself a second cup of coffee, Mrs. Henry, Mrs. Scanlon and Mrs. Tate, the ladies who ran away from me yesterday, rise from their Committee chairs and make their way toward the front. Forming a triplicate clump, Mrs. Scanlon and Mrs. Tate bend their heads in deference to Mrs. Henry, who starts addressing the mayor, quietly at first but slowly approaching fiery sermon levels of loudness. Soon, her finger punctuates her speech, her pitch rises to stratospheric heights and that nose starts pulsing. I can't exactly make out what she's saying, but Mary Ellen Scanlon's face looks so tight that I wouldn't be surprised if it popped right off her neck and rolled out the front door.

Lizzie finishes eating all the grapes then takes my hand. God, Liza's got to teach this child to wash her hands.

"Best to get it over with, Emmie."

She skips on ahead of me, and I follow, the *click-clack* of my Armani pumps echoing in the chamber. The good people of Bethlehem turn to look at me as I pass them on my way to the front table. The mayor folds his arms across his big Santa belly, holds up a silencing hand to Mrs. Henry, and then looks directly at me. "Well, well, Miss Townsend. So nice of you to join us. Seeing as how your family's ruined Christmas."

At this, Mrs. Reilly, with her tinny voice and lacquered black hair, says, "Emma Jane, how could you? How could your family—"

The mayor turns to quiet his wife, and Liza pulls me down to the empty seat beside her and begins furiously whispering in my ear, filling me in on what I've missed. It seems that Mrs. Scanlon, Mrs. Henry and Mrs. Tate have decided that if my parents can bag the fair, then they should be able to, too.

All the people on the left side of the aisle are with them, and Mr. Henry stands at one point to say that it's about time that he had a decent Christmas meal for once, and if his wife can spend Christmas preparing him a ham instead of showing little kids how to plant poinsettias, then he's all for it. This is greeted by angry grumbling from the right, and soon the whole meeting degenerates into a free-for-all shouting match, like British Parliament. To Faire or not to Faire.

All I can hear is Mrs. Reilly squeaking over everybody that without the Faire, there is no Christmas. And that without Christmas, there is no Bethlehem. Mayor Reilly keeps pointing at me and saying cryptic, vaguely threatening things, like

"This is on the heads of all Townsends" and "The character of a town is being rubbed down with oil on that beach
in Jamaica." He's a nutcase.

There's not much I can do, other than insist that the
Townsends have in no way let the town down. Of course,
I'm off balance because I was expecting to argue a song issue,
not fight for the very life of the Faire, not to mention my
family's honor.

In the midst of this hubbub, my cell phone rings, and the
mayor takes the opportunity to malign New York, profess-
ing that I've been tainted by the evil empire to the south.
It's an impressive rant, I'll give him that. Liza grabs the phone
out of my hand, opens and shuts it quickly (effectively hanging up on the caller—I'm going to kill her if it was my travel
agent) and then hands it to Lizzie, who slips it into a large,
fuzzy pink pocket with her sticky grape-hands.

Meanwhile, the noise in the room crescendos until you
can't make out a single word that anybody's saying. Seats are
thrown off to the side as the townspeople rise and point fingers at one another, screaming and arguing. It seems that all
the anger is ripping the lid of some long-dormant dis-
agreements. I'm hearing lots of off-topic verbal volleys. Not
a lot of Christmas spirit in the room.

My mother would be so disappointed in everyone. Or
maybe she wouldn't. She *is* the one who caused all this, by
running off to Jamaica instead of dealing with the fact that
the tradition was changing. And now the whole thing's un-
raveling! Mrs. Scanlon, Mrs. Henry and Mrs. Tate finally
walk down the center aisle, claiming that they are not going
to do what Mrs. Townsend doesn't have to, and that the
whole town can just stuff it. (That is a direct quote.)

Everybody follows them, pushing and shoving their way to the door, Liza desperately trying to keep an eye on her children while talking some sense into the three ladies. The parade continues through the store, and out the door and then, suddenly, everyone stops moving and sinks into an eerie, pregnant quiet as we gather on the sidewalk outside the square. We stop moving so suddenly that I slam into Liza, causing Kimmy to fall out of her arms and onto the sidewalk. The child doesn't even cry. She just tugs at Liza's hand and points into the park, saying, "Pretty, pretty, pretty!" I push past them to the front of the throng, elbow my way to where the mayor has stopped.

From where we stand, you can see into the northwest corner of the square. Midmorning light, while weak, shimmers off the snow, and the twinkle of hundreds of white string lights bounces off the orange trees creating a soft, glowing halo. The disassembled skeletons of the various Faire booths are strewn about the area, marking the location where the dessert, ornament-making and craft stations will be, and in the middle of everything, standing tall and proud and silent, is Tim's ice sculpture. The thin sounds of "We Wish You a Merry Christmas" drift from a small boom box.

Liza and I run out to Tim, who's with Nana and her three friends, pushing snow into a snowman.

"Tim! Oh, my God! Look at it!" I rush forward and put my gloved hands on the ice, which looks like an actual tree, with pine needles and everything.

He stands when he sees me and, of course, doesn't answer. But when he notices the crowd, his whole demeanor changes. He becomes taller, loud—comfortable enough to command, "Hey, everybody! We're making some snowpeople to gather around the tree. Come on!"

All of the fifty or so people stay rooted to their spots, just staring at me. My mouth opens, and I look to Tim for some advisement. Fifty people continue to look at me.

Then Liza nudges me, and whispers, "Only Townsends decorate." Of course. It's never occurred to any of the people of Bethlehem that they could help.

"Uh. Well, traditions are made to be broken," I start out slowly, improvising in my best summation voice. "And this year, uh, we wanted everybody to decorate with our family." Mayor Reilly, standing at the head of the crowd, peers at me. I can practically see the wheels turning in his head, trying to make this offer fit with what he knows about the Christmas Faire.

Mrs. Reilly steps up to his side, and squeaks, loud enough for everyone to hear, "That might be a nice idea. Committee, all in favor of helping with the decorations?" And slowly Mrs. Reilly and two other bundled, rosy-cheeked ladies raise their hands.

Mrs. Reilly scans the crowd for Mrs. Henry, Mrs. Scanlon and Mrs. Tate. They turn their noses up at her and grumble a bit under their breaths.

"Mary Ellen Scanlon, get off your high horse, young lady!" This stunning piece of diplomatic negotiating comes from my nana. Mary Ellen Scanlon looks less than pleased.

But then old Mrs. Scanlon comes round the body of the snowman she's working on and orders, "Mary Ellen, don't just stand there with your mouth open like a fish. Help your mother and Mrs. Townsend right this instant."

Mary Ellen Scanlon starts to melt right in front of me, like the witch in *The Wizard of Oz*. She slowly walks over to my nana and old Mrs. Scanlon, rolls up her sleeves and then turns to Mrs. Reilly and raises her hand in an *aye* vote.

Upon seeing Mrs. Scanlon's surrender, Mayor Reilly shouts, "The Faire is saved! Bethlehem perseveres!" Then all the people, who only fifteen minutes before were ready to kill each other, erupt in joyous rumblings, bursting forth from their spots and flooding into the park. Soon, dozens of people are bent over piles of snow, rolling them into an army of Christmas Faire snowmen.

Lizzie toddles over, her cheeks rosy red and her pink-and-purple snowflake hat covered in frost. She hands me my open cell, saying, "It's for you, Emmie," before running back to JJ and Kimmy and pelting Liza in the butt with a snowball.

"Did you survive?"

"I can't talk, Jeff, but all's well. You wouldn't believe what's happening here." I shut the phone off and seal it away in my inside pocket. I've never seen anything like this—my neighbors shouting gleefully and rolling up their sleeves and working together on snowmen, of all things. This is the first time I can remember anybody having any real fun in the town square.

Tim walks up to me, playfully punches my arm. "It looks good, right?"

"It looks like Christmas."

Tim takes my hand and tugs at me. "Come on. We've got a snowman to finish."

"But—" It's too late. Tim's quite a strong man and I follow willingly. He leads me over to Nana, and she looks up at me.

"Now this is a Christmas Eve, Emma Jane."

Who knew it was possible to enjoy yourself in the Bethlehem town square? Though my feet are rapidly losing sensation and my hair is molded to my cheeks and my nose is running, I proceed to have a really good time, freezing in the snowy cold and helping Tim roll snow into three giant balls. Once we get them on top of one another, Tim takes some of what I assume are his sculpting tools from his pocket and begins to shape our snow creature into an angel.

I look up to see Mr. Scanlon playfully tug at Mrs. Scanlon's braid, and Mr. and Mrs. Henry happily collecting pine cones to form snow-people features. My grandmother gleefully knocks down other people's snow heads, and surreptitiously trades a flask back and forth with old Mrs. Scanlon.

"This is a lot more fun than skiing in Aspen," Tim says over the top of our snow angel.

"How did you—?"

"I've got my eye on you," he says, keeping his focus on the creation of two snowy wings.

I ponder what he means, still confused at how somebody who came from the same background as Eric could be so content playing in the snow, dressed in Wal-Mart clothes, without any sense of propriety. But my musings are cut short by the approach of the mayor, surrounded by his redneck entourage.

"Emma, it appears that the Faire will be going on as planned." He teeters back and forth on his toes, and repeats, "*Everything* will be taking place as planned."

"Mayor, Emma and I are handling all the Townsend duties. So no worries." Tim smiles broadly.

The mayor squints at him. "Well, I'm not taking a Latch's word on it. Have you ever even *been* to a Bethlehem Christmas Faire?"

"What does that matter?" I snap. "Look at his Christmas spirit!"

Tim quiets and touches my arm. "I'm going to go give Helen a hand."

"Okay," I say, and turn my attention back to the mayor, brushing a strand of wet, icicle-covered hair from my face. But before I can say a word, he says his piece.

"Emma Townsend, I am the mayor of this town." He takes a step toward me, and we are closer to each other than I've ever wanted to be. "There *will* be a scene of the Virgin Mother and holy babe tomorrow. Understand me?"

I gulp. "Mayor—"

"I run this town, Emma. Had I known about the Scanlon's plans before, I assure you I would've put a stop to it."

"But—"

"And since your parents aren't here, it's up to you to carry on the Townsend tradition. I expect a beautiful rendition of the nativity scene, Emma Jane. Make your town proud."

I don't even try to say anything, because nothing I could possibly say would matter.

"Well, I'm glad that's settled. I knew you'd be reasonable." He steps back, his face splits into a paunchy grin, and his men fall in line around him. "Now, if you'll excuse me, I have other business to tidy up."

My winter pleasure dissolves as I return to my senses. I had awoken hoping to be on my way to Colorado by the end of the day. I open my fists and let two small snowballs slip to the ground. How did I get so caught up in all this? Over my shoulder, I see Nana and Liza getting attacked by snowballs, courtesy of Lizzie and JJ. Well, good for them. Everybody's happy. Except me.

Stalking away from everyone, I find a bench covered in snow, brush it all off with one annoyed sweep, hit the voice-mail button on my cell phone, and sink down sadly as Eric's hopeful, sweet voice filters down the line.

"Hey. I can't wait to see you. Do you think you can be in some flannel when my mother and I pick you up? That'd be awesome!"

Rats.

Seven

Tim drives me home in his pickup because I refuse to ruin the leather interior of my Lexus by driving home in wet clothes. I complain the whole way, and Tim answers with his customary fragmented responses.

"Who does that man think he is? If the people want to end things in song, then by God, let them end things in song!" I double over to try to get warm. "Jesus Christ, it's *freezing* in here!"

Tim glances away from the road for one second. "Come on, then," he says, opening up his arm to invite me in for a cuddle. There is a marked glint in his eye.

"No, um, that's okay." I scoot farther away from him, but the touch of the frigid window to my face sends me flying back toward the middle of the seat.

"You'd have taken me up on that in high school," he teases.

My head whips over to him. "I think you had your chance with me." I cannot believe I said this out loud.

He quickly glances at me. "What?"

"You know what I mean." I stare at his gloved hands as they rest on the steering wheel. I can't bring myself to look him in the eye.

"Oh. Right."

"Right." I cross my arms in front of my chest and let out a sigh.

"The dance," he says.

"Give the man a million dollars! The dance."

He smacks his lips together. I don't think his nervous habits are very attractive.

"God. Listen, I shouldn't have blown you off like that."

You'd have to examine him with a microscope to see the subtle change in his body language. He reaches out to downshift, and my entire body goes rigidly still. I feel ashamed all over again, just having this thing between us acknowledged after so long.

"I'm totally over it. There's nothing to be sorry about." I wish I was a better actress. I mean, I *should* be over it. It was just a dumb high school dance. But judging from how my nails are digging into the palms of my hands, you might say I'm still feeling it a little.

"I was really snobby back then. And I'm sorry."

I am momentarily stymied into silence and stare past him through the driver side window just as we pass the turnoff for the Latch Chevrolet in Allendale. "Well, you seem to have no problem with the farmer's life now."

He doesn't respond.

"Tim," I say after nearly five minutes pass, "why are you here? Working for my dad when you obviously don't need the money? You have everything anybody could ever want."

He nods and drums his thumbs against the steering

wheel. "Not necessarily." He looks at me as he makes the turn into my driveway. "There's not a lot of room in that world, you know?"

"What do you mean?"

"I mean, like, you can't become a sculptor without making a lot of waves. The finer things come with a lot of, I don't know, rules that…well, they're just confining and they don't guarantee happiness." He looks over at me and smiles, which dramatically lessens the melodramatic tone of the moment. He says playfully, "A trip to Aspen won't, either."

Well, I have nothing to say to this. I try really hard to think of what would make me happier than not having to work while still being able to spend a small fortune on shoes. I can't come up with anything. I suppose this makes me shallow. Well, so be it. I'm officially shallow, and I embrace this part of myself wholeheartedly. And anyway, only a guy who has plenty of money and status can say stuff like this and think it's true. A trip to Aspen most certainly will make me happy. So will the gi-normous ring Eric's going to put on my finger.

The thought of said ring brings a smile to my lips.

"Something funny?" Tim asks.

"Oh, something's funny, all right. You know what, Tim? I am going to go ahead and organize this stupid nativity scene. And then I'm going to fly to Colorado, and find my boyfriend and talk to him about making me 'unhappy' for the rest of my life."

"Okay, Emma" is all I get out of him. He pulls up to the front of the house, drops me off and pulls away.

The rest of my afternoon is spent in a state of panicked planning. After changing out of my damp clothes and cheering myself with a brand-new Betsey Johnson dress, I sit down at my mother's antique wooden writing desk to jot down a list of what to do to organize the stinkin' nativity. Then I call Eric and break the news to him that I won't be able to leave here until after Christmas.

He isn't happy. In fact, he basically hangs up the phone, after saying that I've ruined everything. I cry a bit, but then stop, because I have too much to do to feel sorry for myself. And anyway, Eric can be a little dramatic. As long as I get there before the end of the day on the twenty-sixth, everything will be forgiven.

I take my list out to the ramshackle shed in our backyard. This shed was my favorite place to hide when I was a kid, because I could slip between the wooden slats without ever unlocking the door, so nobody ever had any idea where I was. I could sit in there for hours, thumbing through *Vogue* and *Seventeen* and *Sassy,* ignoring the calls from my mother, begging me to go down and pick some apples. But this time, I use the rusty key that my mother hides above the door frame and bend down to avoid getting clobbered by the bouquet of mistletoe.

In the shed are the bags of costumes for the Faire, and as I pull them out one by one, I make notes on the roles I have to find people to play. You'd think that I would have some kind of recall for this, seeing as I've participated in this thing for the past twenty-seven years.

There's a Mary, a Joseph, an innkeeper, three wise men, three shepherds, and a flock of farm animals. Lovely. My mother and father usually play Mary and Joseph, with Nana playing the innkeeper, and me and Jeff and Liza playing the wise men. My parents would normally round out the cast with whoever was helping out on the farm at the time, but

Tim can't play three shepherds by himself, and the way it's going, I may need to recruit him as my Joseph.

While waiting for Tim to come home, I start phoning around, calling all the people I can think of, looking for volunteers. Nobody's home, of course. It's Christmas Eve, so everyone is down at the square, preparing for Christmas Day. I have no choice but to beg people in person to help me.

As I stare out the window, willing Tim through my psychic commands to come home, the home phone rings. When I pick it up, all I hear at first is steel drum music, then the searching sounds of my mother's voice.

"Emma? Emma?"

"Hey, Mom!"

"Oh, hold on, dear. Yes, yes, two more. David, did you want the peach or the passion fruit?"

"Mom. Hello?"

"Sorry, dear. Sorry. Merry Christmas Eve! Are you having a great time with your grandmother?"

"Um, I haven't really seen her that much. She's a busy woman."

"Yes, well, she's something." Then she speaks to my father again, whose commentary I can hear through the phone. "Your mother. A spitfire. Right."

"Mom, the nativity's back on."

"What, dear?"

"I said, THE NATIVITY IS BACK ON." I am standing in the thicket of hanging paper snowflakes now, screaming my head off.

"What? It is! Oh, no! How'd that happen?" Pause. "David, the nativity's back on."

"Mary Ellen Scanlon must be foaming at the mouth!" my dad shouts in the background.

"The costumes are in the shed, dear."

"I already found them. Listen, Mom. I really wish you were here."

"What?"

"What is she saying?" asks Dad.

"I said, I REALLY WISH—oh, forget it. Are you having fun?"

"Oh, Emma, we should've listened to you and Jeff before this! Do you know how wonderful it is to take a break? I've read two whole books already, and your father is beating everyone he meets at Scrabble. We're having a great Christmas, just the two of us."

"Oh. Well, that sounds good, Mom. But I miss you."

"We miss you, too, dear. Merry Christmas."

As she hangs up, I can hear her telling my dad, "Oh, honey, a limbo contest!"

I hold my head in my hands for a second. I can't believe that they don't sound less happy. Weren't the two of them built for Christmas? I storm into the kitchen, rip the lid off a tin of Christmas cookies and sit down for a good old-fashioned binge. The nerve of that woman—to not even be the tiniest bit sorry that she's not spending the holiday with me.

Tim picks this wonderful moment to come home. He finds me slumped over the remnants of three reindeer sugar cookies.

"Hey," he says quietly.

"Hey."

"So, let's go put on a play!" His attempts to ease the tension with this big, brassy, fake voice fail.

"Fine. I'm ready," I respond through a mouthful of cookie.

"What's up?" Tim walks over to the fridge, pulls out a gallon of milk and drinks right from the carton.

"Seriously, what's happened to you?"

"Aw, don't take it out on me. What happened to *you*?"

"My mother. She couldn't care less about me. Or Christmas." I smash a fourth reindeer with my fist, sending chunks of sugar cookie flying to all reaches of the counter.

"Isn't that what you want? For everybody to not make such a big deal about Christmas?" He wipes his mouth with the back of his hand.

"Oh, what do you know?" I snap, for lack of anything better to say.

The rest of my afternoon—Christmas Eve, let it be said, a day that I have historically spent at the short end of my mother's leash, decorating the interior of our ornament-making booth—is an even bigger than usual exercise in humility.

Tim cheerfully agrees to play one of the wise men, and Nana will play the innkeeper if I promise to help her in our booth for the entire Faire *and* wear the elf costume. Using my crack negotiating skills, I get her to volunteer her white-hair posse of old Mrs. Scanlon, Barney Downing and Norm Bray to play the shepherds. She even convinces Mr. Downing to lend his prize sheep, so that I have a flock by night.

The rest of the casting isn't going so well. I have to find two other wise men, and a Mary and a Joseph, and the people of the town aren't exactly eager to volunteer, despite my freshly applied makeup, beauty pageant smile, tray of cookies and total dedication to the Christmas Faire. Even Tim's hunky looks aren't helping persuade people.

Mrs. Scanlon, of course, is still furious that Joe won't be closing out the Faire, so she withholds her help and persuades Mrs. Tate and Mrs. Henry to abstain, too, despite threats from old Mrs. Scanlon to cut Mary Ellen out of the will.

Next, Tim and I go grudgingly up to the Reillys' circle of dessert booths, where Liza is busy dusting the shelves and lining them with parchment paper while Jake covers them in a fresh coat of purple paint.

"Emmy! Timmy!"

Lizzie leaps out at me when we approach, and I try to avoid her sticky-handed hug, but it's no use. This child is hell-bent on giving me affection. She puts lollipop hands all over my ski coat. Not that it matters anymore. The coat has taken quite a beating over the past day and a half.

Her screech brings Jake Jr. around from behind one of the booths, and a high-pitched squeal from the youngest child, Kimmy, who is jammed underneath the glass case of the booth Liza is cleaning.

"Kimmy's the desserts," Lizzie says, pointing at the baby girl stuffed into the case. "Timmy, you pay me for a dessert, okay?" Tim immediately puts on his play hat and hands the child a *real* dollar bill in exchange for the toddler, who comes springing out of the glass case and lands in Tim's arms.

All these kids do is jump, hug and scream.

"You're not helping!" I say testily to Tim.

"Sure I am," he says, swinging the child this way and that, eliciting cherubic giggles and hiccups from her.

Liza looks over at us and says to Tim, "You need to have your own kids, Tim."

"In due time, Liza, in due time."

I feel really uncomfortable, and could possibly be blushing, because despite myself, there is a second where I picture myself as the mother of Tim's happy, laughing children. But my fantasy is wrong. It's supposed to be Eric playing my society husband, because the vision I have is of a clean-shaven, three-piece-suit version of Tim, and that's clearly not what he grew up to be.

I shake it off. Literally. I shake my head and walk up to Liza. "I have a huge favor, Li. Huge. I need you and Jake to play Joseph and Mary in the nativity."

"What?" Liza wipes her brow with a gloved hand. Her gray hair creeps down onto her forehead from beneath her hat, and her cheeks are bright red from being out in the cold for so long. "Why us?"

"I asked everybody," I say. "Nobody can do it."

"Why can't you play Mary?"

I don't know if it's because of the cold or the desperation I feel, but I can't come up with anything to say but the truth. "I don't want to wear the costume."

Liza slaps the countertop with her hand, and looks me dead in the eye. "You're unbelievable. You know what? Since that's your reason, I definitely can't help you."

Damn it! I knew in this case the truth would not set me free.

"Well, what about Jake?" My voice comes through all mopey and pouty. "Can he be Joseph?"

"Jake?" Liza calls over to where he stands on a ladder. "Emma wants to know, can you stand the costume long enough to play Joseph in the nativity scene?"

Jake doesn't even look up from what he's painting. "I'd love to but can't."

"Jake!" I shout.

"Emma! Reillys do lights. No lights, no scene," he calls down.

"No Joseph, no scene!" I counter.

"You heard the man, Emma. There's no changing his mind when he makes it up."

I look to Tim, who hunches up his shoulders, then down at little Lizzie, who is pretending to scrub one of the booths with a wax-on, wax-off motion while singing to herself, *"Mary and Joseph, sitting in a tree."*

"If only Lizzie could play Joseph." I say, more to myself, out of frustration, than to anybody around me. But Lizzie drops what she's doing as soon as this comes out of my mouth and catapults herself into Liza's arms. That Liza has some good reflexes. She catches her daughter neatly.

"Mommy! Mommy! Let me and JJ play Mary and Joseph! We can play! We can play!"

My mouth drops open and I step back slowly (having stirred up a child's temper, I don't want to make any sudden moves). Being Joan-Crawford bad with children, I don't know how to solve this mess, and so I say nothing. But Liza interprets my silence as encouragement.

"Haven't you done enough?" she demands angrily. "Now you have to put ideas into my kids' heads?"

"What did I do? I was just...I was just talking to myself."

"No, no, no, Emmy. You said I could be Joseph. I want to be Joseph." Then big crocodile tears start dripping down Lizzie's face, and she rubs them away with her sticky hands. And all I can think is that maybe her hands will finally be clean.

"Lizzie, calm down, calm down," I run up to where Liza stands holding her crying daughter, and rub circles into her thin little back. "How about junior wise men?" I ask Liza quietly.

She rolls her eyes. "You're making that up."

Tim pipes in, "No, actually, Emma was saying earlier that she thought Lizzie and JJ should be the wise men—weren't you, Emma?"

"Um..."

"And Kimmy can be Jesus."

"Kimmy cannot be Jesus. The mayor will flip."

Well, this all pleases Lizzie to no end. She wriggles out of Liza's arms and starts running in a circle around the booths shouting "Kimmy's Jesus! Kimmy's Jesus" as JJ tries to tackle her.

"Nice going, Em," Liza says, with only a trace of annoyance in her voice.

"Well, if Kimmy's Jesus, will you please, please, please play Mary?"

So I'm playing Mary.

How bad can it be? If Kevin Costner can direct himself in a movie, then I should be able to handle this.

Fortunately for me, everyone (except Tim and possibly Kimmy) has witnessed this thing a thousand times, so they pretty much know the drill. At six-thirty, after all the booths are up, painted, dusted and prepped, and after Nana and Tim have hauled all of our ornament-making supplies from the farm and the mayor has okayed our booths, and after I've swapped my stilettos for a pair of my mother's sensible snow-boots, we all meet by the Ethan Allen statue in the corner of the square.

Lizzie and JJ and Kimmy are *beside* themselves with joy. As I stand at the base of the statue, with a clipboard in one hand and my cell phone in the other, making notes to my-self into the voice recorder, the three of them dart around me and through my legs, playing freeze tag. It doesn't take but five minutes before Tim joins in, and though I'm stand-ing still, trying to work, Lizzie keeps whacking me in the hip, screeching, "Freeze" loud enough to wake Ethan Allen.

"Everybody?" I say as soon as Nana and Mrs. Scanlon and Mr. Bray and Mr. Downing show up. The kids keep run-ning and shouting, "You're it!" at Tim, and Liza is sitting on a swing drinking a cup of coffee and looking totally ex-hausted, and soon Lizzie runs to Nana and invites her to play. Now I'm desperately trying to rein three children, one rich kid and four senior citizens into paying attention.

Tim sees that I'm getting frustrated and scoops Lizzie up into his arms. "Emma said to 'freeze!'" I watch in utter an-noyance as all of them freeze in various positions: JJ and Kimmy lying in the snow. Mr. Bray kissing my nana's hand. Mr. Downing trying to pinch Mrs. Scanlon's bottom.

"This isn't fun and games, you know! It's serious business to the town!"

"We understand," Tim says, lowering Lizzie to the ground.

"Keep a straight face, Elizabeth, or Emma'll take you over her knee, now," my nana cackles from her position by JJ's snow angel.

"Well, Nana, why don't you help here?" I'm whining. I know it, but I'm cold and I want to go home and rest, and try to find a flight to Colorado, and call Eric and make him not be angry with me anymore. But instead I'm here, orga-nizing these clowns into a parade.

"Oh, for goodness' sakes, Emma Jane. Everybody knows what to do," Liza says, snippily, from her perch on the bench.

"Helen'll trot out there like nobody's business and make

her little speech, then you and phantom Joseph will walk up to the gazebo—" Mrs. Scanlon calls.

"Right," I check my clipboard. "Then you, Nana, you'll meet me—"

"Oh, for crying out loud! I've been doing this since 1943. Get on with it."

"Fine. You all think you know what to do? Fine. Just meet me fifteen minutes before, put on your costumes, and we'll see how it goes!"

With that I stalk off through the square and make my way to my car. Is it too much to ask for a little order? I fumble for my keys, pull out my cell, see that nobody has called, kick my tire, and then slump into my seat.

Taking a deep breath I rest my head on the steering wheel before putting my key in the ignition. And because I'm bound to spend every second in Bethlehem frustrated, the car won't start.

"Son of a—" I scramble out of the car and step right into a puddle.

Even though I'm in my mother's boots, this makes me want to cry.

"Hey, Emma!" Tim comes jogging toward me. "Come with me." He takes my elbow and starts dragging me back toward the statue of Ethan Allen.

"Let me go!"

"No."

Damn his terseness.

"I don't even want to be here! I am supposed to be on my way to get proposed to! But this town doesn't care at all about personal desires. All they care about is a stupid, boring, dumb Christmas—" I lose my train of thought. I can't say what it is that gets me, but something about seeing my nana and her friends in their sacks, and little JJ looking so darling in that ugly brown pullover, and the way Lizzie's hair tumbles down around her shoulders underneath that royal blue shepherd's cap, and how the children are sitting on Liza's knee, pulling at her hair and kissing her cheek, well it's enough to stop someone dead in their tracks. And then Kimmy crawls up onto Liza's lap and wraps her chubby little hands around her neck, and says, "I love you, Mama," and I completely forget about being anywhere but here, watching my family as they model their nativity costumes.

I take a deep breath.

I mean, I've participated in this damn thing for twenty-seven years, and the most I can say about any of my experiences is that the costume was itchy.

But the thing is, this is my family. This is what we do. We wear scratchy burlap sacks and pretend to be wise men and shepherds and the baby Jesus, and the whole town gets to have the moment that I am having right now. A reminder moment of why we celebrate Christmas in the first place.

"See? We can get it together," Tim says with a hint of satisfaction in his voice.

"You guys look really good," I say as I scoop Kimmy into my arms. "I'm sorry about my little tantrum before."

"You're a Townsend. Tantrums comes with the package," says my nana the innkeeper, taking a flask from the back pocket of Mrs. Scanlon, the wise woman.

"It's still a nice package," Tim says quietly.

I turn away from him and blush. Damn his terseness!

Eight

On the morning of my last Christmas in Bethlehem, I stretch myself awake and scramble from my bed out of habit; it's ingrained in me to try to beat Jeff down to the tree and to the presents. But then I remember: no presents. No Jeff. No Mom or Dad. Just me and the rolling echo sound of an empty house.

I get to the kitchen to find no nana and no coffee. I check my cell to see no messages. None from my travel agent (I'm firing her when I get back to the city) and none from Eric, who is so upset that he probably won't even call today to wish me a Merry Christmas.

I wash and make myself beautiful, pinning my blond hair back in two diamond-chip bobby pins that I bought myself for my twenty-fifth birthday. I tiptoe through the quiet house, completely freaked out by the lack of activity, and walk into the living room. It is empty in here, not even a stocking under the tree. I walk over to my father's record player, search the albums, find what I'm looking for and put

it on the turntable. The click of the needle sounds just before an organ introduces the first measures of "White Christmas." Bing Crosby's voice fills the empty room, and I take a
deep breath.

I flip the switch on the train set that rings my mother's
Christmas village. It sputters to life and begins its trip around
the room. Then I turn on the Christmas tree lights and step
back to take it all in, and I think about what Tim asked me
yesterday: "Isn't that what you want? For everybody to not
make such a big deal about Christmas?"

I crumple onto the couch, slip an old afghan around my
shoulders and stare at the tree. It *is* what I always wanted.
And now I seem to have it and I'm totally miserable.

Could it be that I've grown so used to the hustle and bus-
tle of a Townsend Christmas morning that I actually *like* it?
I mean, haven't I spent years plotting my escape from my
mother's antics? My father's lectures on the town?

I reach for my cell phone, which of course is right by my
side. I punch in Eric's number, and listen as it rings. *One. Two.
Three. Four.*

On the fifth ring, he picks up. "Do you know what time
it is here?"

"Eric." When I say his name, I notice a large lump in my
throat, and my eyes tear up. "I was just calling to wish you a
Merry Christmas."

"Merry Christmas, Emma," he says without much feeling.

I don't think he's fully awake.

"You didn't call me back last night."

"I was thinking, that's all."

"Oh." I don't ask what about, because all of a sudden images start going off in my mind, like a picture show. Tim

eating apple pie straight out of the pan. Tim cutting into that block of ice with Dad's chainsaw. Tim stringing popcorn. Tim making a snowman. Tim wearing an old burlap sack and playing a wise man. I don't think I could get Eric to make a snowman with my nana. I don't think I could get Eric to play a wise man. Even if I *really* needed him to.

And the thing is, and this hits me from out of nowhere, if I marry Eric and become a Wesson and give my children a much more comfortable life than I had, I'll *still* have to come home to Bethlehem for Christmas. And I'll still have to string popcorn on the twenty-third. And I'll most likely still have to dress up in costumes to sell apple cider by the side of the road. And I want whoever my husband is to want to do all of these things with me.

"Emma? Are you there?" Eric asks, shaking me out of my own thoughts.

"Yeah." In an instant, I realize that I won't be going to Colorado, after all.

You could knock me down with a fistful of pine needles.

"Actually, Eric, I'm gonna call you back, when I know what I'm doing, okay?" I hang up quickly before he has a chance to say anything else, then stare at the phone in disbelief—

"Hey." The Tim Latch of my high-school dreams stands in the doorway: clean-shaven, in shirt and tie and jacket, with what I immediately recognize as Zegna oxfords.

It's with a debilitating confidence that I sense my crush roaring back to one-hundred-percent strength. And this time, I like Tim Latch for an entirely different set of reasons than I did before.

"Hey," I say. "You're all cleaned up."

"Family breakfast. Kind of a tradition." He walks into

the room and hands me a small package wrapped in red foil and topped with a big white grosgrain bow. "Merry Christmas."

The wrapping is gorgeous, clearly from a high-end paperie, but it doesn't even matter. I'm so touched by the thought, I am speechless. And really, really nervous. My heart is beating fast and my cheeks feel warm and the room is kind of spinning.

"But I didn't think— I didn't get you anything."

"Just open it."

I love presents, so I open his gift with gusto. There's a small jewelry box and inside that is a gold chain, with a small, ornately sculpted pine star that's been lacquered and polished so that it shines like a diamond. "Oh my God. It's gorgeous." I hold it up to my eye level and let the star dance on the end of the chain.

"I made it for you. It's the star of Bethlehem. Like you've been this Christmas."

I turn back to him. "I don't know. You're the one who keeps making it feel like a holiday."

"I thought you should have one nice thing to take from this trip."

Tim has no way of knowing that I have more to take away from this visit than I ever could have asked for. So I don't respond. I attach the delicate chain around my neck and turn to model it for him. "How's it look?"

"Perfect."

I touch the necklace and look into Tim's chocolaty eyes. "This is really special. You've kind of…made my Christmas."

He smiles and stands up. "Well, let's get to it. We've got an elf costume to put you in." He reaches out his hand and leads me to his truck, and we make our way to the town square, and the hundred and eighth annual Bethlehem Christmas Faire.

So I go and run my parents' ornament-making booth with my nana, wearing an elf costume the whole time. Red felt, with Walgreens tights and ten-dollar red boots that Nana bought from Payless.

I don't even mind when Tim comes round to take our picture.

Despite myself, something overtakes me—my mother would say it's the Christmas spirit. Mrs. Tate, Mrs. Scanlon and Mrs. Henry even seem to let the good feelings of the day erase their memories. Mrs. Scanlon brings a tray of maple cookies and the three ladies partake in Nana's twelve-thirty model-crèche-making instructional. Tim Latch, who is making his Bethlehem Christmas Faire debut, has the time of his life. He runs two sessions in a row, showing the men of Bethlehem how to whittle wood into star necklaces for their wives. He uses my Christmas present as a template, and I have to say, I get a little thrill down to my toes each time he calls me over, saying, "Em, can you show the mayor your necklace? See how it's supposed to look, Randy?"

After the two-thirty group leaves, Tim and I are left alone to clean up and prepare for the three-thirty juniors session. Nana has begun her annual schedule of Faire naps. She's snoring in a corner, stretched out on a bench, her face devoured by her peppermint-striped Santa hat, boots sticking up into the cold Vermont afternoon.

"Hey, if you want to check out the other booths, I can handle it here," Tim offers, a garbage bag in his hand overflowing with string and wood chips and empty Elmer's glue bottles.

"That's okay. I've seen it all." I mumble as I set out a miniature pair of scissors and bag of cotton balls at each of twelve different seats.

"That's right. I forgot." Tim grimaces as he stoops to shovel more scraps into the garbage bag.

"No, no! I mean I'm happy to be here, taking care of the Townsend booth."

Tim straightens and looks at me. "Too bad Molly can't hear you say that."

"Well, I'll tell her as soon as she gets back."

"That's in a week—" He looks at me, a hopeful, doubtful expression on his face.

"I was thinking that I'd stay for New Year's. Spend some overdue time with my parents."

He smiles at me, and goes back to cleaning, and I continue setting up for the kids. After a beat, I look up at him and smile. "So. An artist, huh?"

He smiles back. "Don't worry. I still know how to drive a Lexus."

The only thing that puts a damper on my mood is the fact that I have to spend the next forty-five minutes with the children of Bethlehem.

Have I mentioned I'm bad with kids?

When they get to the booth for the session, Lizzie informs me that I need to spend more time with kids if I don't want to be a grouch for the rest of my life. Then she and JJ announce that they would like to be my godparents.

"But you have to be adult to be godparents," I say, handing each of them a bucket full of felt and pipe cleaners.

"We're junior godparents," JJ says.

With my helpers in tow, and Tim's necklace around my neck, I proceed to spend an entire hour passing out glue, not freaking out when the Henry child gets marker on my calf-skin glove and helping Lizzie hand out graham crackers and cups full of cider. I'm no elementary school teacher, but I do okay.

When the session ends, I look up to see Tim standing by the corner of the booth and grinning at me.

"I didn't wring any necks." I walk over to him. "So, since you made me something, I thought I'd give you an ornament." I hand him a twine Rudolph, about three inches long, with a dried-hollyberry red nose.

He holds it up to the generator-produced light. "I like it. Now that's some art."

We begin to walk to the Ethan Allen statue. I tell Tim if he really wants to get on my good side, he'll play Joseph. The corner of his mouth lifts in a smile. "I don't think so, Emma."

When we round the corner, I see Nana and her friends in their costumes and Liza talking to Kimmy, telling her to be quiet while she's Jesus. Lizzie has my clipboard, and she's yelling at JJ, "Don't touch my clothes, Jake Jr. They're from *New York*."

Well, I can't help myself—it's just so cute that I run up and gather her in my arms. She shrieks and laughs from her belly and drops my clipboard on the snowy ground and then I spin her in a circle until we're *both* laughing from our bellies.

"My God. They've replaced you with a pod person."

I shriek and jump back, completely shocked to see Jeff. Dressed as Joseph. And standing right next to him is Jenny Shaw. Dressed as Mary.

"You're here!" I hug Jeff and Jenny with all my might. "How? When? Oh, my God!"

"I couldn't let you spend Christmas all by yourself, with

only this old lady for company," Jeff says with a twinkle in his eye as Nana cuffs his ears.

"I called him and told him to get his skinny behind up to our Christmas scene. He's a good boy."

Jenny throws her arm around me. "That Jeffrey's a big softie. All he's talked about for three months is how he can't wait to miss this Faire, then this morning he has a big breakdown and says that he can't spend a Christmas away from you."

"Hey! Offsides!" Jeff tries to tackle Jenny to shut her up, but it's too late.

"Aw, Jeffrey. Ya big girl!" I play-punch him in the shoulder.

"Nice outfit."

"Oh, shut up."

"Anyway, I really have always wanted to see this town, so here we are! Merry Christmas, Emma." Jenny kisses me on the cheek.

"Enough with all the mushy love junk, ladies," Jeff says. "Nana, after you, my dear."

My grandmother does a wolf whistle, and the sheep and Mr. Bray and Mr. Downing and Mrs. Scanlon, Lizzie, JJ and Kimmy all follow her down the snowy path, moving into the proper order and getting ready for their big moment.

Tim gives me a wink and rubs my cheek with his finger before turning to follow them. Jenny's eyes go wide as she gives me a thumbs-up and makes her own way down the path.

Before Jeff and I can follow, Liza pulls me into a warm hug. "You've done good here, Em." Then she gives me a real smile, wide and bright and gleaming, and walks off toward the light booth.

Jeff slings his arm around my shoulder. "So, the two of us. We're all talk, huh?"

"Apparently."

"Guess we'll both be here next year, too."

"Yeah."

We step up to where the procession will start. Lizzie and JJ are hushed, nervous, peering out at the crowd that's gathered, covered in winter coats, clutching steaming cups of coffee and hot chocolate and powdered doughnuts, craning their necks, waiting for my nana. The expressions on their faces fill my heart up, and for a moment I almost consider the mayor a hero. It's a lovely thing my family does every year, reenacting and making sure we remember there's a reason we're here besides presents and shopping and making pies. I feel something like Bethlehem pride as my nana marches out and recites the nativity story from the book of Luke, from memory, just as she has each year since she was old enough to talk.

"I forgot how much I like this part," Jeff whispers to me.

"I forgot how much I like everything," I whisper back.

"Well, honey, you're home. Merry Christmas." He shifts his robe, grabs Jenny's elbow and leads her and Kimmy out onto the green.

I smile and watch, pull my own brown burlap sack over my head, grab Tim and Lizzie and JJ, and march out to become the first person ever to play a fourth wise man.

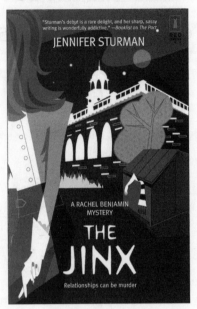

*Pilby Party
Essentials:*
- *Chinese takeout*
- *Ice cream*
- *A video (maybe two.)*
- *Bed*

*All the things
you want, and
no chance of disaster.*

Don't know what
a Pilby Party is?
Read *Carrie Pilby,*
by Caren Lissner,
to find out.

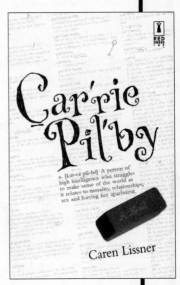

Also by Caren Lissner

Starting from Square Two

by Caren Lissner

Twenty-nine-year-old Gert Healy thought she
would never have to return to the craziness of the
dating world. Would never have to worry about
what to wear and what to say and whether she
was pretty enough. But the death of her husband
two years earlier has forced her to clad up in
miniskirts and leather jackets and brave it…again.
But does Gert have it in her to fight through the
singles crowds in search of a second miracle?

It's back to square one on everything. Well, actually, she's done it all before. Square two, then.

"Debut author Caren Lissner deftly delivers
a novel that is funny, sarcastic and
thought-provoking. (4 stars)"
—*Romantic Times* on *Carrie Pilby*

**RED
DRESS
INK**
TM

RDI03043R-TR